Praise fo...
Jenn...

"Fancy hats an...
delicious cozy read."
　　　　　　　—Rhys Bowen, *New York Times* bestselling author of
　　　　　　　　　　　　　　　the Royal Spyness Mysteries

"A delicious romp through my favorite part of London
with a delightful new heroine."
　　　　　　　—*New York Times* bestselling author Deborah Crombie

"The sharp writing and smart plotting are outstanding,
and the surprising reveal and even more suspenseful
chase will have readers at the edge of their seats. This
stellar mystery sets a high bar for mysteries."
　　　　　　　　　　　　　　—Kings River Life Magazine

"Brimming with McKinlay's trademark wit and snappy
one-liners, Anglophiles will love this thoroughly entertaining new murder mystery series. A hat trick of love,
laughter, and suspense, and another feather in [Jenn
McKinlay's] cap."
　　　　　　　　　　　　—Hannah Dennison, author of
　　　　　　　　　　　　　the Vicky Hill Exclusive! mysteries

BURIED TO THE BRIM

Jenn McKinlay

BERKLEY PRIME CRIME
New York

BERKLEY PRIME CRIME
Published by Berkley
An imprint of Penguin Random House LLC
penguinrandomhouse.com

Copyright © 2020 by Jennifer McKinlay Orf
Excerpt from *Paris Is Always a Good Idea* by Jenn McKinlay © 2020 by Jennifer McKinlay Orf

BERKLEY and the BERKLEY & B colophon are registered trademarks and
BERKLEY PRIME CRIME is a trademark of Penguin Random House LLC.

ISBN: 9781984804723

First Edition: January 2020

Printed in the United States of America
3   5   7   9   10   8   6   4   2

Cover art by Robert Gantt Steele
Book design by Laura K. Corless

This book is for every reader who asked me to write another Hat Shop Mystery. Your devotion to the series inspired me to write just one more . . . for now.

Acknowledgments

No writer works alone, not really, and I am very fortunate to have the best of the best helping me with every single book. Tremendous thanks to Kate Seaver, Christina Hogrebe and Sarah Blumenstock for their support, encouragement and brilliant suggestions. Also, many thanks to Brittanie Black and Jessica Mangicaro for their incredible work behind the scenes in promoting the books. You're amazing!

Chapter 1

If I held my left hand just so, I could see the diamonds catch and scatter the light, even the dreary February light in London, into a million tiny rainbows. I, Scarlett Parker, was engaged to be married. Harry, excuse me, my fiancé, Harrison Wentworth, proposed to me a few months ago when we were visiting my parents in Connecticut, and I don't think my feet have touched terra firma ever since. And it's not just because of my spectacular ring, although this cushion cut Harry Winston did add a little something to the proposal, but rather because after dating all the wrong men, I finally found my Mr. Right.

I held my hand over my heart and sighed.

"She's doing it again," Fee said. She was standing behind the counter in the middle of the hat shop.

"It's like a trance," Viv said. "Or perhaps a fit. It'll pass."

I turned away from the front window, where I'd been arranging a new display of spring hats before I got distracted by my ring, and glanced at my cousin, Vivian Tremont, and her assistant, Fiona (Fee) Felton. They were both looking at me as if they were convinced I'd lost my mind.

Viv's blue eyes, the only feature we shared, were narrowed and her lips pursed. Her long blond curls were piled on top of her head in a messy bun and she was dressed for warmth in a long pale green tunic sweater over charcoal tights and black boots. If I didn't love her so much, I'd loathe her for being so fairy-tale-princess pretty, but I did love her. She was the closest thing I had to a sister and when my life had imploded a few years ago, she was the one who sent for me, insisting I take my place as her partner in the hat shop that our grandmother Mim had bequeathed to us.

Fee, Viv's assistant, had her head tipped to the side. Her chin-length corkscrew curls, highlighted with vibrant streaks of purple, bounced as she nodded in agreement with Viv's assessment. A beautiful woman, Fee was tall and lithe, with dark eyes and skin, and cheekbones you could slice cucumbers on. She'd been Viv's millinery apprentice while in fashion school but had become a full-time employee once she graduated. It was a good thing I adored her, too, because honestly, hanging out with these two knockouts could damage even the most well-adjusted girl's self-esteem.

Despite a rocky start, I'd been in London for almost three years, and I couldn't imagine spending my days anywhere but our quaint little hat shop, Mim's Whims, on Portobello Road in Notting Hill. Being an American, the hat thing had always been a curiosity for me. Even when I came over to stay with Mim during my school holidays, I never quite understood the passion for hats that exists in Britain. Mim told me that wearing a hat is woven into the social fabric of being British. For the royal family, in particular, protocol dictates that they wear hats to all royal occasions. Royal and upper-class women rarely showed their hair in public before the 1950s, Mim explained, and so the hat remains relevant in British society.

Personally, even though I love the beautiful hats Viv and Fee create, I still don't quite get it. Although, I have to admit, there is no better cure for a bad-hair day than one of Viv's exceptional designs.

"I'm not having a fit," I protested. I tossed my straight red hair over my shoulder in my most diva manner and tipped my nose up in the air. "I'm just happy. Can't a girl be happy without everyone thinking she's bonkers?"

Viv and Fee exchanged a glance and then they broke into matching grins.

"We're just teasing you, yeah?" Fee said. Her nose ring caught the light as she turned her head to the side. She jerked her chin in the direction of the front door and said, "And if I'm not mistaken, here comes the reason you're so daft."

I whirled around and my heart gave a flutter at the sight of the tall man with wavy brown hair and bright green eyes who was approaching our shop. Harry! I was so delighted to see my fiancé; I didn't realize he had someone with him until Viv let out a huff of disgust.

"Is that a dog?" she cried. "Is he bringing it into our shop?"

Harry grinned at me as he pulled open the door, and it took all of my brain power to glance away from him and take in the petite woman and the adorable corgi who had entered the shop beside him.

"Yes, that's definitely a dog," Fee said. *"Aw.* Look. It's wearing galoshes and a mac."

I glanced down. It was! As giddy as I was about seeing Harry, the sight of the stubby-legged canine in a raincoat about did me in. *Totes adorbs!* I hurried from the window and dropped to the floor beside the pup.

"Well, aren't you just the cutest thing?" I asked. I held out my hand so we could become acquainted and a cold, wet nose nuzzled my fingers.

"She used to greet me like that," Harry said. His tone was dry, and when I glanced up he was smiling ruefully at the woman beside him.

"By letting you sniff her hand?" the woman asked. She grinned. "That's odd. Is that a new thing you young kids do?"

Harry laughed. "You're a regular card, Aunt Betty."

Aunt Betty! I'd heard stories about her from Harry's parents. Mostly his father since Betty was his little sister. Everyone doted on Aunt Betty.

She was a petite woman but very stylish in a later-year Audrey Hepburn sort of way with her long burgundy wool coat, a jaunty navy and white polka-dot scarf and large

4

sunglasses. Harry gave her a one-armed hug. The obvious affection between them made me smile.

"Aunt Betty, may I introduce you to my friends? Vivian Tremont and Fiona Felton." He gestured to Viv and Fee behind the counter and then said, "And this is my beautiful fiancée, Scarlett Parker. Ginger, this is my absolute favorite aunt in the whole wide world, Betty Wentworth."

"Delightful to meet you," I said. I stood up and shook her gloved hand.

Aunt Betty gave Harry a side-eye. "I'm your only aunt."

"That doesn't make it not true," he said. She laughed and swatted his arm.

"And who is your handsome companion?" I asked.

"She's not talking about me," Harry said. He sounded aggrieved.

"Well, you can't honestly expect to compete with my Freddy, now, can you, dear?" Aunt Betty asked Harrison. "I mean, look at his bum, it's shaped like a heart."

A laugh came out my nose. I took a discreet peek at Freddy's behind underneath the bright yellow raincoat—yup, definitely in the shape of a fuzzy heart. *Aw.* I felt Harry's gaze upon me and tried to save myself.

"Let me clarify to salvage your self-esteem." I winked at him and turned to Betty. "Who is your handsome *four-legged* companion?"

Aunt Betty smiled and turned to Harry. "I like her."

"Everyone does," Harry said.

"His full name is Freddy Darling Wentworth, and he is handsome, isn't he?" Aunt Betty asked. "I mean, just look at him, all honey-colored with ears and a good snout. He's a perfect specimen of a corgi. He's descended from the same line as the Queen's dogs, you know."

"Is he?" Fee asked. She came out from behind the counter and knelt in front of Freddy. A cold wet nose poked out from under the large yellow rain hat, and Freddy licked her fingers.

"Yes, he's a Pembroke Welsh corgi from the same lineage as the Queen's beloved Susan," Aunt Betty said.

"That's incredible," I said. "It's like having royalty in the shop. Last time we were so graced was when the Duchess of Sussex and the Duchess of Cambridge came for wedding hats."

"You did not just compare a dog to the royals," Viv said. She looked utterly appalled.

Viv is a monarchist and the royal family is sacrosanct. Probably because they buy a lot of her hats. Not that I'm saying her loyalty could be bought but there was definitely a fiscal relationship there, if you know what I mean. After all, when the Duchess of Sussex wore a particularly cute confection of Viv's, a pale pink cap with matching feathers and Swarovski crystals, the shop got hammered with orders for the same. I swear Viv made that identical hat for a month straight.

"No," I protested. I glanced at the others—only Harry looked like he was trying not to laugh. "Of course not. I just meant he's very much *like* a royal—you know, he's royal adjacent given that his family tree forks right into Buckingham Palace and all." They stared at me, not moved by my argument in the least. I felt compelled to add, "You know Queen Elizabeth would agree with me."

Fee blew an errant curl out of her eyes. "She does have a point there. The Queen is absolutely mad about her dogs."

"Howling mad, you might say," Harrison said with a mischievous grin.

That seemed to break the tension.

"Pawsitively smitten." Viv chortled.

"She absolutely hounds people about them." Fee laughed.

The three of them were in stitches while Aunt Betty looked at them in dismay. Naturally, I felt obliged to contribute, too, because I can be punny.

"We should call her Queen Elizabark," I said. I chuckled pretty hard. No one else did. Instead, they all went serious. Viv shook her head and Fee sighed. I glanced at Harry, the man who is supposed to have my back, and he winked at me. It was a pity wink. Honestly!

"Nice effort, Ginger," he said.

"Nice effort?" I planted my hands on my hips. "Queen Elizabark—aw, come on, you know that's funny."

Harry looked at Aunt Betty and said, "Americans." Then he shrugged. I swatted his shoulder, knowing it was all in good fun. At least, I'm pretty sure it was. I'd been trying to mix it up in their oh-so-droll British puns for years but with no real success as yet.

"There, there, dear." Aunt Betty patted my arm. "Not everyone has the gift of humor."

I rolled my eyes. Someday I was going to have the last laugh.

"This is all very . . . whatever it is," Viv said. She gestured to us and then to Freddy. "But why is there a dog in my shop, potentially getting hair on my hats?"

"Funny you should ask, Viv," Harry said.

I glanced at him. I knew that tone. This was the voice he used when he was feeling distinctly uncomfortable. Of course, being British, this meant most of the time. I honestly think part of the reason Harry loved me so much was because, being American, I do not have the same overdeveloped sense of unease about all things social.

"The thing is . . ." he began and paused. He put his hand on the back of his neck. I knew this tactic. It was a stalling maneuver Harry used when he was trying to think of exactly how to say something so that it wouldn't come out the wrong way. I crossed my arms. This was sure to be good. "The fact of the matter is, well, we were—"

"The point, dear," Aunt Betty said to Harry. "Get to the point."

Harry looked from her to Viv. "Aunt Betty was hoping you could help Freddy out with his next run at the PAWS dog show."

"The what?"

"PAWS dog show," Aunt Betty repeated. "Freddy's a contender."

Viv frowned. She glanced down at the dog, who was looking up at her from under the brim of his bright yellow hat. "Me? Help Freddy?"

"That's right," Aunt Betty said. She nodded and clapped her hands in front of her chest. Her soft brown eyes sparkled with enthusiasm. "Harry says you're the best milliner in London."

"Well, it would be bad form to argue with the truth, wouldn't it?" Viv asked.

She attempted to look modest but it was a wasted effort. If there was one thing that was true about Viv, it was that she really was the best milliner in London, and I'm not biased because I'm her cousin and we're in business together. She really is extra special. And I can say this as the person who works with the clients and has to convince them that the giant birdcage Viv put on their Ascot hat really will light up their mentions in the society pages in the best possible way.

"Freddy has been runner-up in the PAWS dog show for three years running," Aunt Betty said. "This is his year, I know it. But he needs a little boost."

"Well, given the lack of length in his legs, I can see that," Viv said. "But I'm not sure where I come in."

Fee blew a curl out of her eyes and said, "Don't be thick, Viv, they clearly want you to design a hat for Freddy."

"What?" Viv asked. Her frown stretched into a look of surprise. "I've never designed a hat for a dog before. I don't even know how it would stay on his head."

"Chin strap," I said. She glanced at me. "Sorry, just thinking out loud."

"I don't make hats with chin straps," Viv said. She looked insulted at the thought.

"Sure you do," Fee said. "Remember the darling lace-trimmed bonnets for the youngest flower girls in the royal . . ."

Fee's voice trailed off under the power of Viv's glare.

I figured I'd better mediate the situation before Viv hurt Aunt Betty's feelings and we ended up in an incident. I swear, my job was mostly to mitigate "incidents," which was ironic because it was an incident of my own that landed me here. Thankfully, I wasn't worried about Freddy's feelings, figuring he had enough self-esteem to manage a rejection from Viv.

"Come and sit down," I said to Harry and Aunt Betty. "Maybe if we hear more about what you need, we can help you."

Viv shot me a dark look, which I ignored. I led both Harry and Aunt Betty over to the dark blue easy chairs we had grouped around a glass coffee table on the far side of the shop. This was where Viv did her consultations with clients, over tea and scones, going through our catalog to see what they required for an upcoming event, be it a wedding, funeral, graduation, garden party, you name it.

Freddy trotted after his mama, sitting right at Aunt Betty's feet when she sat on the love seat. Harry sat beside her while Viv and I took the remaining chairs.

"I'm just going to get back to my fascinators, yeah?" Fee said. She gestured toward the workroom at the back of the shop. "I've got a hen party coming in later to pick them up and it won't do not to have them finished."

"Are these the ones with the . . . uh . . ." My voice trailed off. A hen party in Britain was the equivalent of a bachelorette party on the night before a wedding in the States.

"Yes, they're the ones," Fee said. "Pink satin top hats

with a wide black satin band around the crown, finished by a sparkly pink, er, embellishment on the side."

I laughed. I knew exactly what the embellishment looked like. "Classy."

Viv looked pained. "I know the bride is your cousin, Fee," she said. "But promise me we'll never have to make anything that tacky again."

"I promise," Fee said. Then she winked at me. "At least until Scarlett gets married."

A thrill rippled through me and I glanced at Harry and caught him smiling at me, which caused another ripple. A bride. I was going to be a bride. More specifically, I was going to be his bride. I couldn't wait. It was only half a year away now. Mrs. Harrison Wentworth. It never got old.

Fee left and I glanced at Viv to see if she wanted to start the conversation with Aunt Betty. She was too busy staring at Freddy. For his part, he seemed unaware of her scrutiny and emitted a big yawn and slowly slid to the floor. Harrison reached down and loosened the dog's raincoat and took off his hat and boots. Freddy flopped over on his side and began to snooze.

"So, why hats?" I asked. "Are they required at the dog show?"

"Goodness, no," Aunt Betty said. "But Harry and I got to talking about you, dear"—she paused to smile at me—"and your hat shop and the idea just hit me that maybe what Freddy needed was a dashing chapeau to garner some added notice from the judges. It's his fourth year competing and I just can't stand that he's been runner-up three years in a row."

"Always a bridesmaid, never a bride. I can see where that would grate," Viv said.

"The PAWS competition is unique," Harry explained. "The Pet Animal Welfare Society hosts the charity event every year. It's open to all dogs and the purpose is to raise money for shelters all over the country. It has three categories: appearance, agility and obedience."

"There's no conformation category," Aunt Betty said. "So, truly, any dog can enter."

"What's conformation?" Viv asked.

"It's an evaluation to determine how closely a dog conforms to the specific features of his breed," I said. Aunt Betty gave me a surprised look, and I explained, "I never miss watching Westminster."

"In the PAWS competition, they score the dog's overall appearance on how it carries itself, the quality of its teeth and coat, that sort of thing. The dog with the highest combined score in all three categories—appearance, obedience and agility—is declared best in show."

"So the PAWS dog show is more like a beauty pageant?" Viv asked.

"Precisely," Aunt Betty said. She gazed adoringly at Freddy. "He's a natural, don't you think?"

Viv said nothing but I nodded to make up for her lack of enthusiasm.

"I like it," I said. "It's nice that dogs that aren't purebred still have a shot if they can outscore the others. But won't wearing a hat impede Freddy's abilities somewhat?"

I pictured Freddy in a top hat, leaping over rails and racing through tunnels. I didn't think it would go well.

"Naturally, I wouldn't have him wear it for the agility tests," Aunt Betty said. "Just for the initial presentation, so he can make a statement. It's time somebody knocked that pompous blowhard Richard Freestone and his English bull-dog, Muffin, off the pedestal once and for all. The man has won PAWS three years running. Enough."

"And you think a hat from my shop will do the trick?" Viv asked. It was clear from her tone that she had her doubts.

"It will definitely give Freddy's profile a boost," Aunt Betty said. "Freestone has almost one million followers for Muffin and they endorse everything from leashes to bis-cuits. It's galling."

Aunt Betty was petite and fine boned. I could tell she had been a beauty in her youth, as she was still quite lovely. Her hair was white and her eyes were a rich brown, she had an oval face that was faintly lined. My guess was that she was the same age as Harry's parents, who were in their late fifties.

"He does seem to wear a hat well," I said. I gestured to the rain hat Harry had removed.

"He's very agreeable," Aunt Betty said. "I'm sure he'd take to wearing a hat for the show. He's quite smart."

"I can see that," I said. Harry gave me a doubtful look. "It's in his eyes."

"He also recently sired a litter of puppies," Aunt Betty said.

"Puppies!" I cried. I turned to Viv. "Just what the shop needs—a mascot. We should totally get one."

"No," Viv said. Realizing she must sound harsh, she added in a softer voice, "Puppies eat hats, Scarlett."

"They prefer shoes," Aunt Betty said.

"Not helping," I muttered. I glanced at Harry. "Does your building allow dogs?"

"Uh . . ." Harrison glanced from me to Freddy and back. "I've never asked."

"You should," I said. "Then we could get one of Freddy's puppies and it would be like training for when we have babies."

It took everything I had to keep a straight face as Harry's face went pale and he started to sweat. I knew I shouldn't tease him but, oh, he made it so easy.

"Or maybe we should get two or three puppies," I said. "You know I really am hoping we have twins or perhaps triplets right after we marry. Wouldn't puppies be fabulous training?"

Somehow I managed to stay serious. It was Viv who blew it. She snorted. Harry looked at her and then at me.

"You're winding me up, aren't you, Ginger?" he asked. He shook his head but a small smile played on his lips. "Just wait until you come home and there is a puppy."

"Promise?" I laughed.

"No, no puppies," Viv said. "Not here at Mim's Whims. When you move in with Harrison, you can have one."

I glanced at Harry. We had agreed not to move in together until after we were married. Partly it was because

I didn't want to leave Viv to live alone above the hat shop but also because I wanted to save the whole cohabitating thing until after we were man and wife. I figured after he saw the state I habitually left a bathroom in, he would be less able to ditch me once we were legally bound. But a puppy was a new factor in the equation.

"Maybe I should move in sooner than we planned," I said.

"When did you say those puppies were available, Aunt Betty?" he asked. He'd been pushing to live together ever since we got engaged.

"Oh, his litter is already spoken for," she said. "I get my pick of the pups as part of the stud fee but the rest are already bought and paid for."

"Oh." I was surprised at how disappointed I felt. I really do love dogs.

"Don't worry, pet," Aunt Betty said. She patted my hand. "Freddy still has his meat and two veg. He'll sire another litter."

I blinked. Meat and two veg? I glanced at Harry. Even after three years, there were still some British euphemisms that escaped me. He gave me a pointed look.

"Oh," I said. "Oh." Aunt Betty had been referring to Freddy's man parts. A meat and two veg. I tried not to laugh. I failed.

Freddy rolled over so he was belly up. It was clear that he required a tummy rub and I was happy to oblige.

"Look at how sweet he is, Viv," I said. "I think you could definitely make him a hat that would give him some added pizzazz." I turned to Betty. "When would you need the hat?"

"The competition begins in three weeks," she said.

Viv frowned. She studied Freddy, whose tongue was lolling out while he stared at her with his big brown eyes. She was going to crack. I knew it. In five, four, three . . .

"All right, all right," she said. "I'll do it but just this one time."

"Yay!" I clapped. "And who knows? Maybe you'll influence a whole new market, and hats for dogs will start trending."

If looks could kill, yeah, I'd be six feet under.

Chapter 2

"Has Freddy arrived yet?" Viv asked. "He needs his final fitting."

"Not yet," I said. I was perusing the *Evening Standard* I'd grabbed at Notting Hill Gate the night before. There was a charming article about the royal tots, which I devoured, as I was totally enamored with those kids. Apple cheeked and clear eyed. I just adored them all. Thank goodness Harry and Meghan were making more for us all to love.

"Please tell me you're not having baby pangs," Viv said. She leaned over my shoulder and squinted with distaste at the article. Viv wasn't really the maternal type.

I put my hand over where I assumed my uterus was, you know, behind the slight roll of chubby belly that sat between my hips.

"Nope, not even a spasm," I said. "However, I am having some puppy pangs, which are just like baby pangs but for puppies."

I batted my big baby blues at her.

"No." She shook her head.

Darn. Well, it was worth a try.

Woof!

Viv and I both turned to the door. Freddy pranced in, no raincoat today, as if he owned the joint.

"Are you sure you don't want a dog?" I asked. "He'd really add a whole new layer to our advertising. We could feature him on all of our promotions."

"Scarlett, we sell hats," Viv said. "There is no correlation between dog owners and hats. If you can find me statistics that prove dog owners buy five times the number of hats as non–dog owners then I could see where you're going with this, but if you're just wanting to get a pet, we can acquire a fish."

"A fish?" I asked. I knelt down to scratch Freddy's ears. He leaned against me as if he'd been waiting for a good scratch all day. Handsome boy. "You can't cuddle a fish."

"Precisely."

I rolled my eyes and then turned to the door. Harry was holding it open for Aunt Betty. They seemed to be having an intense discussion.

"You didn't say that to him, did you?" Harry asked.

Aunt Betty jutted out her chin in a stubborn pose. "No, but somebody should."

"Aunt B, going after the sponsor of the dog show is not going to help Freddy win the competition," Harry said.

"This is bigger than the dog show," she said. "I think that dog food was making Freddy sick. I don't care if Gerry Swendson is the biggest sponsor of the show. His dog food is bad."

Harry glanced up and met my gaze and shrugged as if he had no idea what to say. I turned to Aunt Betty. "What's this about bad dog food?"

"The winner and the three runners-up for the PAWS dog show get a year's supply of food from Swendson's Dog Food, the company that sponsors the show," she said. "Freddy was a finalist last year, so he won some dog food, but it made him sick and I threw it all out."

"Are you sure it was the food?" I asked. "He didn't get into the garbage or some strange plant at the park?"

"No, I'm quite sure it was the food," she said. "And I think someone needs to talk to Swendson about it to warn him that his quality control is no good."

"I can try and look into it for you," Harrison said. "My company investigates all sorts of investment opportunities. I can see what the word is about the quality of Swendson's Dog Food."

"Oh, would you?" she asked. "It would relieve my mind, knowing someone was doing something. I mentioned it to several people last year but everyone made excuses just because Swendson is a sponsor. Our dogs need better care than that."

"Agreed," Harry said. "Don't think on it anymore."

Aunt Betty turned to Viv. "How did the hat turn out? Did you decide on the bowler? I am just dying to see it."

Freddy abandoned me and approached Viv with a sniff and a small wag. She stared at him, clearly immune to his charm. He sat at her feet and looked up at her.

"That's better," she said. "I'll go get the hats."

"Hats?" I asked. "As in plural?"

She gave me a look. "What? I couldn't decide what he'd look better in—a trilby, a bowler, or a fedora."

"So you made all three?"

She waved her hand. "Don't make it into a thing. He has a very small head. It wasn't that much work."

I waited until she walked out of the room before I looked at Harry. I made a face that I hoped indicated my surprise and he mirrored it, breaking into a grin that I returned. We both loved Viv but there was no question that she was a strange bird. Three hats for a dog? She could deny it all she wanted but she liked Freddy and she liked making the dog hats.

"I hope she hasn't gone to too much trouble," Aunt Betty said. "I certainly didn't want her to tax herself on Freddy's account."

"Don't you worry," I said. "Once Viv gets an idea, well, it's best to just let her run with it. Lucky Freddy. He'll be the most dashing dog at the show."

Aunt Betty smiled but I could see it was forced and she appeared to be fretting.

"Are you worried about the competition?" I asked.

"No," she said. She shook her head and her white hair sparkled in the store's bright lights. "Best in show is Freddy's for the taking, but I am concerned about Swendson's food."

I nodded. My former job in hospitality, otherwise known as a people pleaser, usually helped me find the sunny-side-up or the glass-half-full angle to any situation. I racked my brain, trying to find the silver lining here. It was tricky.

"Harry will figure it out," I said. "He's the best, and I'm not just saying that because I'm going to marry him."

"You're right, dear," she said. She glanced between us. "You two are going to make beautiful babies."

I felt my face get hot. Babies? We hadn't even trained with a puppy yet! When I glanced past her at Harry, he was smiling at me in that way he did when he thought I was adorable in my embarrassment. This was one of the many reasons why I was marrying this man. In a world that frequently considered me odd, my man got me.

Viv, with an armful of hats, came back into the room. Being the mad hatter that she was, Viv hadn't just made hats for Freddy but had pushed on and made matching hats for Aunt Betty as well. To quote my British friends, they were smashing!

I sat beside Harry while Aunt Betty and Freddy did an impromptu fashion show for us. Despite his appearance of being a love lush, wanting never-ending tummy rubs, when Aunt Betty put him through his paces, Freddy was on task. He followed all of her commands instantly and when he pranced through the shop wearing his bowler jauntily perched over one eye, well, I didn't see how he couldn't win the dog show.

Aunt Betty clapped her hands and looked overcome. "These are simply brilliant. Thank you, my dear, thank you so much. We have the cocktail party tomorrow night and I can't wait to put our competition on notice."

She impulsively hugged Viv, who is not a hugger by nature, and to my surprise Viv hugged her back. She even reached down and patted Freddy's hat.

"Yes, I think these will do," she said. "My work here is done."

With that, Viv left us in the front of the shop while she disappeared into the workroom to go shape, stitch and embellish some other client's dream.

Harry rose from the couch, and I joined him. I gathered the hats for Freddy and Aunt Betty and boxed them in nests of tissue paper in our trademark blue-and-white-striped hatboxes with the name *Mim's Whims* scrawled across the lid with a silk braid cord for a handle. Harry was going to look adorable carrying these for his aunt.

"See you at the pitch later?" he asked.

"Pitch?" I asked. I had no idea what he was talking about.

"Rugby pitch," he clarified. "It's the Thirsty Lions' first match of the season. Remember?"

I hadn't but I didn't admit it.

"Oh, right! Of course, I wouldn't miss it," I said. This was the truth. I knew nothing about rugby except that Harry had been playing since he was a kid and he became a little crazed while following his favorite team, the New-castle Falcons. His local club team was sponsored by a pub called the Thirsty Lion, thus the very original team name.

"Freddy and I will be there as well to cheer you on," Aunt Betty said. She looked at me. "You know the old expression—'Football is a gentleman's game played by ruffians, and rugby is a ruffian's game played by gentlemen.'"

I thought about American football. There was nothing gentlemanly about it so I figured she was using the common name for soccer in the rest of the world, which was definitely more apt since they used their feet so much, you know, when they weren't flopping on the ground trying to get a foul. There was no flopping in rugby, thank God. Plus, Harrison in shorts. What's not to love?

The pitch, as it turned out, was in a city park northwest of Portobello Road. Viv, Fee and I closed the shop and took the Underground to the nearest stop. It was a short walk from there in the dreary weather. The high was fifty-seven degrees Fahrenheit or thirteen-point-nine if I was going by Celsius, which my brain even after three years simply couldn't grasp. Thirteen, in my mind, was like crazy Minnesota or Nebraska cold. Of course, having moved to London from Florida, fifty-seven felt pretty cold, too.

We carried a thick, plaid wool blanket to sit on and a backpack full of food, including a thermos of hot tea. As we crossed the tree-lined grassy lawn toward the playing

23

fields, I could just make out the pitch. Harrison's club wore red and black colors, which I knew from seeing him launder his uniform. The other team was in green and white. If we were judging by color, I thought the red and black definitely made more of a winning statement.

When we arrived at the sideline, I saw my two very best friends, Andre Eisel and Nick Carroll, who were already seated in folding chairs with a plaid blanket spread in front of them. They were the first friends I'd made when I moved to London and I simply adored them.

"Scarlett, over here!" Andre stood and waved. He was tall and built, with dark skin, close-cropped hair and a rogue's smile. The diamond stud he wore in one ear flashed at me almost as brightly as his grin. A photographer by trade, he owned a studio down the street from our hat shop, although his partner, Nick, wasn't a photographer but a dentist.

Nick waved a large red and black flag at me and when he stood, I noted he had completely decked himself out in Harrison's team colors, with red pants and a black rugby shirt with a fat, red stripe around the middle. This didn't flatter his rounded figure, but really, who was going to notice when he paired it with an enormous red-and-black-striped velvet top hat, which sat low on his brow and added about a foot to his overall height?

"Nicholas Carroll, where did you get that abomination?" Viv asked. She stared at the hat as if it had done something more to offend her than merely exist.

We were all wearing red and black hats as well, because Viv insisted that we always wear hats when out in public so as to advertise the shop. I really didn't mind today because it kept my ears from freezing. I had chosen a black bucket hat with a big red rose for embellishment. Fee had donned a felted newsboy cap in red with a black band, and Viv wore a festive tam in a Fair Isle pattern of red and black with a large red pom-pom on top.

"Whatever do you mean, Viv?" Nick asked. He doffed his hat, making his thinning reddish-blond hair stand on end as if it, too, were outraged by the insult to his chapeau.

"That!" Viv pointed to the hat in his hand. "Where did you get that? The Non Stop Party Shop?"

"Right in Kensington," he agreed.

Viv gave him a dark look. "I bet it leaves a black sweat ring around your head."

"Ah!" Nick gasped and looked at Andre. He lifted the hat and pitched forward, shoving his head in Andre's direction. "It hasn't, has it?"

"No, love, you're fine," Andre said. He grinned at me and opened his arms for a hug.

Next I hugged Nick, who still looked worried. "Don't listen to Viv," I said. "Your hat is festive and fun and there's nothing wrong with that. You know how she gets about hats in general and her hats in particular."

"Hmm, rather like I am about teeth, I expect," he said. "Exactly."

Fee and Viv hugged our friends, too, while I looked for

my man among his team. Once I spotted him my heart did that fluttery thing it always did when I caught sight of Harry. I used to think it was indigestion back when I couldn't stand him but now I knew better. And today it seemed to do an extra somersault at the sight of him in his rugby attire.

Fee stood beside me and followed the line of my gaze. "Nice kit, yeah?"

"Kit?" I asked.

"Their uniforms," she explained.

"Oh, of course," I said. "There's nothing quite like a man in a rugby shirt, is there?"

"Nope, nothing," she agreed.

We watched as the men warmed up—lots of stretching and strutting, and a few halfhearted attempts to wrestle one another to the ground. Then the referee appeared. Harrison caught sight of us, hard to miss with the hats and all, and jogged over to our blanket. He took his mouth guard out and scooped me close and planted a solid kiss on me, charming me stupid of course, before he let go and exchanged high fives with Nick and Andre.

"Thanks for coming out," he said. He scanned the crowd. "You haven't seen Aunt Betty, have you?"

"No," I said. "She's probably just running late."

A frown marred his forehead. "I'm worried about her. This dog show business is getting—"

"Oy, Worthless, get over here!" a voice shouted from the pitch. My eyebrows lifted in surprise at the nickname, but Harry grinned. Clearly, he'd been called worse. He kissed me quick, put his mouth guard in and then jogged back onto the field.

Fee had opened the thermos and was pouring tea into thick paper cups. I glanced at the basket Nick and Andre brought and saw that they were also drinking hot tea but out of real china. I raised a brow in question and Nick tipped his nose up in the air.

"Just because we're dining al fresco does not mean we're savages," he said.

I kneeled on their blanket and swiped a chocolate-dipped biscuit out of a crystal bowl. Nick wagged his finger at me. "That's not a proper dinner, Scarlett."

"It's an appetizer," I said.

He shook his head and then held up a dish of fat, juicy strawberries. "At least have something healthy with it."

"Nick, you are a better wife than I'll ever be," I said with a sigh.

He patted my hand. "Don't you worry. I offer lessons."

I laughed and he raised his eyebrows and gave me a pointed look. Oh, dear.

A whistle sounded as the match began. Truthfully, I wasn't really sure what I was watching. There was a circular pile of men in the middle and each team had a line of men staggered down their side of the field. Viv was already bored and looking at a selection of pearl beads on her phone, but Fee seemed to know exactly what was happening. In fact, she jumped to her feet and started yelling, although I wasn't sure if she was encouraging our team or chastising them. Nick bounced up out of his seat and joined her. I was impressed that he managed this without spilling any of his tea.

Andre was sitting in his chair behind me and he leaned forward so that he was half over my shoulder and asked, "Do you have any idea what is going on?"

I thought about bluffing, but what would be the point? I glanced at him and said, "Not a clue."

He grinned. "Harrison is shirking his duties to make you a proper English wife."

"Clearly," I said. "Although, I have managed to put the kettle on for tea without burning down his apartment."

He raised a brow. "Look at you, getting all domestic."

I preened just the littlest bit. Cooking had never been my strong suit. Once, I went to heat water in the microwave for tea, and Harrison looked like he'd keel over. I learned quickly that the kettle was the only acceptable way to heat water for tea and this fact was nonnegotiable.

"All right, I'll give you the short course on rugby," Andre said. "That pile of bodies in the center is the scrum."

"Scrum, got it," I said.

"In the center of the scrum each team has a hooker," he continued. I snorted, because I'm mature like that. He gave me a look. I stopped. "The hookers try to hook the ball out to their mates and then the team has to run the ball over the opposing team's line to ground it for a five-point try."

"Well, that seems simple enough," I said. "It's a bit like American football, you know, except for the fact that there are no helmets or pads—or any safety gear, for that matter." I tried not to think about this, as the thought of Harrison with a head injury made me queasy.

"That, and in rugby you can ruck and maul, and you only pass the ball to the side or back. Also, the game doesn't stop at a tackle," he said.

"It doesn't?"

"Nope, whichever team grabs a dropped ball first, can grab it and keep going."

"Dang," I said.

I glanced back at the field. Despite the baggy shorts they all wore, I noticed the muscle-hardened legs and defined shoulders and kicked myself for not being a bigger fan of rugby earlier in my life. I scanned the men I could see and noted that Harrison's friend, or the guy he called his "best mate," Alistair Turner, was in the thick of the match.

Alistair had become a good friend over the past few years as he'd used his lawyerly abilities to help us out a couple of times. Seeing him on the pitch now, grabbing the oblong ball and running with his unruly shoulder-length black hair flying as he sprinted for the line, I had to check and see if Viv was catching this. *Argh!* She was not!

"Hey, Viv," I said. "Look! There's Alistair!"

Viv thumbed through some more pictures on her phone. When she did glance up, it was with a bored look. I pointed. She heaved a put-upon sigh and glanced at the pitch.

I watched to see if her eyes narrowed or widened in

recognition. The woman was stone cold. There was not one indrawn breath of surprise or flutter of an eyelash in appreciation of the man's athletic prowess. Good thing Alistair was soaring out on the field because here on the sideline, he was crashing and burning.

Chapter 3

"Go, Alistair, go!" Fee was shouting loud enough for all of us. I left Viv to her phone and ran over to the sidelines to add my encouragement.

Out of nowhere a player from the other team appeared. He was closing in on Alistair. I watched as Harry sprinted— seriously, I'd never seen him move so fast—running to intercept the player in green and white. He made a diving tackle, well, I assumed it was supposed to be a tackle, but he mostly grabbed the man by the ankle, forcing him to stumble and then drag Harry's dead weight. Finally, the man in green and white went down with a bellow as he shot out an arm for Alistair, who neatly sidestepped and doubled down on his speed.

One more brick wall of a man appeared but Alistair

feinted to the right and then leapt into the air on the guy's left, flying the required yardage over the line to ground the ball and score a try.

Our side of the pitch went crazy. I scanned the field, looking for Harry. He was already up and running and he and Alistair did a very manly, cough cough, chest bump at the end of the field.

"That was amazing! Did you see?" Fee cried. She had her hat in her hand and was swinging it wildly as if it were a flag. Nick was on the other side of her, waving his actual flag, and the two of them started chanting, "Thirs-ty Li-ons!"

When they both mimicked a lion's roar with their fingers curled like claws, I laughed. They were fearsome—not. I turned and found Viv standing beside me. She was frowning at the pitch. Even having known her all my life, I had no idea what she was thinking.

"Impressive, right?" I asked.

"If you like dirty, sweaty, grunting men," she said.

"Check, check and check," I replied.

She gave me a look that I'm sure was meant to discourage me, but when I glanced over to where Harry was lining up with his mates—look at me, using the appropriate lingo—I couldn't help but appreciate the ruddy splotches of color on his cheeks, the sparkle in his impossibly green eyes, and the sweat-soaked hank of hair that fell over his forehead into his eyes. My man was a rugby hottie. Who knew?

The game continued and Andre joined me, taking Viv's place as she retreated to the blanket. The one thing I noticed without Andre pointing it out was how respectful the players were of the refs. No matter the call, it was greeted with "yes, sir" or "no, sir." Gentlemen, indeed.

Fee and I took a breather and ransacked our food. The cold evening air was making me ravenous and the sandwiches we'd brought were calling my name with an insistence that could no longer be ignored.

We'd packed a classic ploughman's nosh of cheese and pickle sandwiches, made with Wensleydale cheese and local pickles nestled between two thick slabs of whole grain bread. It sounds gross, but I'd been converted during my time in London and it was now my go-to sandwich in the middle of the night. Guaranteed to sate the hunger and also give a gal some spectacularly weird dreams.

Just as I was taking my first big bite, I heard a commotion on the field. I chewed quickly as I hurried back to the sidelines. The lights had been switched on and the field had that twilight glow about it where the sky was a soft plush purple and the bare limbs of the trees, illuminated by the field spotlights, reached up toward the sky as if desperate for some springtime warmth.

Running across the patchy dry grass was one player who was clearly shorter and hairier than the others. Freddy! He had his eye on the ball and was not about to give it up to the man holding it. With yips and barks, he hunkered low and raced down the field after the player, who glanced over his shoulder with a look of stark surprise.

I saw Harry and Alistair run after the dog. Aunt Betty was down the field, holding a leash with no dog attached, looking as if she had no idea how that had happened.

"I say, isn't there a height requirement for club rugby?" Nick asked Andre, who started to laugh. "I mean, he's got the speed but he'll be shortchanged if he gets the ball."

Andre clapped his hand on Nick's shoulder and quipped, "That's a low blow."

Nick started to chuckle and so did I. Unable to leave it alone, I just couldn't help myself. I wedged myself in between them and said, "It'll be the height of disappointment for him."

They stopped laughing and looked down at me. Nick shook his head with a pained expression and Andre pressed his lips together. I could tell he was trying not to laugh.

"You know that was a good one." I poked him in the ribs with the hand not holding my sandwich. Then I took another bite.

"Cheese and pickles? Excellent, pet, come along," Nick said. He threw his arm around my shoulders and led me downfield. "You, or more accurately, your sandwich, is going to be bait."

"But I like my sandwich," I protested. "It's my favorite."

"Please, we have Scotch eggs and sausage rolls in our basket and there's plenty for everyone," Nick said.

"And wine," Andre added.

That tipped the scale. We approached the field.

"I say, what's he doing now?" Nick asked.

Freddy was running this way and that. He seemed to be circling the players on both teams, trying to draw them

34

into a tighter and tighter circle, with Harry and Alistair winding in the tightest as they tried to catch him without hurting him.

"I think he's herding them," I said. "Are corgis herd dogs?"

"Judging by this, I'm going to say 'yes,'" Andre said.

"We'd better help them, because I don't think he's going to tire out anytime soon." Nick said. "And by 'we' I mean 'you.'"

"Fine." I lowered my sandwich and cried, "Freddy! Here, Freddy, I have some Wensleydale cheese for you."

Aunt Betty waved to me from downfield. I assumed she was giving me the okay, and I waved back.

"Cheese, Freddy!" I cried again, louder this time.

And don't you know, that dog heard me, even over all the racket of the players and the crowd. One minute he had the big oval ball in his sights and the next thing I knew, he did a flip in the air, impressive for those stumpy little legs and worthy of something from *The Matrix*, and then he was coming at me like a bullet.

Low to the ground, his paws churned up the hard turf as he ran. Any herding of the players was forgotten as he locked in on the cheese.

"Is he going to stop?" Nick cried.

"He's not slowing down!" Andre yelled.

"Ah!" they yelled in unison and abandoned me as I moved the sandwich to my side; just as Freddy was closing in, I tossed it high and wide. Again, he made a midair correction and snatched the sandwich before it hit the ground. He landed on his feet and continued to chomp my sandwich as Harry and Aunt Betty came running over.

Harry grabbed the leash from Aunt Betty and clipped Freddy while he scarfed down the last little bit of my cheese and pickles. It wasn't very nice of me, but I hoped the pickles gave him heartburn.

"Brilliant, love, just brilliant," Harry said. Then he kissed me on the head. "Are you all right? He didn't nip you, did he?"

"No, I'm fine," I said. I looked at Freddy. "I hear there are sausage rolls in the area. Let me be clear, they are mine."

Freddy wagged his tail, and Aunt Betty, wheezing a bit, said, "Thank you, my dear, that was quick thinking."

"No problem."

Harrison handed Aunt Betty the leash and I noticed that her lip wobbled just a bit.

"Are you all right, Aunt Betty?" I asked. "You didn't hurt yourself, did you?"

"No, I . . ." She waved her hand dismissively.

"What a handsome dog," Andre said. He was crouched down beside Freddy, admiring him, while Freddy sniffed his hand. "I bet he could win best in show at the upcoming dog show."

Aunt Betty blinked. Her sadness was forgotten. "Do you really think so?"

"Yes," he said. "I've actually been hired to take pictures at the PAWS dog show this weekend. From what I've seen, not that I'm an expert, Freddy has the right stuff."

"Shut up!" I said. "You're working the dog show? Aunt Betty and Freddy are entering the dog show."

"Maybe," Aunt Betty said.

"Wait," I said. "What's happened? You were so excited to enter."

Aunt Betty glanced up and her eyes filled with worry. "I'm nervous."

"What? Why?" Viv cried. She was standing behind us and moved to break into our tight little circle. "How can that be? He has hats!"

"Hats?" Andre and Nick asked together.

"Yes, and they're spectacular," Viv said.

"We've seen them." Harry gestured between us. "They're top-notch."

Viv visibly calmed down.

Harry turned back to his aunt. "Can you tell us why you're worried? Has something happened?"

"Richard Freestone, among other things," she said. Her brown eyes narrowed and her lips tightened.

Harry raised an eyebrow. "Isn't he the man who won last year?"

"And the year before that and the year before that," Aunt Betty said. She sounded glum.

"Well, then it's absolutely time for someone else to win," Nick said. "No worries, your handsome lad there is a shoo-in."

Aunt Betty took a shaky breath and nodded. "You'd think so but today when I turned in our application, Freddy and I went to the office just like we always do—"

37

"Oy, Worthless, are you playing or what?" one of Harry's teammates yelled.

He turned around and shook his head. "I need a minute. Call in Cal to sub for me."

The player gave him a sharp nod and turned back to the game.

Harry took his aunt's arm and led her over to Nick and Andre's picnic basket. "Here. Have a seat and tell us what happened."

Nick popped open the top of their basket and neatly poured Aunt Betty a glass of chardonnay. She accepted it graciously while Freddy, having filled up on my sandwich, sprawled down on their blanket for a nap. Much to my amusement, Aunt Betty lifted her glass in a toast to us all and then downed it in one long swallow.

Harry didn't look surprised. Nick looked like he was choking back a laugh as he refilled her glass, but I knew from glancing at Andre that my face likely had the same look of amazement as his. The woman was tiny, built like a songbird; she was going to be schnockered.

"All right, here's what happened," Aunt Betty said. She waved her glass while she spoke but her voice was clear and her eyes held a look of ire, which was much preferable to the sad expression she'd worn just a few moments earlier.

"Freddy and I went to register this afternoon at Finchley Park and we ran into Liza Stanhope," she said.

"Socialite Liza Stanhope?" Harrison asked.

"That's the one," Aunt Betty said. "She's the director of the PAWS committee, you know."

Harry nodded as if he did know, but I was pretty sure this was brand-new information. I had never heard of Liza Stanhope, which was weird because most of London's finest came to Viv for their hats. The fact that she had never graced our shop with her presence I found a bit off-putting. Who did this Liza Stanhope think she was, anyway?

"She was there when I filled out my registration and she actually curled her lip at Freddy," Aunt Betty said. "And then she said with a sneer that a corgi would never win best in show, not if she had anything to say about it."

Aunt Betty reached down and patted Freddy's head. She was clearly rattled and I wondered if that had been Liza Stanhope's plan all along, to cause Aunt Betty to be filled with self-doubt.

"Oh, Aunt B, she's just the director, she's not a judge," Harry said. "You can't let her get into your head like that."

"I know, but you didn't see her face," Aunt B protested. "And that's not the worst of it."

I was all ears. This was what I was certain we were waiting for.

"When I arrived home before coming here, I found a note in my postbox that was handwritten and . . . it said . . ." She paused as if trying to compose herself before she continued, "'If you persist in competing in the dog show, I will poison your dog.'"

There was a collective gasp.

"That's horrible!" Nick declared. "What sort of evil person does that?"

"Someone who does not want Aunt B competing,"

Harry said. He frowned and studied her face. "Any idea who it might be?"

She shook her head. "The cocktail party that kicks off the three-day competition is tomorrow night, and I'm worried that someone will try to slip Freddy something. I can't risk him but I hate that I'm being intimidated."

"Will Freddy be attending the cocktail party?" Harry asked.

"Of course," she said. "All the dogs go. They have dog-friendly mocktails, it's adorable and Freddy loves it."

"Well, then Scarlett and I will go with you and make sure nothing untoward happens," Harry said. "Don't you worry, Aunt B, we've got your back."

"Nick and I will be there, too," Andre said. "I'm the official event photographer, after all."

"That's perfect." I turned back to Aunt Betty. "See? We'll all be there to protect you and Freddy from harm. It's probably just an idle threat. We should see if anyone else got the same note. Also, we should bring it to the police."

"She's right," Harry said. "Did you save it, Aunt B?"

"I did," she said.

"Then we'll follow up at the party tomorrow and visit the police, too," Harry said. "Everything is going to be just fine."

"Thank you, my dear." Aunt Betty smiled at all of us. She reached down and patted Freddy's head. "Did you hear that, Freddy-bottoms? You are going to have an entourage."

"Exactly!" Harry said. "With all of us there, what could possibly go wrong?"

He kissed my head and then jogged back to the pitch and I felt a shiver start at my spine and ripple all the way through me. I refused to believe it was anything more than a response to the cold. Certainly, it was not my intuition warning me that things were about to go catawampus, or would that be dogawampus?

Chapter 4

"I don't see why I have to go," Viv said. "It's not as if I'm entering a dog in the show."

"No," I agreed. "But Freddy is wearing your hats and having you there might give him the profile boost Aunt Betty needs. And besides, given the threat to Freddy, we need all eyes available."

"If I'd known a public appearance was involved, I would have charged Aunt Betty more for the hats," she said.

"You made them for free," I said.

"Exactly."

We were walking toward Notting Hill Gate, to catch the train that would take us to Finchley Park, where the cocktail party and the dog show were being held. It was just on the other side of Kensington, in a slightly posher neighborhood than ours—okay, a vastly more posh neighborhood, but why quibble?

It was a cocktail party so we were in our favorite minidresses under our thick wool coats. Mine was a royal blue number that fit at the hips and flared at the knees. Viv had insisted I wear a matching blue cocktail hat with an ostrich feather that curled around the back of my head. Fabulous! Viv was outfitted in red, a deep blue–toned scarlet red that she enhanced by wearing a matching fascinator with an explosion of tulle and shimmering beads coming out of it. Her lipstick was on point in the same shade of red as well. Judging by the heads that swiveled in her direction as she strode onto the train, she was killing it.

Even in the bright blue dress, I felt thrust into the shadows next to Viv. When I was younger, I would have envied her extraordinary beauty, but now that I was older, and wiser, I wouldn't change a thing. Not being a knockout, I had learned to get by on my personality, and I knew that was ultimately what had turned Harrison's head my way.

He'd crushed on me when we were kids because of my overt friendliness, and when we'd reconnected as adults, that was what brought him back to me. If I had grown up looking like Viv, tousled long blond hair and delicate features, I most likely never would have developed my essential people skills, which would have been tragic. Because unlike Viv, who was an artist at heart with a marketable skill set as a milliner, I am hopeless in the creative arts. I simply do not have the imagination or the attention span for that sort of thing. Managing people is my gift and I love it.

Viv cleared a path onto the train and two men jumped out of their seats to offer them to her. She nodded her thanks and we took their seats with our backs to the windows as the train shot through the tunnels of the Underground.

"Who knows," I said. "Maybe we'll win over Liza Stanhope and she'll come to our shop for her next hat."

Viv shrugged. It was clear she could not care less. This was a part of her artist charm. She didn't give a flip who bought her hats. She was all about the creation. The forms, the fabric, the shape, the embellishments, these were the things that twirled through her head in a constant kaleidoscope. She had no use for the people who bought her hats. That was my job. To keep up the publicity, the public awareness and the fawning over our clients. Good thing I liked that sort of thing. I am an excellent hat ambassador, if I do say so myself.

Weirdly, I hadn't started out as the manager of our millinery empire—okay it's one shop but a girl can dream, can't she? My arrival in London had actually begun on the heels of my life's greatest humiliation, because you can never really succeed until you have failed spectacularly, or at least that's what I like to tell myself.

About three years ago, I was working for a resort hotel in Tampa, Florida, using my hospitality degree to its maximum potential as a manager. I was also dating the owner of the hotel. It was a glorious relationship, or so I thought. Because while I was under the impression that my beau was divorcing his wife and planning to make me his missus, he was contentedly married and considered me his side bit. How did I find out? Well, I inadvertently crashed the extravagant fifth-year wedding anniversary party he planned for her and ended up fastballing anniversary cake at him, which unbeknownst to me had a seventy-five-thousand-dollar diamond necklace in it. Oops.

Naturally, these being the times we live in, someone got video of the episode and I went viral, dubbed as the party crasher. I essentially had to flee the country to get away from the bright hot spotlight of the paparazzi. Viv reached out to me and sent me a one-way ticket to London, insisting that I take up my half of the hat shop our grandmother Mim had left to us when she passed. I agreed and the rest, as they say, is history.

We jostled along on the train. People got on and got off. Viv acquired more looks and stares of appreciation, and I enjoyed watching her completely ignore them all. Men did some pretty amazing things to get her attention. There was one man who was so impressed with his own bum, he made sure to stand so it was right in her face. Viv turned to me with a look of disgust.

"Really?" She didn't bother to lower her voice when she gestured to the empty air around us and asked, "Does he not see all of the available space?"

"I think he's trying to impress you with his glutes," I said.

She frowned. Then she took her umbrella out of her lap and pointed it right at his behind. "Well, I'm not impressed and he's in for a hell of a poke if he leans back."

The man, clearly eavesdropping, glanced over his shoulder. When he noticed the business end of Viv's umbrella pointed at his posterior, he let out a small yelp and moved away.

You'd think the other men in our car would get the idea. Nope. Into the vacuum left by the bum guy stepped a charmer who locked in on Viv and asked, "Can I sit in your lap because my knees are suddenly weak?"

Viv didn't deign to answer him. She just frowned and made a shooing motion with her hands. With an indignant huff and a softly muttered insult, he gave up and moved away.

"Honestly," Viv said. "Are there no decent single men in the entire city of London?"

I looked at her. To meddle or not to meddle, this was the question.

"What about Alistair?" I asked.

"No."

"What do you mean, 'no'?" I asked. "He's the whole package. Hot, employed, brilliant and he adores you."

Truly, it boggled how she could turn up her nose at the man.

"He is relationship material," she said. "I am not looking for a relationship."

I glanced around the train car to see if the men were about to attack. "Say that a little louder, why don't you?"

She waved a hand dismissively.

"Viv, what's wrong with a relationship?" I asked.

"I'm not very good at them," she said.

"Just because your husband—"

"Don't talk about him," she said. "I can't bear it."

I studied her face. Despite her eccentric artistic temperament, Viv's emotions ran close to the surface and the pain on her face was genuine. She'd had a rough patch in the relationship department, no doubt, but that was no reason to shut down a guy who was one in a million, was it?

"But Alistair—"

"Asked me out last night after the rugby match, and I said no," she said. "So, that's dusted and done. Let's move on."

She brushed off the lower half of her wool coat even though there was nothing there and turned away from me, indicating that this conversation was over. Honestly, it was as if she didn't even know me! There was no way I was going to let it go. Men like Alistair were rare, like super rare, up there with spotting a unicorn or a yeti. I would be failing in my cousinly obligation of not letting her screw up her life if I just let it go.

That being said, I know Viv, and when she decides she isn't going to listen, there is no making her hear what you have to say. No, changing her opinion about Alistair had to be done in a sneaky underhanded covert-op sort of way, which meant I absolutely needed a consult with my besties, Nick and Andre, to determine how best to go about changing Viv's mind.

Before I could get a good brood about it going, our stop came up. When the train slowed and the doors whooshed open, we hurried out. Standing on the platform, I glanced up to get my bearings but Viv was already off and moving through the crowd. Thank goodness she was in red, so I could follow her like a cat tracking a laser.

She crossed the platform and headed through a door that took us to another waiting area. I glanced up and read the digital display sign that showed the arrival time for the next train was in two minutes. I stood beside Viv, pulling my own coat more tightly about me. February in London was damp and chilly—oh, who was I kidding? Pretty much every month in London was damp and chilly, but February was particularly rude about it.

The train arrived and this time we went only two stops before hopping out and climbing the stairs to the neighborhood above. The wind swept down the street and we both clapped a hand onto our hats to hold them in place.

"Finchley Park, right?" Viv asked.

"Yes." I nodded.

She turned on her spiky heel and strode toward a small green at the end of the street. When we arrived, I saw the park was bigger than it appeared. It was completely fenced in with thick hedges inside wrought iron with an imposing gate. At one side of the park was a large redbrick building where events were held, in this case where the dog show would take place. PAWS had signs all over the side of the building, advertising the show.

Viv pulled the gate and held it open for me. I paused, waiting for her to shut the gate behind her so that we could stroll up the walkway together. As we approached, a door opened in the building in front of us and out through the wooden door shot a white dog with brown spots, who was wearing a frilly little pink dress with sparkles on it. Despite the skirt, she hit the grass like a firecracker was attached to her backside and she flattened herself low to the ground as she ran in big loops around the yard, her tiny legs eating up the turf as she sped by.

"Coco!" a woman called to the small dog. The woman was dressed in a deep purple coat with a jaunty scarf tied around her neck. She had short, silver hair which was pushed back from her face by a pair of eyeglasses that perched on her head like a hairband. "Coco!" she cried again. The dog paid her absolutely no mind. The woman sighed and turned to us.

"I could have had a cat," she said. "Or a fish. But no, I picked her."

I laughed and glanced at the dog, who wore the happiest expression I'd ever seen. "True, but you'd never get a cat in a dress."

"Or a fish," Viv said.

"Fair point," the woman agreed. The dog, done with running, came back and collapsed at her feet.

"I'm Scarlett and this is my cousin, Viv. Do you know if the PAWS cocktail party is in there?"

"Yes, it is," she said. "I'm Sue, by the way, and this is Coco."

"Nice dress," Viv said. She pointed to Coco's outfit. Sue scooped the dog up into her arms and Coco propped her chin on her shoulder and blinked at us, the picture of innocence.

"Do you think so?" Sue asked. "I was thinking I should have put her in her blue dress, but pink just seemed so cheerful, plus it's her favorite. Of course, I don't suppose it matters since Betty Wentworth and her dog, Freddy, are in matching hats. Matching bowler hats, no less, can you believe it? Who could compete with that?"

"No one. Since I'm the milliner who made them, yes, I have to say that," Viv said.

"Oh, really?" Sue asked. Her delicate eyebrows rose over her pretty hazel eyes. "Are you looking for any more clients? Coco does love her hats."

Viv glanced from Sue to Coco with a thoughtful look. "Maybe. Stop by our shop, Mim's Whims in Notting Hill, and we'll talk." She strode into the party without another word, leaving Sue staring after her in bemusement.

"Yes, she's like that with everyone," I said. "Personally, I'd love to see Coco in a pink hat to match her dress." I reached into my clutch purse and found a card. "Stop by anytime."

"Why, thank you," Sue said. "I think I will."

I turned and followed Viv into the party, leaving Sue to discuss the merits of a hat with her dog. I had a feeling we'd be seeing them sooner rather than later.

The party was everything a dog cocktail party should be. There were several food stations, some specifically for the dogs in attendance, serving dog-friendly appetizers. There were also several self-filtering water stations.

Just inside the door there was a coat check where Viv and I unloaded our heavy wool coats. I'd been a little afraid we'd be overdressed but we were on point. People were dressed to impress and, in my opinion at least, the outfits worked. This was obviously a high-society event, as diamonds sparkled, shoes gleamed, suits ranged from black to blue to one sassy burgundy number. Viv and I were not the only two women in hats. In fact, hats were most definitely in the majority and everywhere I looked there were dogs. It was glorious!

Tall dogs, short dogs, pudgy dogs, slim dogs, old dogs, young dogs, it was a canine cornucopia. Most of the dogs were leashed and well behaved, sitting or standing beside their person. I could see now why Coco had likely been taken outside to run her wiggles out. Unruly behavior was definitely frowned upon at the party.

"It smells like dog in here," Viv said. She wrinkled her nose. "I need a drink. How about you?"

"Yes, please," I said. I followed her, pulling my phone out of my bag to see if Harry had sent me a text. There was nothing. The room was so thick with people and dogs; I couldn't spot him or Aunt Betty anywhere. For that matter, I didn't see Andre or Nick either. I wondered if they had Andre set up someplace specific to take pictures of the dogs or if he was wandering around the room with his camera. I looked up and scanned the crowd.

No sign of him. Darn. A skittish whippet leaned against my leg while I sent a quick text to Harry and then another to Andre. I gently disengaged the dog with a smile at her person and found Viv was already at the bar, frowning at a list of cocktails.

"Okay, it looks like our choices are of the canine variety," she said. "Personally, I'm going to have the Greyhound—and you?"

I blinked and took the list she handed me. It was a list of cocktails all named after dogs, such as the Salty Chihuahua, the Frosty French Bulldog, and the Pomegranate Pomeranian. I smiled at Viv, but she didn't look amused.

"Sorry, I'll have the Pink Poodle, please," I said. It was vanilla vodka, lemon-lime soda and a splash of grenadine. Yum.

Viv was just handing me my drink—it was in a large martini glass with a circular slice of lime impaled on the edge—when we heard a commotion on the far side of the room. I'm not sure why but my intuition told me that our people were involved.

"Let's go," I said to Viv. She grabbed her drink, not nearly as pretty as mine, and followed me as I used my elbow to snowplow through the crowd. We crossed the massive high-ceilinged room until we reached the opposite entrance.

The voices got louder and I turned a corner and found Aunt Betty, standing with Freddy, waving her finger in the face of a man who looked like he wanted to strangle her. He was tall and thin, dressed in a black suit that was clearly bespoke, on his wrist gleamed a gold Rolex and on his hand sparkled a ring with a diamond the size of my head. Truly, the guy was wearing enough bling to rival a rapper. His thick head of white hair was unruly in a product-infused way. He was obviously a very wealthy man and there was no dog at his side so I assumed he was one of the sponsors of the PAWS dog show.

People all around them were listening in, but Betty was oblivious, continuing her tirade regardless of the audience. She'd even pushed back her charcoal gray bowler with the exquisite aqua ribbon stitched around the outer edge of the brim, which matched the one Freddy was wearing, so she could give the man her full glare.

"You have to have a full investigation into the process," Aunt Betty was saying. "A quality control measure is clearly lacking somewhere in the chain. You can't ignore it when dogs are made ill by your product—"

"You can repeat your lies as often as you want," the man snapped. "That doesn't make them true."

"How dare you! I am not lying," Aunt Betty protested. In one hand she had Freddy's leash and in the other a drink, which was tall and clear but stuffed with limes.

"I can assure you that everything you have said thus far is wrong," the man said, bristling. If he'd been a dog the hair on his scruff would have stood up. Freddy must not have liked his tone because I noticed his ears went back and his fur was beginning to rise. "And if it is wrong then it is a lie."

"My dog was sick, I tell you," Aunt Betty said. "Your

dog food made Freddy violently ill. I had to throw it all out. A year's worth!"

"That was stupidly shortsighted on your part," the man snarled. "My dog food is of the highest quality."

I gasped. This had to be Swendson, the sponsor of the show. Oh, God. This was bad, so bad. I scanned the area, looking for Harry. He was supposed to be with her. Where was he? He needed to do some damage control on his aunt.

"It's poison, that's what it is," Aunt Betty said. She stiffened her spine and glared at him. "You'd better be careful; some dog owner is liable to do unto you as you've done unto their dog."

"Are you threatening me? With poison?"

I noticed several people were openly watching the exchange with mouths agape and eyes wide. One of them was even filming it with their phone. Oh, no.

"I'd say it's more of a promise," Aunt Betty snarled.

"I'm sorry, Ma'am, what was your name again?" Swendson asked. His look was calculating and I knew he was going to use his sponsorship power to check her. This wasn't going to go well for Aunt Betty or Freddy.

"Time to jump in," I said to Viv. I gave her a nudge forward, harder than I should have, I suppose, as she careened forward and bumped hips with Swendson, breaking his stare-off with Aunt Betty.

"Hey, there you are," I said. I looped my arm through Aunt Betty's and tugged. "Harry is looking for you. Let's go!"

"Wait, I'm not finished yet," she said. She turned back to Swendson, whose attention was on Viv and, like most men did when she crossed their path, he stared at her with a slightly slack-jawed look of disbelief. "It is imperative, Mr. Swend—"

He tore his gaze away from Viv and focused on Aunt Betty. I could see the veins in his neck begin to throb. Uh-oh.

"Harry! Yoo-hoo!" I shouted over Aunt Betty, trying to lure Harry in from wherever he was. "Over here!"

"Hello," Viv said. She placed her hand on Swendson's arm. "I'm Vivian." She looked at Mr. Swendson from under her eyelashes. He forgot about Aunt Betty.

"Ginger, there you are!" Harry pushed through the crowd. Nick and Andre were right behind him. Unfortunately, this brought Mr. Swendson back around, too.

"Hey, there, Freddy old chap," Nick said. "Aunt Betty, where did you go? We were supposed to stay together to protect Freddy."

I saw Mr. Swendson's eyes go from Aunt Betty to Freddy. Damn it, even if he didn't know Aunt Betty's name, now he knew her dog's. I was willing to bet he could deduce who Aunt Betty was from that. If he complained, it could make the judging very difficult for Freddy. Viv's hats or no, the competition could be lost before it even began.

"You mean Cedric," I said. I tried to project my voice over the rumble of the crowd toward Mr. Swendson. "That dog's name is Cedric."

My friends all looked at me as if I were mental. Why was no one playing along? Clearly, if I had renamed the dog, I had done it for a reason.

"Scarlett, how many of those bevvies have you had?" Andre asked with a half smile. "Freddy is his name; it always has been."

Mr. Swendson's eyes narrowed. He removed Viv's hand from his arm, glared at Aunt Betty and stalked away from our rambunctious group without another word. Damn it.

Chapter 5

"What was that all about?" Harry asked me. With one eyebrow raised in inquiry he glanced from Mr. Swendson's retreating back to me.

"That was Mr. Swendson," I said. "Of Swendson's Dog Food."

Harry's head snapped in the direction of the man in the sharp suit, and his mouth formed a small O.

"Did Aunt Betty . . . ?"

"Yes," I said. "With a finger in his face and everything."

"Oh, no."

"I tried to distract him by throwing Viv in his line of sight but Aunt Betty was not to be deterred."

"Thus, the new name Cedric," he said. A smile lifted

the corners of his mouth and I basked in the glow of his amused affection. "Nice try, Ginger."

I shrugged. "For all the good it did," I said. Then I downed the Pink Poodle in one big gulp.

"Aunt Betty." Harry turned to his aunt. "I thought we talked about not confronting Mr. Swendson, knowing that it might adversely affect Freddy's chances at winning best in show."

"Pff." Aunt Betty puffed out a breath. Then she lifted her own glass to her lips. She was about to upend the contents when Nick deftly lifted the glass out of her hands. She protested but he raised it to his nose and gave it a sniff.

"Gin," he said. "A double, if I'm not mistaken."

"It was to settle my nerves," Aunt Betty said. "You know, in case the bad person who left the note showed up."

"How many?" Harry asked.

"Nerves?" Aunt Betty asked. "Well, quite a few, I'd say."

"That's not what I meant, Aunt B, and you know it." Harrison kept his gaze steady and Aunt Betty tipped her nose up and turned away.

"I'm not a child, Harrison Wentworth," she said. "And I would appreciate it if you didn't treat me as one."

Her indignation, while well played, didn't move Harry in the least.

"Aunt Betty, I think it would be best if you and Freddy called it a night," he said. "There's just too many people to keep track of and I don't like the risk that someone could slip something to Freddy without us seeing. Plus, Swendson didn't look pleased and if he points you out to the

BURIED TO THE BRIM

PAWS chairpersons, you might find yourselves bounced from the competition."

Aunt Betty blinked. "But we already paid. They can't do that."

"Trust me, when money talks—" he began but Nick interrupted him.

"Bulldogs walk."

We all looked at him. "What? It's true."

Viv, who had finished her drink as well, reached out and straightened Aunt Betty's bowler.

"I'm getting ready to leave, too," Viv said. "I'll walk out with you."

"Me, too," I said.

"Well, I have to take more pictures," Andre said. He held up his camera and then stepped back to take a few candid shots of Aunt Betty and Freddy.

"And I have a commitment to drink more at the bar," Nick said. He and Andre waved as they walked back into the crowd.

"I will escort you all home," Harrison said. "I have my car and can give everyone a lift."

"Oh, that's sweet of you," Aunt Betty said. She patted his arm and handed him Freddy's leash. "Be a dear and carry Freddy, won't you? He's tired from the long day."

Harry gave me a wry glance and I tucked my laugh into my cheek. When he bent down and picked up Freddy, the happy corgi took advantage and licked Harry's face. This time I laughed out loud.

Viv and Aunt Betty walked ahead, leading the way

through the crowd, and I fell in beside Harrison. He carried Freddy, who was a sturdy little fellow, as if he weighed nothing at all.

"What say we drop everyone off and you come back to my place?" Harry asked.

Of course I was going to say yes, duh, but I liked to keep Harry on his toes.

"I don't know," I said. "I have to sort my socks tonight."

"I have gelato in the freezer," he countered.

"Tempting, but I've been thinking I need to learn to cook and tonight is the night."

"All right, I'll just have to catch up on the latest episode of *Bodyguard* by myself." He adjusted Freddy in his arms and heaved a sigh.

"Playing the Richard Madden card is dirty pool."

A slow grin spread across his lips. "So, you're in?"

"Natch," I said. Then I grinned at him and said, "Actually, I was in all along. I just wanted you to work for it a bit."

"One of the many reasons I love you," he said. Then he kissed me and we slipped out the door that Viv held open for us and into the night.

I arrived home from Harry's bright and early. The shop wouldn't open for a few hours but Viv and Fee were already in the workroom. I could hear the radio broadcasting BBC 2—we all enjoyed the human-interest aspect to the reporting—and I tried to slink to the stairs before Viv or Fee saw me.

I glanced across the shop at my grandmother's favorite cabinet. It was an old wooden piece with a bird, I called him Ferd, carved across the top with wings open and head pointed down. He had freaked me out when I was a kid. In truth, he still gave me the shivers. I swear, he watched everything that was going on, but I had begun to talk to him when I first moved back and the habit had stuck. I held my finger up to my lips in a *shh* gesture. Ferd said nothing, so I figured we understood each other.

"G'mornin', Scarlett," Viv called from the back. "Have a nice night with Harry?"

I slumped over, glaring at Ferd as if it were his fault. Hoping that Viv had a pot of coffee or tea going, I trudged to the workroom. I knew I looked a wreck with no makeup and a scorching case of postshower, air-dried hair, but at least I kept some of my clothes over at Harry's so I had a fresh outfit on and wasn't arriving in last night's cocktail dress. That would be entirely too walk-of-shame-ish.

"Cup of coffee?" Fee asked me as I entered the room.

"Yes, please." I nodded. All was forgiven.

I dumped my purse on the table and slid onto one of the short stools that were scattered around the steel-topped worktable where Viv sat. She was attaching a large rosette in a pale pink silk onto a delicate straw hat of the same color. Ribbons had already been fastened and the rosette sat atop the bows. I knew that this particular hat was being made in a variety of spring colors for the Easter crowd. I also knew these hats would go for five hundred and twenty-five pounds each or, at the current exchange rate, six hundred eighty-one dollars American. For. A. Hat. It boggles, doesn't it?

Fee poured me a cup of coffee from the carafe on the counter and slid it across the table to me along with a spoon. Then she delivered the cream and sugar containers. I do love her so.

I had slept late at Harry's and was still fuzzy, as I'd raced out of his apartment without any magic bean or leaf juice. Harry drank tea in the morning, which was all right but it just lacked the punch to the face that coffee offered. I had yet to bring him over to the dark side of java, but I had cracked Fee and Viv, so I knew it was just a matter of time.

"Did Harrison come with you?" Viv asked. "I was hoping he'd feel like cooking us breakfast."

"No, he hurried off to rugby practice," I said. "We'll have to make do with cereal."

None of us could cook. Technically, I suppose we could if we wanted to but so far none of us were inclined to learn.

"I'm so tired of cereal." Viv pouted. "I clearly need a spouse."

It was on the tip of my tongue to point out that Alistair probably loved to cook, but given how snappy she'd been about it before, I decided not to say anything.

"Or a live-in cook," Fee suggested. "Much less annoying than a spouse, yeah?"

Viv let go of her hat and tapped her lips with her index

finger. "You might be onto something. Especially when Scarlett moves out to live with her hubby."

"Or you could date someone, say a hot, rugby-attorney-type someone," I said. Okay, my filter is clearly faulty, and I really didn't mean to say that out loud. I swear.

"Are you talking about Alistair?" Fee asked. "He was spectacular on the pitch, wasn't he?"

"Yes, he was," I said.

Viv shrugged and looked back down at her hat. She was obviously ignoring my suggestion. So annoying.

Fee was fiddling with the velvet trim on the brim of the hat she was working on. It was another spring creation. The white straw hat had been shaped into a fedora style and then she'd attached a lavender velvet ribbon around the brim, which complimented the spray of multihued feathers that decorated the crown. It really was spectacular and I marveled at how her talents had developed in the years she'd been Viv's apprentice and now assistant.

"So, are you not interested in Alistair?" Fee asked. She gave Viv a side-eye as if she didn't want to look her directly in the eyes when she asked.

I sipped my coffee and stared over the rim of the mug at the two of them. Was Fee interested in Alistair? What would Viv make of that? Oh, dear, this could get seriously complicated.

"Why do you ask?" Viv glanced at Fee.

"No reason, just . . ." Fee's voice trailed off and I found

myself leaning forward to hear what she had to say. *Just what? Don't leave me hanging like this!*

Viv frowned. Fee looked back down at her hat. "No reason. He's just a brilliant rugby player, is all."

She picked up her hat and turned away from us as she went to store it on a stand on the far wall where they kept all of their hats in various states of doneness. Viv looked at me and she blinked and then widened her eyes. When I shrugged, she pointed at Fee and mouthed the name *Alistair* and then held her hands up in a *what does this mean?* gesture.

I glanced at Fee, who was retrieving her next project, a pretty cap with netting, both of which were dyed the color of grass in spring. I quickly shook my head at Viv to indicate I had no idea. Was Fee interested in Alistair? It certainly sounded like it and given that Viv had been ignoring Alistair for the better part of a year, I thought Fee should go for it, but I didn't say this out loud.

"Will Harrison be—" Viv began but my phone sounded from my bag, cutting her off. I pulled the phone out of the side compartment and glanced at the screen. It was Harry.

"Speak of the devil," I said. I held up my phone and Viv waved her hand at me, indicating I should answer. "Hi, Harry, how goes practice?"

"I've got a situation, Ginger. Can I borrow you from the shop for a bit?"

I felt the blood rush out of my head. I braced myself against the table. "Are you hurt?"

"No, nothing like that," he said. "It's Aunt Betty."

"Aunt Betty?" I asked.

"Yes, she's at the dog show," he said. "They're refusing to let her in."

"What?" I gasped. "Why?"

"I'm betting it has something to do with how she tore into Swendson last night," he said.

"Oh, no," I said.

"I'm too far away to get to her, but she called me and she's distraught," he said. "Is there any way you can head over there and keep her company until I can get there? I want to talk to someone before she throws in the towel on Freddy's chance to be best in show."

"I'm on my way," I said. I ended the call and rose to my feet, downing my hot coffee. "We have a situation. Aunt Betty is at the dog show and they are refusing to let her in. I'm going over to sit with her until Harry gets there."

"What?" Viv snapped. "But she has hats."

I had to fight my smile. With Viv it would always come down to the hats.

"Care to come with me?" I asked. "You can advocate for the hats."

Viv picked up her work in progress and placed it on a blank mannequin's head. She turned to Fee and asked, "Can you handle the shop for a bit on your own?"

"Of course," she said. "Go rescue Aunt Betty."

The dog show was at the same place the cocktail party had been so Viv and I took the same route on the Tube. It

67

was quicker today with less of a rush-hour crush. Halfway there, I realized I hadn't eaten breakfast and my stomach made its unhappiness known with a righteous grumble that was thankfully drowned out by the sound of the train.

When we approached the big brick building, we found the crowd was just as thick today but there was an air of anticipation that was palpable. Dogs and their handlers were everywhere and, looking for Aunt Betty, I scanned the crowd. She was so petite; it was impossible to see her in the throng of people.

"Over there," Viv said. She pointed toward a massive registration table.

It was festooned with a big banner that had the PAWS logo on it. Tucked off to the side in the corner was Aunt Betty with Freddy at her side. They wore matching light brown trilby hats with a dashing green ribbon around the crown and a matching one on the edge of the brim. They looked very smart and had their hats tipped at the same jaunty angle. Fun fact: historically when a woman's hat is worn at an angle it always tilts to the right to accommodate her escort, a man, who would walk on her left between her and the street traffic.

Unfortunately, even the hat couldn't hide the look of despair on Aunt Betty's face. She looked so tiny and sad and rejected, like a kid looking for a friend on the playground, that I felt my temper heat. What had they done to her?

I began to stride forward and Viv fell in beside me. I imagined we looked like Beyoncé and Kelly Rowland in a GIF taken from one of their Destiny's Child music videos, strutting forward and looking like we were about to kick some serious tail. I certainly felt like it. No one put Aunt Betty and Freddy in a corner.

"Aunt Betty!" I climbed the short steps up to the dais and stopped in front of her. "What's happening?"

"Oh, Scarlett." Aunt Betty reached out her free hand and grabbed mine as if she needed me to give her strength. "They've kicked me and Freddy out of the show. Even though I already registered and paid, they said they can't find my paperwork and that's that. They won't even let me reregister, as if I'd be willing to pay that exorbitant fee twice."

"Did they actually look for your paperwork?" Viv asked.

Aunt Betty turned to her and smiled, obviously grateful to have our support, and then shook her head, her smile fading. "No. The woman over there with the cowlick and the scowl flipped through some papers and said she couldn't find it. I don't think she really tried."

"Well, she will this time," I said.

I am a people pleaser, this is true, unless you are in a position of service and you refuse to serve. Then I'm going to call you out and badger you until I get what I want. I approached the woman with the short gray hair that did indeed have a cowlick that made it stick up. She smiled at me in greeting until she noticed Aunt Betty beside me and then she scowled.

"May I help you?" she asked.

"Yes, we are looking for our entrance papers," I said. "The name is Betty Wentworth and the canine is Freddy."

"I already looked. We don't have those names." Her chin jutted out.

"Well, since the registration fee has been paid, I suggest you quickly make some new papers," I said.

"Prove it," the woman said. She crossed her arms over her chest, looking very pleased with herself.

I silently prayed that Betty had brought a receipt with her and then I turned to her with a smile and said, "Any chance you have . . . ?"

Betty held up a receipt. I almost hugged her. Viv grinned, and I took the paper and turned back to the surly gal.

"You were saying?" I asked. I slapped the receipt down in front of her.

Her lips twisted into a little puckered-up moue of displeasure. This should not have given me as much satisfaction as it did. But it did.

"Ms. Stanhope, we have a situation," the woman said. She rose from her seat and turned away from us to address a woman who was standing several feet back behind the registration table.

Stanhope. This must be the socialite Liza Stanhope, who had been there when Aunt Betty had registered, the one who had said a corgi would never win. I studied her.

She was tall and thin, and everything about her seemed pointy. Her nose, her chin, the wicked narrow tips of her shoes. I was betting her elbows and knees could be lethal if she put in some effort.

She approached us, with her reading glasses perched on the end of her nose. Her face looked as if it had been stretched and lifted until it maintained a glossy sheen that resembled plastic. It was not a good look. Her hair was dyed an inky shade of black and was styled in waves that should have softened her features but didn't. Large black pearls adorned her ears and a string of the same circled her throat. She wore a white blouse with the collar up, framing her face, over a pin-striped skirt in browns and greens with a wide brown leather belt.

She was holding a pen in one hand, and her fingernails resembled red talons. She looked as if she would poke out the eye of anyone she was displeased with and I feared that someone was going to be me.

"What situation?" Ms. Stanhope asked. Her voice was low and soft and yet we could still hear her over the crowd. The hair on the back of my neck began to prickle.

"Hello, Liza," Aunt Betty said, stepping out from behind me.

Liza Stanhope's eyebrows lifted up on her forehead. "Betty."

"Apparently, there's been a mix-up with my registration," Betty said.

"No, there hasn't," Liza said.

The two women watched each other and I glanced between them, back and forth, waiting to see who would make the next move.

"No?" Betty asked. She gestured to her receipt. "Then why do I have a receipt for payment and yet am not registered to be in the dog show?"

"Your registration has been misplaced, there's no mix-up," Liza said.

I felt myself sag with relief. I glanced at Viv and gave her a relieved smile. This was good, we were going to be able to figure this out and get Aunt Betty and Freddy into the dog show. Harry would be so relieved. Heck, I was so relieved. Viv didn't return my smile. Instead, her head tilted to the side as she studied Liza Stanhope as if expecting more. She wasn't wrong.

"And your registration is going to keep getting misplaced," Liza said. Her gaze on Betty never wavered.

Uh-oh!

"I'm sorry," I said. "I don't quite understand."

Liza didn't bother to acknowledge me.

"You can't do that," Aunt Betty huffed. "You were right there when I filled out my paperwork. I gave it to you—"

Liza smiled. It was a slow shift of her lips, like a poisonous vine unfurling in the sunlight. "Huh, I have no recollection of that. How odd. I guess this is what happens when you threaten to poison our main sponsor in a drunken tirade."

"Ah!" Aunt Betty gasped. "I was not drunk and it wasn't a tirade. I was merely informing Mr. Swendson about some quality control concerns I had with his dog food."

Like me and Viv, Freddy was glancing between the two women as if it was a volleyball match. He was seated at Aunt Betty's feet, looking adorably confused. I reached down and patted his head. Viv glanced from Freddy to Liza.

"You almost lost us our biggest sponsor," Liza snapped. "Now you are out of the show and so is your mongrel."

"That was completely uncalled for," Aunt Betty seethed. I really thought she was going to clap her hands over Freddy's ears. "Say what you want about me, but leave Freddy out of it."

"He's with you," Liza snarled. "So you bet I'll leave him out. I'll leave him out of the dog show for good."

I was a little afraid the two women were going to come to blows. I glanced behind me to see if Viv thought the same and, if so, how did she think we should get Aunt Betty out of here before the whole situation got out of control. She wasn't there.

I scanned the crowd of dogs and their people behind us. I didn't see Viv anywhere. How could she have wandered off *now*? Wasn't that just like her? Always disappearing when things were getting dicey. I don't mean to complain but, honestly, I was so tired of having to figure everything out by myself. It was just exhausting.

"You can't do this," I said to Liza Stanhope. "She has a receipt. She paid. You need to let her compete."

"Who are you?" Liza asked. She starred at me over the tops of her reading glasses.

"Scarlett Parker," I said. "I'm a friend."

"Well, Scarlett, if you're such a good friend, you should have stopped her from accosting Mr. Swendson last night. He's threatened to pull his sponsorship of the dog show if she's in it," Liza snapped. She looked in irritation at Aunt Betty. "What were you thinking? Do you have any idea how much money is at stake if he pulls his sponsorship?"

"And if his dog food makes dogs sick?" Aunt Betty countered. "That's okay? We're supposed to be helping dogs, not harming them."

"What seems to be the trouble, Liza?" The woman who joined us was sturdily built and dressed in jeans, hiking boots and a hand-knit sweater. She had ruddy cheeks and her white hair was tousled as if she'd just stepped inside after striding across a moor in the wilds of Yorkshire.

"It's nothing, Mary," Liza said. Her voice was tight.

"It doesn't sound like nothing," Mary said. Her voice was mild but I sensed a note of authority behind it. Liza must have heard it, too.

"It's just a registration mix-up. We'll take care of it," Liza said.

It hit me then that Mary must be Mary Swendson, Gerry Swendson's sister and co-owner of the dog food empire. I thought it was interesting that Liza didn't want to out Aunt Betty as the woman who had accosted Gerry the night before. I wondered why. In true administrative style, Liza just wanted to pretend nothing had happened and make it go away. Pro tip: that never works.

"Here you are," Viv said. She popped up on the other

side of Aunt Betty and Freddy. She held a packet of papers in one hand, a badge on a lanyard in the other. "Freddy is entered in the dog show—"

"What?" Liza Stanhope gasped.

Viv looped a lanyard around my neck. "There now. You and Freddy are all set."

"Excuse me?" I asked. I looked from the badge to Viv.

She looked from me to Aunt Betty. "Given the circumstances, I think it's best that someone unknown enters with Freddy."

"And you chose me?" I asked.

"You're the one who wants a dog," she said.

"Who did this?" Liza fumed. "How dare they? I'll have their jobs."

"Given that they're volunteers, that seems rather counterproductive, doesn't it?" Mary asked. "And what's wrong with this Freddy that you disapprove of him so?"

Liza's upper lip curled up on one side, and I thought I heard her growl. "Nothing."

Mary glanced over the table at Freddy, who was still sitting like a little gentleman. "Hello, there," she said to him. "You were in the show last year, weren't you?"

I wondered if she expected him to answer.

"Yes, he was," Aunt Betty said. "Last year and the two years prior as well."

Mary smiled at her. "Well, I hope this is his year, then."

"Thank you," Aunt Betty said. "I do, too. He's entered

with Scarlett this year, so maybe that will change his luck."

I felt my insides twist with nerves. I was so out of my depth; I was surprised I didn't drown on dry land.

"You look nervous," Mary said. Her voice was kind.

"A little," I admitted.

"Dogs are pack animals. Freddy will follow your lead so long as you establish your dominance," she said.

"Dominance?" My voice squeaked. How mortifying.

"You need to be his alpha," she explained. "The dog hierarchy is alpha, beta and omega, with the alpha the dominant above all others, the beta subservient only to the alpha, and the omega subservient to everyone. With you and Freddy, you need to be his alpha so he can be your beta."

I glanced down at Freddy. His pointy ears had swiveled while he listened and I wondered what he made of this. His tongue hung out the side of his mouth and he looked like he wanted to please. Maybe this would work.

"I'll see what I can do," I said.

"Good luck."

Mary left us and I noticed Liza's face had turned a mottled shade of red. She looked like she was about to have security called to escort us out of the building.

"So glad this is sorted," Viv said. She gestured to the exit. "Shall we?"

"This isn't over, Wentworth," Liza called after Aunt Betty.

Aunt Betty paused and gave her a haughty stare and

said, "Of course it isn't. It won't be over until my Freddy has won."

Then she turned back around and gestured for Viv and me to fall in behind her and Freddy, which we did. Talk about your natural alpha. If they expected me to be able to do that, we were so screwed.

Chapter 6

"But I don't know squat about dog shows," I protested.

"Aunt Betty can coach you," Viv said. "Now I'm done with this sea of humanity and canines. We have our schedule. Let's go."

I glanced at Aunt Betty. "Is this okay with you? I don't want to take your place, especially if it will upset Freddy."

She glanced over her shoulder at Liza Stanhope, who stood staring after us, looking like she was going to have a screaming hissy fit.

"Yes, I think you will do nicely," Aunt Betty said. She took off her hat and plopped it on my head, then she tipped her nose up in the air and turned on her heel. I followed after her, trying to look more confident than I felt.

Harry met us outside the hall. Despite the chilly late-February temperature, he was still in his practice clothes, baggy shorts, a sweat-stained T-shirt, over which he wore a gray hooded sweatshirt. His hair was mussed and he had dirt on his knees. He looked fantastic and I had the sudden urge to take a bite out of him like he was an apple.

Viv jostled me with an elbow to my side. "Scarlett, are you all right? You have a weird look on your face."

"Huh? Me?" I blinked. "Yeah, sure, I'm fine, good, great."

Harry's left eyebrow cranked up on his forehead as he studied my face. "What's going on, Ginger?"

I took the opportunity to slip my arm around him and hug him to my side. Then I held up my lanyard. "Apparently, Freddy and I are competing in the dog show."

"What?" He hugged me back while studying my fancy credentials as if he was waiting for the punch line.

"I've been banned from the competition," Aunt Betty said with a sniff, making it clear how she felt about the situation. "But Vivian had the brilliant idea to sign up Scarlett in my place. So, we have a lot of work to do. The first competition is the agility test this afternoon and while Freddy can manage this himself, you do need to present him properly."

My stomach twisted and I felt a coating of sweat cover my palms. I did not want to screw this up. How was I supposed to be good to go in a matter of hours?

"Don't worry, love," Harry said. "You've got this."

* * *

It turned out, I did not "got this." We practiced in a nearby park, so Freddy could get used to me giving him commands. The commands were simple, "over," "through," "under" and so forth, but not knowing the course, I had no idea if I was going to give the right command on the right apparatus.

"This isn't going to work," I cried. "Unless I can see the course ahead of time and memorize what command to give when."

"That won't happen," Aunt Betty said. "In fact, I am quite certain Liza will make sure you go first in your division just to make it as difficult as possible for you."

I groaned. I turned to Harry and said, "Help."

He gave me a tender smile and then he cupped my face and said, "You can do this, Ginger, I know you can."

As one, we trooped back to the hall in Finchley Park. When we arrived, the crowd, there to observe the event, had filled the fold-out bleachers that lined the perimeter of the large room. Viv looked for seats, while Aunt Betty and Harry walked me to the corridor that led to the competitors' waiting area.

"We can't go into the waiting area with you," Harry said. "It's reserved for the dogs and their handlers only."

"Oh, okay," I said. My nerves ratcheted up to the breaking point. I wasn't a shy person, not even a little, but I really didn't like the idea that Freddy's success or failure was dependent upon me when I had no idea what I was doing. Plus, there was still the possibility that whoever had threatened to poison Freddy was lurking in the shadows. If anything happened to him, it would be all my fault. Panic made my brain go fuzzy and suddenly I couldn't remember even the simplest of commands. How did I tell him to jump or leap or crawl? Oh, man, it was all gone!

My terror must have been on my face, because Aunt Betty reached over and squeezed my hand. "Just let Freddy lead the way. He knows what to do." Then she bent down and cupped Freddy's face. He stared into her eyes and Betty said something to him that I couldn't hear but I could see Freddy's ears move and his tail wag. It must have been quite the motivational speech.

"We'll see you after the competition," Aunt Betty said to me. She glanced down at Freddy. "Make us proud."

Freddy barked as if promising to do so. Weirdly, this made me feel a smidgeon more confident.

Harry kissed the top of my head, "Go get 'em, Ginger."

"Right," I said.

I straightened my shoulders and pulled the double doors open. I gave my people one brave smile before we stepped inside. The door swung shut behind me and I took a moment to get my bearings.

A PAWS representative checked my credentials and Freddy's at the door. With a nod and a smile of encouragement, she checked her clipboard and said, "Scarlett Parker and Freddy. You're just in time. You're first in the second round of agility tests, which will start"—she paused to check the time on her cell phone—"in thirty minutes. Please wait with the others and we'll call you when it's your turn."

Oh, jeez. It took everything I had not to turn around and run out the door. Locking my knees, I moved forward. I walked down the dark hallway to a large open room at the end of the building. It seemed to me that all of the other dog handlers appeared perfectly at ease, while I was scanning the area for a wastebasket so I could throw up. While I stepped cautiously inside with utter trepidation, Freddy, on the other hand, began to prance as if he fed off the energy of the room.

I took a moment to get the feel of the place. There was definitely a manic energy pulsing. Dogs were being brushed, clipped and perfumed as if they weren't supposed to go and race madly around a bunch of equipment. I felt as if I were walking into a children's beauty pageant. I glanced down at Freddy. He was good-looking, cute as a button, in fact, but could he beat the dogs around us?

There was a white standard poodle with the traditional showy cut that looked as if the only thing missing was a crown perched on its pompadour. It even lifted its snout in disdain as Freddy and I walked by. Then there was a German pointer. He was a beauty, no question, but he was also chasing his own tail in a tight circle and when he stopped he staggered, so not the sharpest tack in the box. Lastly, there was a very handsome Weimaraner. The eyes on this one were intelligent and soulful. I had the sudden urge to hug him, which I was sure would be frowned upon.

JENN McKINLAY

Did my short-legged, friendly companion stand a chance at beating any of these dogs? I was abruptly hit with the fear that his feelings might be hurt. Did dogs understand when they didn't win? Then, of course, the anxiety rolled right into frustration, as it does. I was going to kill Viv for getting me into this.

"Scarlett!"

I spun around, hoping that I was about to be spared this public humiliation. Was Aunt Betty going to be allowed back into the competition? Was my moment over before it began, please God? My heart soared with hope and then plummeted when I saw Andre coming at me with his camera.

"Oh, it's you," I said.

Andre paused. "As greetings go, I have to say that is lacking in, well, everything."

"Sorry." I bit my lip. "I'm delighted to see you, really, I was just hoping you were someone offering me an escape route."

He glanced at my badge. "You've taken Aunt Betty's place? Why?"

"The chairwoman, Liza Stanhope, made a fuss and was refusing to let Aunt Betty compete. This was Viv's doing," I said. "In fact, I was just plotting her early demise."

A small smile tipped the corners of his lips. He glanced around the room. "It is a bit intense, isn't it? I don't know that I would have taken the job if I'd known it was going to involve so much fur and drool." With a tragic expression he pointed down at his brown leather loafers. "A mastiff got slobber on my Alexander McQueens."

"More than you bargained for, I'm sure," I said. I was suddenly grateful that I was dressed in my Saturday best, sneakers, or trainers as they liked to call them here, and a sweat suit, which was clearly a misnomer because I never did anything that made me sweat; in fact, I wasn't even sure I could sweat other than the nervous sort of flop sweat that happened when I was terrified, like right now.

"When are you up?" he asked.

"In thirty minutes," I said.

Andre checked the paper schedule in his hand. "Right, you're first in the next round. Speaking of which, I had better get out there now and prepare."

"You're leaving me?" I asked. Panic made my voice squeaky.

Andre squeezed my hand and then bent over to pat Freddy's head. "Don't worry. I'll see you out there. Just meditate or something, you'll be fine. I mean, look at this boy. He has 'champion' written all over him."

Freddy barked as if he knew exactly what Andre had said. It made me smile and I felt a burst of confidence. If Freddy was this smart, maybe we would be all right after all. I watched Andre leave and then found a spot against the wall to while away the next thirty . . . no, a glance at the clock gave me twenty minutes. Why did that feel like an eternity and yet not nearly enough time to mentally prepare to be humiliated in front of the crowd? Gah!

I closed my eyes and willed away the sound of the contestants talking, the whimpers, growls and barks of the dogs, the muted sound of the crowd applauding whatever was happening on the course at the moment. Freddy, bless his heart, leaned against my leg. His trust in me made me feel nervous and at the same time confident. He believed in us, how could I not? But also, what if I let him down? What if I said "over" when it was supposed to be "through," or "under" when it was supposed to be "over"?

"Freddy?"

I opened my eyes. Who was talking to my dog?

"Is that Betty Wentworth's Freddy?"

I turned my head and saw a middle-aged man, rather soft around the jawline and middle with thinning gray hair and wire-rimmed glasses, staring at Freddy as if trying to place an acquaintance who was out of context.

"Yes," I said. "I'm competing with Freddy on her behalf today."

"Oh." He glanced up at me then. He looked me over and extended his hand. "Richard Freestone and this is Muffin."

This was the man Betty had mentioned as the previous winner, the pompous blowhard she wanted to knock off his pedestal. Being in the fashion industry, sort of, I noted that his clothes were all high-end designer stuff, pointy shoes and tapered pants with a shirt cut to try and reduce the slight pudge he had going. I shook his hand and then glanced down to see an English bulldog sitting beside him. It occurred to me that the old expression was true:

dog owners and their dogs did resemble each other, and in the case of these two, they both had some rather impressive jowls.

"Is Betty all right?" he asked. I met his gaze. There was genuine concern there, which made me like him more but I still didn't feel the need to enlighten him about the situation with the registration. Then again, I thought of the threat Betty had received. Freestone was the reigning winner. If someone wanted Betty out, surely they wanted him out, too. This was my chance to do some information excavation.

"She's fine," I said. "She just wanted me to have a go at the dog show, and there was . . . well, a thing."

He gave me a speculative look and then said, "A thing?"

"A note that gave us some concern," I said.

"In her postbox?" he asked. "Telling her to withdraw or they would poison Freddy?"

My eyes went wide. "How did you know?"

"I got one, too," he said. "And so did two other high-ranking competitors. There could be more but those are the ones I know about."

"But you're still here?"

"As is Freddy," he said.

"We weren't sure if it was a scare tactic or not," I said.

"I'm betting it was," Richard said. "But, of course, I am ever vigilant. Muffin takes no food or treats unless they're from me."

"Same," I said.

We were both silent, glancing around the room as if a

person was going to leap out and say, "Ha! It was just a bad joke" or "Aha! Now I've got you!" Neither of these things happened. Richard finished surveying the room and turned back to me.

"I did hear one other rumor," he said. He looked troubled.

"Oh?"

"Yes. I heard that Liza Stanhope said she was going to ban Betty from competing because of an incident at the cocktail party."

I did not confirm or deny.

After a moment, he said, "How fortunate that Betty had planned to have you compete with Freddy in her stead."

"Indeed," I agreed. I could feel the hot flush of embarrassment at the fib color my face. Still, I didn't give any details. Technically, Aunt Betty did want me to compete with Freddy in her place, since she was banned and all.

"May I offer a word of advice?" he asked.

"Sure," I said. He could offer it, but that didn't mean I would listen.

"Muffin and I have won this competition three years running," he said. "The best in show is ours to lose."

I stared at him. There was some breathtaking arrogance there.

"If anyone can best us, it's Freddy," he continued. "He knows what to do, just let him lead."

Okay, that was nice of him to say. I felt myself warm to the man. He did have kind brown eyes and he seemed to genuinely care.

"Thank you," I said. "I appreciate—"

"Richard, Richard, Richard," a voice interrupted, saying his name, drawing out each syllable, making each one more filled with contempt than the last. "Do you really think that you and that dried-up old prune of a dog have a chance at this competition? It is Henry's year and everyone knows it."

Richard's jowls shook as he spun around to face the person who approached us from behind. It was a couple, a man and woman, who were leading a Jack Russell terrier. Perhaps it was my instant dislike of his people, but I thought the Jack Russell had a sly look to him as if he was just waiting to make trouble.

Richard turned away from them without acknowledging the woman's words. He looked at me and, in a low voice, said, "The Youngs. Awful people. Their Henry is a thug, keep Freddy away from him."

"Ah!" the woman gasped. "I heard that."

"It's no secret, Penelope," Richard said. He made a hand gesture and Muffin scurried to stand behind him, using him as a sort of human shield protecting herself from Henry. I took a step forward, placing myself in front of Freddy. "You and Jasper treat Henry like he's your baby. He's spoiled, ill-mannered and not fit for competition."

The man, presumably Jasper, holding Henry's leash, looked like he wanted to punch Richard. I sidestepped, not wanting to get caught in the fracas. But Jasper reined in his temper and jutted out his chin in a defiant manner.

"We'll see," he said. "Come along, Henry, Penelope."

We watched as Jasper and Penelope began to walk

away but Henry stayed. As if he understood that Muffin and Freddy were his competition, he sat and stared at them as if trying to intimidate them.

"Henry, come," Penelope commanded. Henry ignored her.

"Henry, now," Jasper snapped. Henry didn't budge, not even in response to a yank on his leash. Jasper was forced to bend down and pick him up and carry him off.

"Let's hope those two never have children," Richard said.

I'd been thinking the same thing and laughed.

"Scarlett Parker and Freddy, you're next." I heard my name called and my laughter caught in my throat like a dry cracker.

"Good luck," Richard said.

I glanced quickly at his face. I couldn't tell if he meant it or not, but I decided it really didn't matter. It was showtime. I tightened my grip on Freddy's leash as we approached the doors that led out to the arena. The personnel at the door signaled for me to wait. I could hear the crowd applauding. I wondered where Harry, Viv and Aunt Betty were in the crowd, and I hoped we didn't let them down.

"All right, Freddy," I said. I adjusted my hat and his and tried to sound more confident than I felt. "Let's do this."

Chapter 7

The spotlights were the first thing I noticed. They were very bright and very hot. We approached the judges' table, and I presented Freddy as Aunt Betty had shown me. The consummate charmer, Freddy gave a small bow, lowering himself on his forelegs while leaving his rump in the air, as he glanced at them from under the brim of his hat. They should have just handed him the trophy right there because, honestly, he was too much in the best possible way.

There were five judges, and I noticed that they each took a second to make a note before the stern-looking woman who was the head judge gave me the nod to proceed.

The agility course looked like the craziest sort of maze and frankly if one of the volunteers hadn't been standing at the entrance, I would have had no idea where to go. Freddy did not seem confused at all and trotted right over to the start line. I saw there was a large digital clock and a timekeeper stood next to it.

The PAWS volunteer next to me said, "When I say, 'Go,' you may begin."

She was a young woman, probably a few years younger than me, and she gave me a reassuring smile. I nodded and removed both Freddy's hat and my own, leaving them on a nearby bench. We took our places at the start line. I scanned the tunnels, jumps, a small pond and series of standing hoops in front of us and thought I might pass out.

I bent down next to Freddy, unclipped his leash and said, "It's all on you, buddy, no pressure, but seriously, I don't have a clue. Just run your cute little butt off, okay?"

Freddy turned his head so we were nose to nose. He licked my face and then barked. I took that to mean he understood.

I straightened up and the volunteer shouted, "Go!"

Freddy took off like there was a steak dinner ahead of him. I bolted after him, trying to look like I knew what I was doing, but seriously, since I run only if someone scary is chasing me, I was pretty winded after the first series of hoops, the tunnel and a series of short rails. Freddy did not wait for me. He dashed through the course as if it were what he was bred to do.

Halfway through, my nerves were forgotten as I marveled at how brilliantly Freddy was attacking the course. He didn't just jump, he soared. When he ran fast, it was fast and low to the ground, like a high-speed train with no brakes. At the apparatus that required crawling, he looked like a commando attacking an enemy line. I found myself jumping up and down beside him, cheering him on as more of a spectator than a handler. Freddy paid me no mind. When he sped for the finish line, I was right behind him. Okay, not right behind, but pretty close.

He sat proudly in front of the judges' table, and I collapsed to my knees beside him. I was sucking in huge gulps of air while Andre snapped our picture. I hugged Freddy, thrilled that we had survived and he had kicked butt.

When our time score came up, the crowd erupted. Freddy had moved into first place on the leaderboard, which so far ranked only the agility course. I laughed as Andre looped an arm about me and hauled me to my feet.

"You did it, Scarlett!" he cried. "That was brilliant!"

"Freddy did it," I gasped. "I was just along for the run."

Aunt Betty, Harry and Viv waved to us from their spot behind the judges' table. I shot a double thumbs-up at them. The look on Aunt Betty's face made it all worth it. She was thrilled.

I reached down to pet Freddy, but he wasn't there. I glanced up to see that he had trotted back onto the course. Not wanting him to undo his fabulous run with some misbehavior, I hurried after him, calling, "Freddy, come here, boy."

Freddy ignored me. I glanced at the judges' table. They were watching him with what was clearly disapproval.

JENN McKINLAY

Damn it! I put on some speed even though I was pretty sure I was going to pass out from lack of oxygen.

"Freddy!" I called. He ignored me.

At the end of the arena was the cloth-draped podium where the winners would be showcased at the end of the competition. Did Freddy think he had already won? Would points be deducted for his overconfidence?

I had almost reached him when he ducked under the festive bunting. Nuts! I knelt down and called him through gritted teeth, "Freddy, come out here right now."

I hoped Jasper and Penelope Young were not privy to this scene as I didn't want them to think Freddy was anything like Henry, although at the moment there was a marked similarity in the stubborn department.

Was this what parenting a toddler or teen was like? I was going to have to do a big rethink on children if I couldn't even get a well-trained dog to listen to me.

"Freddy!" I hissed. I could feel the eyes of the crowd on my back and hear the titters of laughter that people were trying, not nearly hard enough, to suppress. I glanced over my shoulder to see the head judge, a woman who looked to have absolutely no sense of humor, frowning at me.

Just as I was about to forcibly yank Freddy out from under the dais by his heart-shaped behind, he came trotting out with a man's shoe clamped in his teeth. I rocked back on my heels. What the hell?

He trotted toward me and dropped the brown shoe in my lap. It was a high-end designer shoe, camel-colored in what appeared to be crocodile. Freddy sat down, panting

94

with his tongue hanging out, as if waiting to see if I would throw it for a game of fetch. Aware of the crowd watching, I picked it up and, with a shrug, held it in the air.

The audience seemed to find Freddy's shenanigans amusing and I heard a man shout, "Oy, is that a part of the agility test?"

This was met with a low rumble of laughter from the crowd.

"I think he should get bonus points for that," a woman shouted, and the crowd applauded.

Freddy looked pretty pleased with himself and I glanced, again, at the judges and they seemed amused, too. Okay, maybe this wouldn't hurt his score.

I put the shoe on the dais and clipped Freddy's collar with the leash. I was about to walk away when it occurred to me that the quality of the shoe wasn't the sort that would become a dog toy when it had served its purpose as footwear. The brown leather was soft to the touch, the hand stitching impeccable, there wasn't much wear on the leather or the sole, so why the heck was it under the dais?

"I think you're good to go now, Scarlett," Andre said. He handed me our hats. "The crowd seems taken with Freddy's cleverness."

I glanced from Andre to the dais and back. "There's something wrong here."

His face, which had been wreathed in a jovial smile, fell, plummeting into an expression of dismay and possibly a little horror. He backed away.

"No."

"Hold Freddy," I said. I shoved the leash and the hats at him.

"No."

"Andre, we may have a situation here," I said.

"Why?" he asked. "Let's just walk away and pretend that everything is fabulous, because if we pretend hard enough it could be. It really could."

I stared at him, waiting. With a sigh of resignation, he let his camera hang from the strap around his neck and took the leash and the hats. I couldn't blame him for his reluctance. Shortly after we'd met for the first time, he and I had discovered one of Viv's clients murdered. The trauma had cemented our friendship for life, but it was an experience Andre never wanted to live through again. Well, neither did I . . . but the shoe.

I knelt down and lifted the cloth of the dais. It was pitch-black under there. I threw the heavy fabric up onto the dais to get more light. I could hear the crowd getting restless, wondering what I was doing, and I sensed several people approaching. I wondered if they were planning to forcibly remove me for tampering with the property of the competition.

When enough light shone into the space, I saw, to my horror, another shoe that matched the one Freddy had brought me. Only this one was still attached to the foot inside of it. And it wasn't just a foot. An entire person had been crammed under the dais.

My gaze moved over the body. The clothes were expensive just like the shoes. One hand was visible and I noted that the fingernails appeared bluish. That was bad. I didn't need a medical degree to know this person was in trouble. I reached forward to put my fingers on the person's wrist. The skin was icy to the touch. I jerked back.

"What is the meaning of this?" the head judge snapped. I rocked back on my heels, wiping my fingers on my sweat suit as if dead was contagious.

She was an older lady with thick silver hair that was styled away from her face in waves. The cut flattered her sharp features and distracted from the deep wrinkles around her mouth and eyes. A festive red scarf was tied around her neck and she wore a light blue dress shirt under her official judges' navy blazer. She looked very authoritative. Her bright blue eyes were narrowed as she studied me. Her name badge read *Claudia Curtis*.

"There's . . ." I gestured to the darkness beneath the dais. "A person under there."

"What?" she snapped. She knelt down beside me, using the dais to lower herself to her knees, and peered into the shadows, taking in the other shoe and the foot and the hand at a glance. Her face went pale and she whipped around and snapped her fingers at a few security personnel. When they rushed over, she said, "There's a man under here. Lift him out."

The authority in her voice had the volunteers moving without question. I stepped aside to be close to Andre, who had his eyes clamped shut as if he could wish it all away. The sound of the crowd was rising with curiosity mingled with some high notes of alarm.

It took only moments for the security team to pull the body out from under the dais, and when they did, the glaring brightness of the overhead lights shone down on the body of Gerry Swendson. There appeared to be some bruising on the side of his head, and around his mouth was a thick trail of dried spittle. It was easy to see from the stiffness of his form, the pallor of his skin and the blue tinge to his fingernails and lips that he was dead.

Chapter 8

There was a high-pitched scream. I wondered for a moment if it was me, but no. A woman in the crowd was the shrieker. I jumped at the sound and turned to see a tall, curvy, blond woman, wearing a fur coat and lots of diamonds, faint, right into the lap of the person beside her.

Mayhem ensued. Thankfully, Harry was able to get to me and Andre, and he pulled us aside as the competition officials descended. Relieved of the dog and the hats, Andre had the presence of mind to snap a few pictures of what was enfolding before the Finchley Park security people barricaded the area, using the apparatus from the course and the bunting off the dais.

"Come with me," Harry said. He took my hand and Freddy's leash and led us away from the scene. At the side of the floor, Viv and Aunt Betty were waiting. Harry whispered to me, "We need to get out of here before someone remembers Aunt Betty's altercation with Gerry Swendson last night."

I nodded. I'd been thinking the same thing. I'd gotten only a quick glance at Gerry Swendson but I hadn't seen any blood or any signs of blunt trauma; the bruising on the side of his face looked more like the sort that happened when you fell, which didn't leave a lot of options for his death. If he'd been having a heart attack, would he have crawled under the dais? Highly unlikely. The only reason for hiding the body would be because he'd been murdered. A shiver winnowed through me.

Swendson could have been strangled. I hadn't seen his neck and didn't know if there were any marks, but if it was the cause of death it would surely rule out Aunt Betty. He was a big man and she was tiny. She'd never be able to choke him out. But if it was poison . . . oh, jeez, what had she said to him at the cocktail party? It had been about his dog food being poison and how he'd better be careful because some dog lover was going to do to him what he'd done to their dog.

Oh, this was bad. *So bad!*

We scuttled as a group toward the exit, but the crowd made it impossible. I could hear sirens growing louder. Obviously someone had called the police. An announcement was made over the loudspeaker that no one was allowed to leave the building until the authorities said so.

"Let's go back to the waiting area," I said. "Maybe we can still leave from there."

Harry nodded and he guided us along the perimeter of the room to the corridor entrance that led to the waiting room. There was no one posted at the door, so we slipped inside the competitors' area. Inside, the people and dogs awaiting their turn looked at us in surprise.

Richard Freestone was the first to ask, "What's going on out there?"

Harry and I exchanged a look.

"Are you supposed to be here?" Penelope asked Aunt Betty. "I heard you were banned from the competition."

Aunt Betty bit her lip and looked at Viv. It was clear she had no idea what to say.

"She still owns Freddy," Richard said. "Of course she should be here. How are you, Betty?"

His tone sounded full of affection. I noticed Betty looked flustered. If it was because of what was happening beyond the doors or because of Richard, it was hard to say. Either way, we had no time for this.

"Freddy has to go out," I said. "Make way—doggy with a full bladder!"

The crowd parted and we surged toward the door. I had my hand on the metal handle. I was so close to pushing it open and freeing us from this nightmare, when a voice barked, "Not so fast!"

I dropped the handle and turned around. Standing there with her arms crossed over her chest and glaring at us was Liza Stanhope. She pointed a bony finger at Aunt Betty and said, "It was you!"

To her credit, Aunt Betty wasn't even fazed by the false accusation. Instead, she looked down her nose at Liza, which was impressive not just because Liza towered over her by about a foot but also for the wave of disdain that poured off Aunt Betty when she did it. She was obviously gifted in the art of contempt.

"Don't be ridiculous!" she said.

The absolute confidence in her voice gave Liza pause but then she shook it off, like a dog shedding water. "I'm not being ridiculous. You threatened to poison Gerry Swendson last night and now he's dead."

There was an audible gasp in the room.

"I did no such thing," Aunt Betty snapped. She planted her fists on her hips and I wondered if she was going to take a swing at Liza. Harry stepped in between the two women, obviously thinking the same.

"Now, now, we have no idea what happened to Mr. Swendson," Harry said. He raised his hands in the universal signal to calm down. "So everyone needs to take a deep breath and—"

"What do you mean? What happened to Mr. Swendson?" Penelope Young interrupted. "Is something wrong? What's going on out there?"

"Yeah, what's the holdup?" another dog owner demanded. "We should have competed by now." He turned and glared at me. His precisely clipped mustache perfectly matched that of his salt and pepper schnauzer, whose name tag read Otto. "What did you do?"

"Me?" I asked. "Nothing! I swear."

"Then why are you back here?" Jasper Young asked. "Once you've run the course you're supposed to sit in the stands with the other competitors. Why aren't you out there?"

"There was a thing," I said. "And it required me to come back here." There, now, that was nice and vague.

This didn't satisfy Liza Stanhope. "You will not move until the police have spoken to you." She gestured to a security guard to block the doors and then turned on her heel and shoved her way through the gathering crowd.

"The police?" Penelope gasped. "What is going on? I demand to know."

"I think that's a reasonable request," Richard Freestone said as he turned to our group. "What is happening, Betty?"

Given that he was Aunt Betty's biggest rival, his tone was surprisingly gentle. It did nothing for Aunt Betty. She gave him a dark look and turned away from him.

"Betty, come on, now." Richard was undaunted by the icy rejection. Instead, he looked sad and full of regret as if he wished their relationship could be different. "Clearly, something is happening. Won't you put aside your frustration with me and tell us what it is?"

"They're going to find out in a moment anyway," Harry said. "It might be best to come from us."

"Fine." Betty turned to face the people surrounding us. She took a deep breath and said, "I am sorry to report that

Gerry Swendson was found dead under the podium in the arena."

A collective gasp of shock rippled through the handlers. It grew in volume as it moved through the crowd until it was a low roar. Betty looked agitated by the attention and Richard blinked and took her hand in his. He gave her fingers a gentle squeeze and then let go. Surprisingly, Aunt Betty didn't slug him.

"I trust you're all right, Betty?" he asked.

"Yes, thank you, it's just the shock," she said. Her voice was stiff but there was a softening in her eyes as she met his gaze.

I was riveted. Was there a truce happening between Aunt Betty and Richard? They were of an age, they both loved dogs, but they'd been rivals for years. Could their feelings for each other run deeper than I'd expected? Huh.

"Stop that," Harry whispered in my ear.

"Stop what?" I asked.

"Romanticizing the two of them," he said. "They are not a thing. There is nothing between them."

"What makes you think I'm romanticizing them?" I asked.

"You practically have hearts floating out of your eyes," he said.

"Hey, are you two seeing what I'm seeing?" Viv asked as she jerked her thumb over her shoulder at Aunt Betty and Richard. She wagged her eyebrows and Harry muttered an oath.

"No, no, we're not," he said. He pushed forward and

took Aunt Betty by the elbow, turning her away from Richard and pulling her into a huddle with the rest of us. "We need to focus. Because of Aunt B's dustup with Swendson last night, there's going to be attention on her. We have to do everything we can to keep her from becoming a person of interest. I'm calling Alistair."

"Is that really necessary?" Viv asked. "I mean, we don't even know what happened yet."

Harry looked at her and she had the grace to look away. He took out his phone and opened his contacts. He looked at me and said, "Keep an eye on Aunt B."

I gave him a thumbs-up and moved closer to Aunt Betty, who had taken Freddy's leash, while Viv closed ranks on her other side. Freddy, for his part, stayed at her feet and gazed up at her adoringly. I knew he was an exceptional dog, but seeing him like this really made me want a dog of my own. I glanced from him to Viv.

"No," she said.

I sighed. How could she resist that face? Then again, this was a woman who had resisted Alistair Turner, one of the most eligible bachelors in London. Of course, that thought brought me back to Fee. Did she fancy Alistair? Did Alistair know? What would happen to our circle of friends if she declared her interest and Alistair took her up on it? Would it cause a rift between Viv and Fee? I could feel my anxiety spike. I wanted to talk to Viv about Fee and Alistair, most likely because it kept me from thinking about Swendson's dead body, but I suspected she wouldn't be receptive.

"Scarlett Parker," a loud voice boomed over the murmuring crowd.

I turned toward the voice. A man in an overcoat stood with two beat cops. Clearly, the detective inspector had arrived. I glanced at Harry. He ended his call and stepped forward, taking my elbow.

"I'm sure they just want to get your statement," he said.

"Right," I agreed. I'd been questioned by the police before. More often than your average hat shop owner, I'd be willing to bet, so I wasn't as freaked out as I might have been.

"Aunt Betty, stay with Viv and do not talk to anyone until Alistair gets here," Harry said. "This should only take a moment."

"We'll be fine," Viv said. "Just hurry so we can get out of here, please."

Harry and I moved through the crowd. I could feel dog noses press up against my legs, trying to take my measure in dog fashion. I wondered if they smelled Freddy on me or, more accurately, fear on me? Did that make them like me more or less?

Harry raised an arm and waved at the detective to let him know we were working our way there. The man was tall and broad-shouldered with an intelligent face. His hair, a reddish blond, was thinning on top and he wore a hand-knit scarf, in a shade of deep blue that matched his eyes, draped around his neck. I took that to mean he was married. Only a man who was married would be wearing a hand-knit scarf that was clearly made specifically for him—either that or he still lived with his mother.

When we joined him, I glanced at his left hand. Wedding ring. Bingo. Between the dead body and the married detective, I felt as if my investigative skills were kicking butt today.

"Hi," Harrison greeted him with a handshake. "I'm Harrison Wentworth and this is my fiancée, Scarlett Parker."

"Detective Inspector Bronson," the man said. Up close, I could see he was somewhere in his midthirties. There were crinkle lines in the corners of his eyes but they were more suggestions than actual wrinkles as yet.

"How do you do?" I asked as I took his hand in mine. His grip was warm, dry and firm. A perfect handshake.

"I think the more pertinent question is, How are you, Ms. Parker?" he countered.

"I'm fine," I said. I realized my voice sounded somewhat blasé but it couldn't be helped. Compared to some of the grisly things I'd seen over the past couple of years, Swendson's unmarked body hadn't really been that traumatizing. Still, I didn't want to sound callous. "What I mean is, I'm better now, thanks."

He nodded as if he understood. "I'm sorry to have to put you through it again, but are you willing to answer some questions and tell me exactly what happened?"

"Of course," I said.

"Let's find a quieter place," he suggested. He directed Harry and me through the door back into the corridor that led to the arena. There were a couple of rooms off the hallway that I hadn't noticed before and Bronson led us into one of those.

We found ourselves in a small office with a plaque on the door declaring it the office for the head of security. One of the uniformed officers stationed himself outside the door and Bronson let the door shut behind us. He gestured to the two available seats across from the desk.

"Mr. Millbank, the head of security, has offered us the use of his office while he and his people are canvassing the crowd to ascertain whether anyone saw anything."

"How many people were in the crowd?" I asked.

"Four hundred, give or take a few dozen," he said.

I felt my eyes go wide. With the spotlight on us, I hadn't really gotten a good feel for the crowd in the stands. I was extremely grateful that I hadn't known at the time how many people were watching the potential catastrophe. It made me want to find Freddy and give him a hug and a big juicy bone.

"Can you tell me what happened as you remember it, Ms. Parker?" Bronson asked. He took his phone out of his pocket and asked, "Do you mind if I record our conversation?"

"Not at all, and please call me Scarlett," I said.

He nodded in agreement and I waited until he had the recorder on his phone going. Then I told him exactly what happened from the moment Freddy ran back to the dais to the discovery of Swendson's body.

Bronson made a few notes on a small pad on the desk. When I was finished speaking, he steepled his fingers in front of him and then tapped his mouth with his index fingers. His blue gaze locked on my face as if he was trying to figure out how to take my words and hold them up to the light to look for cracks or flaws. Finally, when my nerves were getting stretched to the breaking point, he spoke.

"Why were you competing in the show?" he asked.

"Excuse me?" I said. I felt like it was pretty self-explanatory.

"Liza Stanhope told me you weren't the original entrant for this competition," he said. "Why are you here?"

There was no accusation in his words but I felt it regardless. Harry stiffened almost imperceptibly beside me and I knew he heard it, too.

"I'm not sure what you mean," I said. Yup, I was stalling. I wanted him to spell it out for me.

"What don't you understand?" he asked. His face hardened. "You were a last-minute entrant. Why?"

"How is that relevant?" Harry asked. He sounded defensive, which was not going to help us.

DI Bronson ignored him and kept his gaze on me. His look was stern. This was the face of a man who sifted through lies to find the truth. He wasn't going to be fobbed off with half-truths or distractions. That being said, I was not about to offer up Aunt Betty on a platter to him.

I let a coy smile turn up the corners of my mouth. Then I leaned against Harry in the chair next to me and took his hand in mine. I gazed up at him with all of the affection in my heart, there is a lot, and I said, "We should tell him."

Harry's green gaze met mine. He kept his face clear, betraying nothing. You've got to love a man who errs on the side of caution.

"Should we?" he asked.

"Yes," I said. My voice was decisive. I turned back to the detective inspector. "The truth is, Harry and I are looking to get a dog of our own and Aunt Betty has been teaching me the ropes of the dog show circuit."

I felt Harry's fingers tighten around mine in approval.

"Is that so?" Bronson's voice was dubious.

"Yes," I said. "There's a litter that Freddy, Aunt Betty's dog, sired and we have our eye on one of the pups."

It was a slight, very slight, exaggeration. I really did want a puppy, and I would take one of Freddy's litter. I just didn't mention that Viv had forbidden it and that the puppy was already taken by Aunt Betty. I also left out the part where I had really taken Aunt Betty's spot because she'd been bounced by Liza Stanhope. I told myself that they were just details that would not play out well for Aunt Betty.

"Is that the only reason?" Bronson asked. It was clear he knew about the hullabaloo from the cocktail party.

"No," Harry said. I looked at him in surprise. Was he going to tell all? "I also asked her to take my Aunt Betty's place since Aunt B is getting up there in years and I thought it might be too much for her."

Bronson nodded. "Indeed? So it had nothing to do with Liza Stanhope banning your aunt from the competition?"

"Ban her?" I asked. "That's news to me. Given that Aunt Betty was here coaching me I don't see how she could be considered banned. As I recall, Ms. Stanhope expressed a dislike of corgis, if you can believe that, and she made her preference clear to everyone at the registration table. Still, here I am." I glanced at Harry. It occurred to me, we needed more than this, so I went there. "Also there was a note."

"A note?" Bronson asked.

I glanced at Harry out of the corner of my eye. He nodded in agreement. Our best line of defense was sharing the information about the threatening note Aunt Betty had received.

"Aunt Betty received a note that read, 'If you persist in competing in the dog show, I will poison your dog.' We turned it in to her local police but they had no idea what to make of it," I said.

"The officers I spoke to were Read and Colby at the Notting Hill Police Station," Harry said.

"Seems to me someone is out to harm Aunt Betty," I said. "And she's not the only one. Richard Freestone received a note, as well as some other competitors. Maybe these situations are related."

Bronson stared at me as if taking my point into account. He was quiet for a moment and then he nodded. When he rose to his feet, Harry and I did as well.

"Thank you for your time, Ms. Pa—Scarlett," he said. "If you could leave your name and phone number with the officer at the door, I'd appreciate it."

"Of course," I said. I waited a beat and then asked, "We are free to go, then?"

"Yes," he said. He glanced at Harry. "But first I'll want to talk to your aunt."

Chapter 9

To his credit, Harry didn't flicker so much as an eyelash. "Certainly."

Bronson left us with the officer in the hallway and disappeared into the room holding all of the contestants. Oh, man, what if he asked Aunt Betty about Swendson and she went off again?

"What if—" I started to say as much to Harry, but he was already on his phone.

I turned to the officer, who looked to be somewhere in his twenties and way out of his element, judging by the mildly panicked look in his eyes, and gave him my name and number. When I turned back, Harry was ending the call.

"It's fine," he said. He pulled me close and whispered

in my ear, "Alistair is here with Aunt Betty. I told him not to let her answer any questions and informed him of our deep desire to adopt a puppy."

"Smooth," I said. With our backs to the officer, I felt confident enough to give him a discreet knuckle bump.

In a matter of minutes, Bronson returned. Viv and Alistair flanked Aunt Betty, and Freddy trotted by her side as if they were on their way for a walk in the park. Aunt Betty looked nervous but when she saw Harry, her expression cleared.

"After you, Ms. Wentworth," Bronson said, gesturing to the open office door. He went to follow her and Freddy, but Alistair slipped in between them. Bronson frowned and closed the door after them, making it clear that the rest of us were to wait here.

"Is she going to be all right?" Viv asked.

"She's with Alistair," Harry said. "She'll be fine."

Viv nodded. I wondered what she was thinking. I also wondered what she'd said, if anything, when Alistair arrived. Knowing Viv, she had said nothing.

I supposed that I needed to let it go. Just because I saw all that was good in Alistair didn't mean she needed to date him. Honestly, he deserved better than a woman who was lukewarm about him at best and if that woman was Fee, well, good on her.

Aware that the officer standing by the door was watching us, none of us spoke. Harry, being the restless sort, began to pace. He had to navigate his way around people who kept entering and leaving the corridor but he didn't seem to care. Viv and I stepped out of the way and leaned up against the wall on the opposite side of the hall.

The cement was cold against my back and I shivered. Viv pressed closer to my side as if to share body heat. I said nothing and neither did Viv. I shifted my weight from foot to foot as the time dragged on, and I began to feel the stirrings of unease.

"They can't honestly think that Aunt Betty harmed Swendson," I said. "It's preposterous."

"True, but they could theorize that she had someone do it for her," Viv said. She cast a side-eye at me. "Someone younger and stronger."

"Me?" I asked. I was outraged. How could she even suggest—

Viv snorted. "No, not you." She tipped her head in Harry's direction. "But a scrappy rugby player might fit the bill, don't you think?"

I felt my heart drop into my shoes. "No, they can't possibly think Harry would have anything to do with it."

Viv shrugged.

"It makes no sense," I insisted. "Besides, there wasn't a mark upon him—Swendson, I mean. If Harry had hurt him, he would have been banged up or bruised."

"Well, that means he was killed by other means, like poison or suffocation," Viv said. "Anyone could have done that to him, including a petite, elderly woman."

"Oh, no," I said. The ramifications of Aunt Betty's situation were slowly sinking in.

"Exactly," Viv agreed.

My mind raced. We needed to know what had killed Gerry Swendson and when, so that we could make certain Aunt Betty had an alibi that stuck. It occurred to me that Bronson wasn't likely to make any details, like cause of death, public for precisely this reason.

Harry paced by me. He turned on his heel at the end of the hallway and came back the same way. His expression was grim and I knew he was worried.

"Hey," I said. I grabbed his hand and held him in place. "It's going to be all right."

"Maybe," he said.

"She has Alistair," Viv said. "He'll look out for her."

I gave her a look, and she tipped up her chin.

"Just because I don't want to date him doesn't mean I don't think he's a good attorney," she said. It was on the tip of my tongue to ask why she didn't want to date him but now was not the time.

"He is that," I agreed. I squeezed Harry's fingers with mine. "Aunt Betty is your father's sister, right?"

"Yes," Harry said. "His little sister. She never married or had kids of her own, so she always made time for her nieces and nephews. She's like a second mom to us all."

"Why didn't she marry?" Viv asked.

I was surprised, as Viv is not one to ask anyone personal questions. We both turned to Harry.

"I don't know," he said. "She never found anyone she fancied enough, I expect. I know there was one tragic love affair in her twenties that held her enthralled for years but then it ended and I don't think she ever dated again."

"Ever?" Viv asked.

"I imagine it becomes a habit," I said. "Keep rejecting offers and eventually it's just second nature to say no even when it's someone you might actually like."

Viv let out an exasperated breath and turned away.

I leaned into Harry. "Was I too obvious?"

"Subtlety is not your gift, Ginger." He gave me a small smile. "I'm dreading telling the family about this."

"Maybe you should wait and see how it goes," I said. "Perhaps Gerry Swendson died of natural causes."

"And stuffed himself under the award dais?" he asked.

"He might have had a stroke and thought he just needed some shut-eye. Maybe he got confused and crawled in there for a nap," I said. It sounded as flimsy as cardboard even to me. Both Viv and Harry gave me a pitying glance that I tried not to take personally.

The office door opened and Alistair stepped out, holding it wide for Aunt Betty and Freddy. I glanced past them to get a look at DI Bronson's face. His eyes looked grim and his mouth was set in a hard line. Whatever had happened in there, he hadn't gotten what he wanted.

I shot Alistair a grateful look but he was busy staring at Viv, who, per usual, ignored him. He ripped his gaze away and turned to Harry.

"Let's go," he said.

Harry nodded. He stepped up to Aunt Betty and asked, "Are you ready, Aunt B?"

"Yes, please," she said. She reached out with an age-spotted hand that trembled and handed him Freddy's leash. She was definitely rattled. Viv, Alistair and I fell in behind them. We decided not to go back through the contestants' room but rather to exit out a side door at the end of the hall.

We were almost there when I heard my name called and felt a tug on my arm. I turned and there was Andre, still holding his camera but looking much better than he had when we'd discovered Swendson.

"Did you hear?" Andre asked.

"Hear what?"

"Liza Stanhope has decided to carry on with the dog show," he said.

"What?"

"She just made the announcement," he said.

Our group staggered to a halt.

I looked at Harry, who had clearly heard Andre's news as his eyes were wide. We exchanged a look of understanding and I knew without him saying it that I was going to have to continue to compete because to withdraw now would make me, or more accurately Aunt Betty, look guilty, as if our only motive to be in the competition had been to murder Gerry Swendson. Damn it.

When Viv and I got back to Mim's Whims, it was to find Fee helping four customers at once. We jumped in to assist and as soon as the last lady had left with her newly boxed hat, we collapsed onto the navy blue upholstered chairs while Fee rushed to lock the door.

118

"Not that I'm not thrilled with the business but it was nonstop today. Who'd have expected such a rush in February?" she asked. She slumped into her chair and put the back of her forearm on her forehead. "Never leave me again, yeah?"

"Not until tomorrow, at any rate," I said.

"What?" she asked. She dropped her arm. "Explain."

I glanced at Viv and asked, "Where to begin?"

"So many choices," she said. "Aunt Betty getting banned? Finding the dog food king's dead body? Being questioned by the police?"

"Or being told the dog show is continuing and that I'll have to continue taking Aunt Betty's place?"

"What?" Fee sat up. "Wait. I need tea. Anyone care for a cuppa?"

"Me," Viv said.

"Me, too," I said.

"Let's take this to the workroom," Fee said. "I think I'm going to need a biscuit or four to listen to this tale of woe."

We rose as one and turned toward the workroom, which had a small kitchenette that we kept fully stocked for our late-afternoon tea. There was a knock on the shop door, and I glanced back to see Harry there. He had a key but it was just as easy for me to let him in.

He had taken Aunt Betty home, saying he would meet me here to talk about the situation after he got her settled. I hurried across the room and turned the dead bolt, pushing the door open to let him in.

"Hi," I said. He had clearly stopped at home to change and was wearing jeans and a Fair Isle sweater in shades of blue under a thick black wool coat. As soon as he stepped inside, bringing a burst of cold air with him, I shut and locked the door and then turned around to hug him.

The bite of cold clung to him but I brushed it off as I wrapped my arms around him and pressed my warmth against him. He held me close and kissed the top of my head. Then he took me by the upper arms and held me away from him. He looked into my eyes as if to assure himself that I was okay.

"I'm fine," I said. I hoped I removed all doubt. "How's Aunt Betty?"

"Worried," he said. "She even talked about dropping out of the dog show."

"Really?" I asked. "But that might look suspicious, plus Freddy is at the top of the leaderboard."

Harry grinned. He threw an arm around me and said, "Look at you, getting all competitive. Don't worry. Her friend and neighbor is with her and they're going to talk it out over some cottage pie."

"Are you two joining us for tea?" Viv called from the workroom.

"On our way," I said. I had recently bought some decadent All Butter Viennese Swirl biscuits from Marks & Spencer, and I felt as if today was the day to bust them open. I shrugged off Harry's arm, took his hand and half led, half dragged him into the back room.

"What did Alistair have to say about the situation?" I

asked. "Does he think they'll come after Aunt Betty? Should you call your parents? What about Freddy? Should he be subjected to going back to that place? What if it damages his dog psyche?"

"Oy, easy there, Ginger," Harry said. "I already forgot the first question."

We entered the workroom to find Viv plating all manner of biscuits, including mine, fruit and cheeses. It was a light tea but it would hit the spot. Fee was in charge of the kettle, which was just beginning to steam. When it reached optimum whistle, she poured the hot water into the teapot and covered it with a cozy while it steeped.

I nudged Harry into a seat at the table Viv had cleared, while I went to retrieve plates and napkins from the cupboard. I passed out the plates and took the seat next to Harry. Fee poured the tea into cups and I took mine, adding just a bit of sugar and milk. The cup was warm in my hands, which I hadn't realized were so cold.

I reached for a buttery swirl and dipped it into my tea. The biscuit absorbed just enough tea to make it crumble in my mouth, releasing the hot tea on my tongue.

"How is Aunt Betty?" Viv asked Harry.

"She's all right," he said. "I don't think she completely realizes the severity of the situation."

"That she's a person of interest?" I asked.

"Exactly," he said. "They don't know the cause of death yet, but the fact that Swendson was shoved under the dais makes it look as if someone murdered him and tried to hide the body."

"Who was the woman who fainted in the stands?" Viv asked. "She seemed quite overcome."

"That was his wife, Tilly Swendson," Harrison said.

Viv and I exchanged a look. I'd seen the woman for only a moment but if I remembered right, she'd looked to be at least twenty years younger than Swendson. I knew from the cousin mind meld Viv and I sometimes shared, particularly when we were being catty, that she was thinking the same thing.

"Maybe his death was a natural cause because she tuckered him out," Viv said.

I snorted some tea and then had a coughing fit. Harry patted my back.

"Let me guess, younger woman?" Fee asked. We both nodded and she said, "So predictable."

"Wouldn't she be a suspect?" I asked. "I mean, it's usually the person closest to the victim if it's murder, right?"

"I'm sure they're considering her," Harry said. "I did some quick research after I dropped off Aunt Betty. Swendson's Dog Food empire is co-owned by Gerry and his sister, Mary. I don't know if Mary will inherit it all or if Tilly will inherit her husband's half, but it should make the dog show really interesting since they're the biggest sponsor and it's going forward."

"Speaking of the dog show," I said, "how are they going to make up the missing agility tests from this afternoon?"

"They are doing them tonight," Harry said. "I was hoping Aunt Betty would stay away, but since Freddy's in the lead, she has a vested interest if Freddy stays in and wants to watch his competition."

"I'll say she does," I agreed. "What time do we need to go back?"

"You're coming?" he asked.

"Of course I am," I said. "Freddy and I are a team."

"You are?" Fee's eyebrows went up.

I explained about Aunt Betty not being able to compete and Fee tipped her head to the side and said, "I'm sorry, but a person, who is in fact the sponsor, has been murdered. What are you thinking to stay in the competition? Harry, tell her she has to drop out. She could be in danger!"

"She's right," Harry said. "I don't want you in harm's way, but . . ."

"If I drop out, it will look suspicious," I said. "I appreciate the concern but I don't want to create undue scrutiny for Aunt Betty."

"But what if the murderer comes after you?" Fee asked.

"Pshaw," I said. I waved my hand in the air. "I'll be fine. Plus, I'll be able to mingle with all of the competitors and find out who might have wanted Swendson dead."

"See!" Fee cried. She pointed at me and glared at Harry. "That, right there, is why she needs to stay out of it!"

"I agree," Viv said. A frown marred her forehead. "I don't like this, Scarlett."

"And what about the hats?" I asked. I thought maybe I could win her over by using the business. "We're already getting interest from the other competitors over our hats. This could be a whole new market for us."

123

"I'm not having you put yourself in danger in order to drum up some business for dog hats," Viv said. She sounded thoroughly exasperated.

"Really? One of the dog owners told me she'd pay five hundred pounds for a hat like the one Freddy was wearing," I said. "And just think about all of the people who watch the dog shows, who would be inspired to buy a hat for their beloved Fido. I'm telling you, this is a whole new market for us and it could be huge."

"I think she's gone mental," Fee said behind her hand to Viv, which was pointless because she didn't exactly whisper.

"What's next?" Viv asked. "A line of fezzes for cats?"

"A cat in a fez would be stupid cute," I said.

"Or a giraffe in a bowler," Harry said. He grinned at me.

"How about a hippopotamus in a tiara?" Viv asked.

"Or an otter in a top hat?" Fee suggested.

"All right, I get it. We don't want to corner the market on animal millinery," I said. I tapped one of Mim's Whims distinctive blue-and-white-striped containers. "But you don't have to be so harsh. I'm just thinking outside the box."

All three of them looked at the hatbox and then at me. Not one smile. Not even a quiver of a lip at my punniness. Tough crowd.

"You're right, you should come with Aunt Betty and me tonight, but promise me you'll try to keep a low profile," Harry said.

"No problem, I can totally fade into the background," I said.

Harry gave me a dubious look. "Really, Ginger?"

"You'll see," I assured him.

The arena was packed. Whether it was because more people could come in the evening or because of the scandal of Swendson's body being found, it was standing room only in the Finchley Park auditorium. I followed Harry, who managed to secure a seat for Aunt Betty in the back, which was good because she was less likely to be noticed. He and I stood against the wall at the top of the bleachers with all of the other people who were seatless.

The evening news had run a story about Swendson's body being found but hadn't said whether the police believed foul play to be involved. It seemed likely to me, but I knew it could be my own paranoia making me think this.

From what Harry had discovered about the dog food company, it was worth billions. Tilly Swendson stood to inherit an awful lot if Gerry had left his share of the company to her. Not surprisingly, she wasn't in attendance at the dog show. At least, when I scanned the special VIP seating behind the judges, she wasn't there. Interestingly, I did see Mary Swendson. She was right behind the judges. Her face looked puffy and her eyes red. Her shoulders drooped and I got the feeling it was taking every bit of her British stiff upper lip to remain and not dissolve into a heap of tears.

"I'm going to go do some recon in the contestants' room," I said.

"What?" Harry asked. "No."

"But I have access," I said. I held up my badge to remind him of my status.

"I don't want you wandering off by yourself," he said. "We don't know if or how or why Swendson was murdered. You could walk right into danger and not know it."

"I promise I'll be careful," I said. "I'm just going to eavesdrop to find out what everyone is saying. Besides, Andre is back there taking pictures. I'll stay with him."

Harry opened his mouth to say something but the loudspeaker cut in with a burst of music and then the announcer introduced Mary Swendson. I watched her rise from her seat and approach the microphone. She looked so different from this morning. There was a fragility about her that made it seem a harsh word or a strong breeze would shatter her into a thousand pieces.

The room was silent as the gaze of every person in the room was on her. She cleared her throat and then did it again. She leaned closer to the microphone and looked up, her eyes sweeping from one side of the room to the other. It seemed hard to believe that just ten hours had passed since I'd first seen her behind the registration table, greeting Freddy with kind words and a warm smile.

"Good evening, ladies and gentleman," she said. Her voice was soft and the crowd grew silent as everyone strained to hear what she had to say. "The PAWS dog show meant everything to my brother, Gerry." She took a steadying breath. "It is for him that I am here now, recommitting our company to its charitable contribution to the dog show he loved so well and the many shelters that will benefit from the money raised here. In fact, in Gerry's memory, Swendson's Dog Food will be matching all contributions made to the PAWS Foundation for the duration of the competition."

I choked. Even I knew that the dog show raised several hundred thousand pounds every year. This was a huge sum of money. A murmur rippled through the crowd and then the applause started. It became deafening. Mary raised her hand in a small wave and then brushed a tear off her face. She looked overcome by the crowd's response. Without another word, she turned and sat down.

"Wow," I said to Harry.

"Indeed," he agreed. Before he could argue, I kissed him quick and scampered off, taking the opportunity to hurry down the bleacher steps, allowing the crowd to fill in behind me, effectively keeping Harry in place while I went to chat up my fellow dog show crowd to see what I could find out.

I showed my credentials and was able to leave the arena behind and slip into the waiting area. If there had been a manic energy this morning, now it was at a fever pitch. I saw the Youngs with Henry. They were both bent over, speaking to him while he sat looking up at them. I couldn't figure out if they were giving him a pep talk or a lecture. I just knew that his ears were back and his tail was not wagging. He was not enjoying the conversation, whatever it was.

I moved among the people prepping their dogs. I tried

to look as if I had a purpose to be there, which was a flagrant fib because I didn't have a dog with me. I hoped that no one would notice and call me out for having competed already that day.

I really didn't know what I was looking for. Did I really think someone was just going to pop up and confess? No. But I knew the gossip would be off the rails. When I worked in the hotel industry, managing the staff, I was always amazed at how fast the tale of the bad behavior of one guest or sometimes an employee could circulate through the building. I knew the dog show would be no different. If there was info to be had about Swendson's death, this was where I'd hear it.

I felt my phone vibrate in my pocket. It was a text from Harrison asking about my progress. Well, that was easy to answer with a thumbs-down.

I looked for Andre but he was out on the course, snapping pictures of the dog that was competing at the moment. I heard a collective groan from the crowd so I figured the dog had messed up something. The bad part of me was happy because it meant Freddy would keep his number one spot at least for a little while.

I scanned the room. I saw several people grooming their dogs as if getting them in the right Zen frame of mind. Some were warming up on special apparatus, like hoops or steps, and others were just hanging out, killing time until their name was called. I stayed out of the middle of the room and worked the perimeter, listening to the chatter.

"I think his wife did it," one woman said to the person standing beside her. They were ignoring their dogs while they chatted and I noticed that one dog, a tall hound, was trying to nip the other, a German pointer, who was perched on a chair, but the women were oblivious.

"Nah, I heard she got cut out of the will," the other one said. "It's all going to the sister."

"Speaking of which, can you believe she's here?" the first woman said. She pulled her dog away and gave him the command to sit, which lasted all of five seconds before he stood on his back legs and tried to put his mouth on the other dog's neck. "What sort of deep freeze is her heart in if she's not even grieving the death of her brother enough to miss the dog show?"

"Well, they do spend a fortune sponsoring it. She's likely trying to keep an eye on her investment."

I nodded. I had to agree with that.

"Beg pardon, can we help you?" one of the women asked.

I felt myself go still. Had they seen me nod? Had they caught me listening? I could feel my face get warm with embarrassment. Curse this fair freckled skin!

Chapter 10

Pretending to misunderstand, I glanced over my shoulder as if looking for whom she might be speaking to. I probably overdid it just a smidgeon. When I turned back around, they were both staring at me—okay, glowering might be more accurate.

"Aren't you the woman who took that corgi through the course this morning? The one that found Gerry's body?" the taller of the two asked. She had dark hair and wore way too much makeup. Personally, I like makeup, as it makes my nonexistent eyebrows and lashes show up, but this woman had made her brows angry and her lipstick was a vibrant shade of purple not found in nature anywhere.

"That's right," I said. Then because I'm a jerk, I couldn't resist bragging. "We're in first place."

"Not for long," the shorter and curvier of the two said.

Since her dog had given up trying to defend itself and was slowly being mawed by the other woman's dog, which was now in the chair with it, I didn't really think it had the gumption to beat Freddy but I didn't say as much. I merely glanced at the dogs and then back up.

"Good luck," I said.

She glanced at the dogs and let out a frustrated sigh. "Julia, get Buck off my poor Archer, right now."

The last part was said as a wail and I hurried away, not wanting to see what would happen if Buck refused to get off Archer. I didn't think it would go well.

I was making my way across the room to poke my head out and see how the dogs who had competed had done—okay, yes, I was going to check that Freddy was still on the top of the leaderboard—when I saw Richard Freestone, three-time champion and person to Muffin the bulldog, talking to Liza Stanhope.

I tried to blend into the faded wallpaper with limited success. Primarily because the wallpaper was beige and I was wearing a bright blue coat, you know, because it brought out my eyes. Thankfully, the conversation between Freestone and Stanhope was looking intense and I didn't think they'd notice me. I sidled closer, keeping my back to them and hoping they didn't recognize my hair.

"I don't care what Swendson said," Freestone was saying. "Betty Wentworth was right. There was something off about the dog food that was distributed to the winners last year. It's almost as if it was tainted for a reason."

"I don't know what you're talking about," Liza said.

"Don't you?" he asked.

"Why would Swendson do that?" she asked. "Having all of the dog finalists get sick after the big show would defeat the purpose of all of the advertising Swendson does, wouldn't it?"

"Unless he was desperate to get rid of the usual suspects," Richard said. "I'm thinking of withdrawing Muffin from the competition."

"Don't you dare!" Liza hissed. "Muffin has a huge social media following. It could ruin the dog show if you withdraw. It's bad enough we have Swendson's death to contend with, if anything else goes wrong, the show might not recover. You have to stay in."

"I don't know. Betty was right—"

"She was not. She's just a pathetic old woman who is bitter because her corgi hasn't won," Liza said. "She was making up lies to cause trouble."

I felt my temper begin to heat. Aunt Betty didn't lie and it took everything I had not to interrupt and curse at the vile Ms. Stanhope.

"Betty's the same age as me, so thanks for that." Richard's voice was dry. I desperately wanted to turn around and see his face but I resisted the impulse. "Listen, Muffin will eat anything, literally anything, and she refused to eat the food that we won from last year's competition. Also, I know about the lawsuit."

Liza jumped as if he'd set off a bomb.

"Shush," she hissed. "Not here."

"Why not?" he asked. "What are you afraid of? It's a bunch of people from last year's show, suing Swendson for making their dogs sick. What does that have to do with PAWS?"

"Nothing, except Swendson is our biggest sponsor," Liza snapped. "We're trying to keep the lawsuit quiet. Personally, Swendson's legal issues are not my problem but the bad publicity that comes with it is, so hush."

"Aren't you concerned that the people suing Swendson are former PAWS dog show competitors?" Richard pressed. "Aren't you worried that one of them went rogue and got revenge on Gerry? Maybe you're next. You should probably hire some more security."

"Stop it. You'll start a panic," Liza said. "Just because you've won this competition for the past three years, Richard, doesn't mean you have the right to advise me about how I run things." She sounded furious.

"I have every right," he said. "You have used my dog as the face of this show and I have gone along with it but I won't continue, not if I find out that Swendson is harming the winning dogs with poor-quality food."

"Stop that," Liza said. "You know that Mary is in charge of the production of the food. She would never let anything but the best ingredients into the food. You know this."

Richard sighed. "I do trust Mary, but something happened last year. Swendson needs to be investigated and since he's dead and now you're going to be staying on—"

"What did you say?" she asked. Her voice sounded wary.

"I'm sorry. I hate to be blunt, but I know about Swendson's plan to replace you as the chairman of PAWS," Richard said. "It was a vicious thing for him to do, to go after you like that. How long have you been running the dog show for charity? Fifteen? Twenty years?"

"Seventeen," Liza said. Her voice sounded strained. "It was a hollow threat. Swendson felt that we needed to shake things up a bit. He wanted the light more on him as the sponsor and less on . . ."

"The winning dog," Richard said. He shook his head. "What a narcissist."

"Be that as it may," Liza said. "He's dead, whether by his own hand or someone else's—"

"He did it to himself," Richard said. He sounded awfully sure of himself. I wondered if he knew something.

"Then why was he found under the dais?" Liza asked.

"Who knows?" Richard shrugged. "The man clearly had issues. Trust me, the police will discover it was suicide."

"As coldhearted as this sounds, I hope you're right," Liza said. "For the sake of us all." She gave him a sharp look and strode off.

I started to slip away but Richard's voice stopped me. "How is Betty?"

I thought about pretending I didn't hear him. There was enough background noise in this room that I could have gotten away with it but I was curious as to what he knew so I did a slow turn instead.

"Betty is fine," I said. "She's here, in fact. Out in the arena, watching Freddy's competition."

"Of course she is." Richard smiled and I noticed he looked younger when he did so. I had thought he had at least ten years on Betty but having heard him say they were the same age, now I could see it.

I studied his face. "You like her."

He lifted one eyebrow. "I find her to be a worthy opponent."

"And you like her."

"I do like pretty things, and Betty is certainly that," he said. He glanced down at his dog and then back up. His expression was chagrined. "She's the reason I enter the competitions."

My eyes went wide. Okay, I totally hadn't expected that. He smiled, obviously pleased to have caught me off guard.

"That's the irony, isn't it?" he asked. "I don't even care if we win. In fact, I'm pretty sure that's working against me with Betty."

"It is." I nodded.

He laughed. "I entered the first time just to spend some time with Betty. We met at our veterinarian's office. Did you know?"

I shook my head. This was brand-new information.

"Betty is the one who talked me into entering the dog show. Turns out Muffin is a fierce competitor." He shrugged. "It all snowballed from there. I'd been posting online about Muffin since she was a pup. She has a lot of personality."

BURIED TO THE BRIM

I glanced down at the bulldog.

I glanced down at the bulldog. She wagged her head and her jowls shook and spit flew. It was hard for me to believe that was more endearing than Freddy's heart-shaped bum. Then Muffin looked up at me and I swear she smiled. Okay, I got it. She was a drooly charmer.

I glanced down at the bulldog. She wagged her head and her jowls shook and spit flew. It was hard for me to believe that was more endearing than Freddy's heart-shaped bum. Then Muffin looked up at me and I swear she smiled. Okay, I got it. She was a drooly charmer.

"But when we won the first dog show, her popularity went global. The next thing I knew Betty had declared me the enemy and there went any chance I had of asking her out."

"But you kept competing," I said.

"I figured she and Freddy had to win one of these days."

"Well, if it's any consolation," I said, "I don't think she's immune to you either." What I did not say was that I was pretty sure Aunt Betty would have happily stepped right over his maimed body to get to the winner's circle with the trophy.

"Oh, I know that," he said. "Unfortunately, I think it's a hostile regard that I can't seem to charm out of her."

"Richard Freestone and Muffin!" one of the volunteers called from the front of the room.

"You're up," I said. "Break a leg."

He gave me a look that said I was daft and I cringed.

"Sorry, I was thinking in American theater talk, you know, because of the superstition against saying 'good luck' to a performer."

"Ah," he said. He gave me a small smile. "This is a bit of a spectacle. I can understand the confusion."

With a small wave, he and Muffin trotted off toward the door.

I waited a bit before I followed. Yes, I admit it. I wanted to see how a three-time reigning champion attacked the course.

The first person I saw when I slipped into the arena was Andre. He was adjusting a camera on a tripod that he had focused on the equipment. I bet he was getting some spectacular shots of the dogs. I didn't want to interrupt, so I stayed back so as not to distract him.

Richard and Muffin hit the course like a force of nature. Much like Freddy, Muffin knew exactly what to do. She hit all the tricks, bending and twisting on her feet, never losing a second. When she broke into a run for the finish line, I had one eye on her and one on the clock, hoping Freddy's time would hold.

Richard was right beside her as they crossed over and the crowd went wild. I scanned the crowd for a glimpse of Harry's face. He was staring at me, looking wide-eyed and nervous. Aunt Betty was just down the row from him. Her hands were clasped in front of her as if she was praying very hard. And then Muffin's time came up. She was two-tenths of a second off Freddy's time. He retained the lead.

I let out a whoop, which I immediately tried to stifle by clapping a hand over my mouth. Instead, I stamped my feet, feeling the need to let the emotion out. I met Harry's gaze and he grinned, clearly delighted. Aunt Betty had risen from her seat and was doing some sort of dance that looked like a very bad "Gangnam Style." I gestured to Harry that he needed to nip that.

He gave me a quick nod and started to make his way to Aunt Betty. I wondered if I should go back to the competitors' room and see if I could learn anything else. I couldn't imagine that I would.

Honestly, finding out that Richard had a thing for Betty was probably the most interesting tidbit, even though I had no intention of telling her. If Richard wanted to make a move, it was up to him. I wasn't about to help him, especially during a competition when Aunt Betty, and by association Freddy, could be thrown off by such a declaration.

Also, there was the info that Swendson had been trying to get Liza removed from the board. I wasn't sure what I would do with it, but if Liza continued to make things difficult for Freddy, I might have to mention it to the powers that be.

I watched the rest of the competition but it was clear that so far the big crystal bowl of kibble was going to be won by Freddy or Muffin. Henry was an outlier who stood a chance but the rest of the dogs seemed way out of their league. Yes, of course, I was totally biased but that doesn't mean it wasn't true.

By the time the competition ended, I was sagging against Harrison as we walked to his car, which was parked in a small lot down the street. The day's events had been utterly exhausting and I couldn't wait to be tucked up in my bed with my book. I needed something to take me completely out of my present mental state and the historical mystery I was presently reading, C. S. Harris's

Sebastian St. Cyr series, was just the ticket. It would be hard to retain my current level of anxiety if I was kicking butt and taking names in Victorian London.

As Harry ushered us down the sidewalk, he whispered in my ear, "My place tonight?"

"I would," I said, "but I have to be back here bright and early with Freddy for part two of the competition. Apparently, tomorrow is the obedience portion and then there's a parade."

"Yes, it's just fabulous," Aunt Betty cut in. "The obedience segment is not nearly as exhausting as the agility tests, but you do have to have him answer your commands. And as for the parade around Finchley Park, you simply have to wear the hats Viv made. You and Freddy will look amazing, but it's very important that he not get off task, so you'll have to be wary of rats, snakes and anything else your competition can throw at you."

"Like, literally throw at me?" I asked. I tucked my chin in and looked at her from beneath my brow. "Why wasn't this mentioned to me before?"

"Don't worry," she said. She patted my hand. "Only humans have died while competing in PAWS."

"Humans plural?" I asked. We reached Harry's car and he opened the front passenger door, waiting for Aunt Betty to climb in.

"Well, if you include Gerry Swendson, yes, there've been two," she said.

I did not find this reassuring. I knew I shouldn't ask but I did anyway. "How did the other person die?"

140

"It was a freak accident when they were crossing through the park in the parade," she said. "A car jumped the curb and ran the person over. The dog was heartbroken and had to be taken out of the competition, naturally."

"How long ago was this?"

"Three years ago. The very first year Freddy and I competed," she said. "The dog, Annie, a beautiful brindle, was a sure thing, too. So sad. I heard she went to live out her days with a family friend in Devon, but she never competed again. You know, I used to just come and watch the shows, never dreaming that I would one day be entered, but now here I am and Freddy is a contender. Dreams can come true."

I glanced at Harry. Yes, they could, I thought. The return smile he sent my way made my heart kick up a notch and I was almost tempted to ditch my book for him, but I was exhausted and I did not want to be accused of neglecting my fictional boyfriend St. Cyr.

"Shall we meet at Finchley Park at eight o'clock in the morning?" I asked. "You can drill me on the obedience commands."

"No. Aunt Betty, Freddy and I will come collect you at the shop," Harry said. "I think until we know exactly what happened to Swendson, it's best if we stay in a group."

"I think you mean a pack," I said. "A dog pack. And just so we're all clear, I'm the alpha."

"Of course you are, love," Harry said. He kissed me on the head, not giving me a chance to see if he was being sarcastic or not.

"But I do agree. We need to remain vigilant, especially since Freddy remains in the lead," I said. "You never know who might want to change that by any means possible."

"You're not selling me on the idea of keeping you in the competition, Ginger," Harry said.

"Sorry."

"Oh, don't you worry," Aunt Betty said. "This girl can handle herself. No worries."

I grinned. I wondered why Aunt Betty had never married. She was cute and funny and clearly had a lot of love to give. I wondered, again, if I should mention Richard Freestone's interest in her. For some reason, I was hesitant, which was extraordinary because I am something of a meddler; just ask Viv about Alistair. But perhaps it was because I didn't know Aunt Betty or Richard Freestone as well as I knew Viv and Alistair. I'd wait until the end of the competition and see.

When Freddy handed Muffin her first loss, I'd have a better idea what sort of man Richard Freestone was and then we could ascertain if there was something worth pursuing.

"Are you sure he knows what 'sit' means?" I asked.

We were standing in Finchley Park, freezing in the bitter morning cold, while Freddy, who appeared to have woken up on the cranky side of surly, stood staring at me with the look of a toddler who was willfully ignoring everyone around him.

"Of course he does," Aunt Betty said. "He just doesn't like the cold."

"That makes two of us," I said. I shivered in my wool coat. I couldn't feel the end of my nose and my toes were rapidly losing feeling as well.

Harry had gone inside the building to see if there'd been any news about Swendson, but he hadn't returned.

"Freddy, you are being a very naughty boy," Aunt Betty said. Freddy turned his head away as if he didn't want to hear it. The canine equivalent of a teenage eye roll.

"Let's go in," I said. "Maybe it's just too cold out here for him to think. I know it's too cold for me."

Aunt Betty glanced between us and then nodded. She took his leash and led him toward the building and I fell into step beside her.

We were about twenty yards away when the doors were thrust open and Harrison came charging out. Beside him was DI Bronson. Neither of them looked happy, but Harry looked less so. Oh, dear.

"Ms. Wentworth," Bronson said at the same time Harry called, "Aunt Betty!"

Instinctively, I moved closer to Aunt Betty.

"Yes, what is it?" Aunt Betty glanced between them.

"Alistair is on his way," Harrison said.

"I'd like to ask you a few questions," Bronson said at the same time.

Aunt Betty stopped walking. She looked up at me and said, "Do you mind, dear?"

She handed me Freddy's leash.

"No, not at all," I said.

She stiffened her spine and said, "I'm happy to answer any questions you have, Detective Inspector."

"Thank you," he said.

"After Alistair gets here," Harry insisted.

"No, now," Aunt Betty said. "Scarlett and Freddy are competing soon and I'm not going to miss it."

"Speaking of which, could we go inside?" I asked. "I'm frozen."

"Of course," Bronson agreed. "We'll head right to the office."

He led the way and Betty followed him. I shrugged at Harry while Freddy tugged on his leash until he was right beside Betty. I did admire his loyalty.

Harry frowned and pulled out his phone. He thumbed a contact that I knew would be Alistair. I could hear him grumbling into his phone as we followed. The hall was still mostly empty but volunteers were setting up the judges' table and the small arena where the obedience portion would take place.

There was an air of expectation about the place, which was odd given that the owner of the sponsoring company had been found dead just yesterday. I would have thought there'd have been a pall over the event, but no. I wondered how liked Gerry Swendson was. I was guessing not very. How sad. All that money and success and yet no one really mourned him.

Once in the office, Bronson gestured to a chair and Aunt Betty sat down. I took the vacant seat beside her while Freddy sat between our feet. Harry had ended his call and was pacing.

"I really think you should wait for Alistair, Aunt Betty," he said.

"No need," she said. "I'm sure Detective Inspector Bronson is just going to ask me about the poison that killed Gerry Swendson."

We all froze. The clock ticking on the wall behind Bronson was the loudest sound in the room.

"I'm sorry, Ms. Wentworth, did you say 'poison'?" Bronson asked.

"Yes." Aunt Betty met his gaze as if it were the most natural thing in the world to know the cause of death without being a medical examiner.

Bronson blinked. "How did *you* know he was poisoned?"

Chapter 11

Harrison let out a very rude, very loud curse. Aunt Betty looked at him in dismay. "There's no need for that sort of language, Harrison."

"I'd say there's every need," he muttered. Then he looked abashed and said, "I'm sorry."

"That's better," she said.

"How did you know?" Bronson asked again. The frown was getting deeper as if the unhappy vee between his eyes was now permanent.

"Don't answer unti—" Harry said but Aunt Betty interrupted.

"Common sense," she said. "He was clearly murdered, otherwise why hide the body? And it had to be poison because as Scarlett remarked after she found him, there wasn't a mark on him except for the bluish tinge to his fingertips and lips."

"So, you're saying you just deduced that it was poison?" Bronson asked.

"Exactly," she said.

"What sort of poison?"

"Well, I'm sure I don't know that," Aunt Betty said. "I mean, it's not like *I* poisoned him." The three of us stared at her. She put her hand over her mouth. "Oh, is that what you thought?"

Harry rubbed a hand over his face and Bronson pinched the bridge of his nose between his thumb and his index finger as if to squeeze away a headache. I blew out a breath. This was turning into quite the pickle. Aunt Betty looked so distraught that I felt the need to make her feel better.

"Actually, I was thinking the exact same thing," I said. Harry looked at me with wide eyes while Bronson narrowed his eyes at me. "Well, I was."

The office door banged open and we all turned.

"Oy, what's this?" Alistair Turner stood there, looking impeccable in a dark gray suit and white shirt with a bold blue necktie. "Aunt Betty, I thought we agreed that there would be no interviews with the police unless I was present."

"That was fast," I said.

"He was already here, planning to talk to Aunt B before meeting with another client," Harry explained.

Aunt Betty looked at Alistair and then leaned forward and whispered to me, "Why won't Viv date him? He's adorable."

Of course, her whisper wasn't a whisper and everyone heard it. I saw Alistair close his eyes for a second as if searching for patience and I decided to throw caution to the wind, because that seemed entirely appropriate.

"Because she's thick," I said. "However, I happen to think that our assistant, Fee, who's rather stunning herself, would be delighted to date him."

"Ginger, it's not really the time or place for matchmaking," Harry said.

I shrugged and glanced at Alistair to see what he made of what I said. He gave me a considering glance.

"As fascinating as the love life of your attorney is," Bronson said, "how about we get back to the matter at hand?"

Alistair stepped all the way into the room and closed the door behind him. I vacated my seat so he could sit with Aunt Betty, and moved to the back of the room to stand beside Harry.

We listened as Bronson asked where Aunt Betty had been yesterday morning before the agility competition. Since we were with her all morning, it was easy to verify her alibi. Bronson accepted our timeline of events from the unfortunate encounter with Swendson at the cocktail party right up to when I stepped in to take Aunt Betty's place.

"When was Swendson poisoned?" I asked.

Bronson's face closed. It was clear he had no intention of discussing the pending investigation. Like that was going to stop me.

"It had to be after the cocktail party," I said. "In fact,

if I think about it, it had to be early morning, before the agility tests."

Bronson's face closed up even more. I remained undaunted.

"Why do you say that, Scarlett?" Alistair asked.

"Because I saw him at the cocktail party and he was in a dark suit, clearly bespoke, with shiny black dress shoes," I said. "The brown crocodile shoe that Freddy brought to me when he discovered his body means that Swendson had clearly changed from his clothes the night before and dressed for the day's events." I looked at Bronson. "So, I'm assuming it was a fast-acting poison that was administered that morning."

He frowned, his dark brows forming one line across his forehead. "Again, I will not discuss a pending investigation."

"Since we've answered your query, may I assume my client is free to go?" Alistair asked.

Bronson gave a slow nod and said, "For now."

They rose from their seats and Harry and I waited for Alistair and Aunt Betty to leave first. I had fallen in behind Harry when Bronson's voice stopped me.

"Ms. Pa—Scarlett," he said. I turned to find him watching me. "A word of caution. You're in the competition. Since we have no idea who might have poisoned Swendson, it could be dangerous. If I were you, I'd keep my theories to myself until we know for certain that Swendson was murdered."

"Duly noted," I said. "I'll be careful." He looked relieved so I felt compelled to add, "But I'm still going to try and figure out who wanted Swendson dead."

He sighed. "Of course you are."

When I met the others in the hallway, Harry looked at me with concern. "All right, Ginger?"

"Since no one got arrested, I'd say we're as good as can be expected," I said. "I should check in and see what time the obedience trials are."

"I have the schedule here, dear," Aunt Betty said. She held up a piece of paper. "You and Freddy are scheduled to compete in an hour."

"Any idea what the FME reported when they examined Swendson?" Harry asked Alistair.

"FME?" I asked.

"Forensic medical examiner," Alistair explained. "They're general practitioners contracted by the police to do initial investigations. I don't know what they reported but I do know that Swendson's body was turned over to the coroner for a postmortem. A more detailed report won't be released for a few weeks, but my sources at the coroner's office did confirm that they're screening for poisons."

Harry looked at his aunt. "That was a good guess, then."

She shrugged. "It just stands to reason, given that his food was making the dogs sick. If someone was going to get revenge, wouldn't poison be the natural choice?"

"Do you think there's any way to find out if someone's dog has died because of Swendson's Dog Food?" Harry asked Alistair.

"I'm sure there must be," he said.

"Last night, I overheard Liza Stanhope and Richard Freeman talking about a lawsuit," I said. "I think some of the former competitors are suing Swendson over the bad dog food."

Alistair looked at me with approval. "Well, I guess I know what I'll be doing this afternoon." He glanced at his watch. "In the meantime, I do have another client to meet with. Aunt Betty, do not talk to the police without me, not even about the weather, am I clear?"

"Like a crystal trophy," she said.

"We're all meeting up at our place above the shop after the competition today. Join us?" I asked him. Alistair hesitated and I wondered if it was because he couldn't bear to see Viv. I decided to bring in my secret weapon. "Nick is cooking curry."

"Well, in that case, how can I refuse?" he said. With a small wave he turned and left, making his way down the hallway and out a side door.

"Let's go find a place to practice, dear," Aunt Betty said. "You and Freddy need to be perfect."

"No pressure," I mumbled to Harry. He smiled and fell into step behind me as Aunt Betty led us down the hallway to a door that would bring us back into the cold for more practice. I hoped Freddy was more into it this time because I'd just gotten the feeling back in my feet.

I wish I could report that the obedience portion of the competition went as well as the agility tests, but I can't. Because it went even better! On our second practice session, Freddy relieved himself in the bushes. I'm not saying that lightening the load helped his powers of concentration, but the dog who walked into the obedience competition did so with a swagger that was unbreakable.

When I said, "sit," he sat. When I commanded him to roll over, he dropped and rolled like he was putting out a fire. Shaking hands was no big deal and then when I asked him to dance, he popped up on his back feet, and I swear he was attempting to do the Electro Shuffle. The crowd went nuts and I was just so proud. And lastly when I asked him to fetch our hats, which I had purposefully left on a bench on the other side of the arena, he did so with alacrity. He was, in short, perfect.

My heart was in my throat as we awaited his score. When it was announced, it took everything in me to nod my head in acceptance with no expression other than a very tiny smile on my face. The score was the highest of the obedience competition so far and Freddy maintained his lead position by an increased margin of one point. Naturally, as soon as we left the floor and were safely in the hallway, I did a fist pump and a little shimmy-shake of my own.

Andre came running toward me, his camera gripped in one hand. "You did it!"

I jumped up and down and clapped. "Technically, Freddy did it, but I'll take my due."

"Let's get a picture," Andre said. "The light is terrible in here, let's go back in the warm-up room."

He led the way and Freddy and I followed. He positioned us against the wall and snapped a serious picture and then I commanded Freddy to dance and I kicked up one leg behind me in a silly pose.

Andre checked the display screen on his camera and laughed. "That one is going to go viral!"

"Oh, no," I said. "My fifteen minutes of online fame is more than over."

"I'll make sure it's just Freddy, then." He gave me a one-armed hug, kissed my head and said, "I'm back on duty. See you at dinner tonight!"

The door shut behind him and I glanced down at Freddy. "See that?" I asked. "You're going to be famous."

"You think you're so precious, don't you?" a scathing voice asked from behind me.

Was that a trick question? Because, duh, of course I think I'm precious. But I also have good manners and know that it would sound very arrogant if I answered "yes," but I balked at saying "no." I mean, why wouldn't I like me? I'm stuck in here, aren't I? How miserable would life be if I didn't think kindly of myself? Regardless, I decided to go with "no" for an answer.

I turned around and found Penelope Young standing there. She had Henry on a leash and he was curling his lip at Freddy. Being the smarty-pants that he is, Freddy moved to sit behind me and ignored him.

"Can I help you, Penelope?" I asked. Not that I intended to help her in any way but it seemed polite to ask.

"You can withdraw your mongrel from the competition," she said.

"No."

"Then I fear you leave me no choice," she said.

I frowned. "No choice?"

"I'll have to report what I overheard to Detective Inspector Bronson," she said.

I stared at her. She looked so smug. I don't like smug.

"Fine," I said. I was calling her bluff and I hoped she was annoyed enough to clue me in as to what the heck she was talking about. She didn't. Pride be damned, I cracked. "What did you overhear?"

She smiled but it didn't reach her eyes. She seemed so sure of herself, I suddenly knew exactly how a mouse felt wedged between the paws of a playful cat.

"That's for me to know—for now," she said. "Enjoy your short time at number one. It isn't going to last. In fact, there's going to be a real shake-up at PAWS when I become the chairman and take Liza Stanhope's place."

Even as I tried to show no reaction I felt my eyes get wide.

"Not so sure of yourself now, are you?" With a toss of her hair, she walked away. Sadly for her, Henry wasn't done growling at Freddy. He refused to budge. Penelope stamped her foot and said, "Come, Henry."

He leaned against the pull of the leash.

"Henry!" she hissed. "Now."

He was doing a fine impression of a boulder. With a

frustrated flap of her arms, she bent over and scooped him up, storming away. I looked down at Freddy. "Is it just me or do you think obedience isn't going to be his thing?"

Freddy barked, and I laughed. "Come on, let's go fuel up before the parade."

At the end of the obedience trials, Freddy was still in the lead but Muffin was breathing down his neck by one half of a point. Still, it was a strong place to be going into tomorrow's judging. It was to be very hands-on but Aunt Betty had an entire grooming regimen prepared for Freddy the next morning that she assured me would put him in peak form.

The parade was mercifully only one lap around Finchley Park with Freddy and me in the lead since he was in first place. Muffin and Richard were right behind us and then came a pretty black standard poodle named Lucy, and after her a mixed breed named Sachewa. Henry had been relegated to fifth place out of the seventy or so contestants, which caused Jasper and Penelope to complain loud enough for everyone to hear. Ugh.

People surrounded the makeshift promenade and they applauded and cheered when we trotted by. Viv, in some utterly crazed scheme, had made Freddy yet another hat last night. It was a top hat and it was ridiculously cute on him. She'd also begged Harry for one of his bow ties to complete the look. She had not made me a matching top hat, instead opting to braid my hair in some complicated twist on which she then placed a sparkly tiara. Not gonna lie, I was rocking the bling.

There was a very small grandstand, and the judges and sponsors watched as we promenaded in front of them. Aunt Betty said this was not a scored event, but I still felt that it was imperative that we give a good performance. She'd shown me how to properly gait Freddy, meaning he needed to walk at my side, at the speed I chose, showing off his breed's style to its best advantage. Doing this in the parade was dicey because there were so many distractions—smells, sounds and such—that the dogs were challenged to stay on task. We were instructed to have our dogs stack in front of the grandstand, which meant they stood still and didn't move.

Freddy was solid at the free stack, which means he stopped and stood still all on his own, as opposed to a hand stack where I could use my hands to assist him. We posed for several seconds and I glanced up at the stands. The judges were all there, as well as Liza Stanhope, Mary Swendson and, much to my surprise, Tilly Swendson. She was still covered in diamonds and furs, but her face was pale and her eyes red-rimmed.

I heard Andre's camera clicking and when I glanced over he gave me a nod, signaling that we could continue. Freddy and I turned and resumed our walk around the park, with my short-legged escort on my left side, maintaining a perfect gait. He really was a gem.

When the parade finished, the competitors all waited in the back room to be dismissed. Being the first one in there, I took the opportunity to watch everyone as they filed in after me. There was a huge variety of dogs in this competition, which included two other corgis. Freddy in his top hat outshone them all, not that I am competitive or anything, but I absolutely am.

While waiting for Harry to come and collect me, I saw Detective Inspector Bronson talking to Liza Stanhope. Her features were pinched, which on her pointy person did not enhance her looks. Mary was standing with them, looking alarmed. I wondered if they were getting new information about the cause of Gerry's death. I led Freddy closer, in a futile attempt to eavesdrop. It didn't work. As the cavernous room rapidly filled with dogs and people, it was impossible to think, never mind listen in on conversations. Rats!

I was about to text Harry when Mary Swendson caught sight of me. She said something to Bronson and Liza and made her way over to Freddy and me. She knelt with her hand out, letting Freddy become familiar with her scent before she petted him.

"You are doing brilliantly," she said to him. "You captured the lead and look to be maintaining it. Good job, old fellow."

Freddy looked ridiculously pleased with himself and if I'm being honest I enjoyed the praise more than I deserved as well.

Mary rose to her feet and said, "Congratulations to you, too, Ms. Parker."

"Thank you—" I began but was interrupted by a woman who staggered right up to Mary and shoved her face in hers until they were just inches apart. It was Tilly Swendson.

"How dare you?" she hissed.

Mary went very still. "Tilly, you are making a scene."

"Of course I am," Tilly cried.

Tilly Swendson. I'd seen her only from a distance before. Up close, she looked older than I expected. Not significantly older but not the twentysomething she appeared to be from a distance. She was solidly in her thirties with the beginnings of middle age marking the skin around her eyes and mouth.

"Are you drunk?" Mary demanded. She looked disgusted.

"Not yet," Tilly said. "But I'll keep trying."

"I thought you were trying to get clean," Mary said.

"I'm off the pain pills, but . . . oh, what do you care?" Tilly hissed.

She threw her arms wide and it was then that I saw the wineglass in her left hand. She wore her blond hair scraped back from her face and styled in a ball on her head, showcasing the enormous diamond-encrusted hoops in her ears. She was no longer wearing her fur coat. Her blouse was sheer and loose over a satiny camisole. Her pants were wide-legged and she wobbled on spiky heels, giving her the look of someone who should be an entertainer on a cruise ship with a pile of fruit on her head and a daiquiri instead of wine in hand.

"Why are you even here?" Tilly demanded. "I'm the widow. I'm the one who should speak for Gerry."

Mary's eyes became hard. I got the feeling this was not the first time they'd had this argument. Her voice when she spoke was soft and low but no less firm for being so.

"If he'd wanted you to speak for him," she said, "he would have left you shares in the company. He did not."

"No, instead, he left me a half-built castle and a mountain of debt," Tilly sneered. "What am I supposed to do with that?"

"This is not the place to discuss this," Mary said.

"Well, I'd talk about it in my home, but I can't because it hasn't been built yet," Tilly said.

"If you hadn't demanded that he build you that monstrosity," Mary said, "you wouldn't be in this predicament."

They both seemed to have forgotten that Freddy and I were there. I said nothing, hoping they'd keep forgetting.

"Oh, so it's my fault your brother was in debt up to his ar—"

"That's quite enough, Tilly," Mary said.

"No, it isn't," Tilly said. "In fact, I haven't even begun. I want my share of the company."

"I'll see you in hell first," Mary said.

"I'm already there," Tilly hissed. "I've lost everything. The will should have been changed. Gerry promised me he'd take care of me. It's your fault, I know it is; you made him shut me out!"

"I did no such thing," Mary said. "Your greed did that. You had him build you a castle, wasn't that enough?"

Tilly's face turned red. "But without any income from the company, how can I pay for it?"

"That is not my problem," Mary said. "Perhaps you should get a job."

"Ah!" Tilly gasped as if the suggestion of working for a living was the gravest insult Mary could send her way. "Gerry loved me. He wanted to take care of me. I can't believe he left me nothing. It was supposed to be mine, all mine!"

"Well, it isn't," Mary said. "I suggest you ask your lover to step up and help you out."

"How dare you," Tilly said. But her gaze didn't meet Mary's. In fact, it shifted across the room to where the judges were clustered in a circle, talking to Detective Inspector Bronson. Was she worried that he'd heard the exchange?

"If you'll excuse me," Mary said icily as she pushed past Tilly. "I have to meet with the judges."

"That's supposed to be my role," Tilly said. The drink sloshed in her hand as she waved wildly about the room. "You've just inserted yourself in everything that was Gerry's. I bet you're thrilled to finally step into the spotlight. In fact, I'll bet you're not even sorry that he's gone, are you?"

I opened my mouth to gasp but nothing came out. I was completely flabbergasted. What a horrible thing to say to a woman who'd just lost her brother.

Mary whirled around. She looked like she wanted to strike Tilly. Honestly, I wouldn't have blamed her if she had.

"Don't you dare question my feelings for my brother," Mary hissed. Her eyes glistened with tears. "He was everything to me. My brother, my best friend, my confidant, my hero and my business partner. I am dead inside right now without him, which is a depth of feeling one such as you can't fathom. The only person who had anything to gain by my brother's death was you."

"How do you figure that?" Tilly screeched. "I've lost everything."

"Right. Everything except your castle and your lover," Mary snapped.

"You can't prove anything." Tilly licked her lips. Her face was pasty white and I thought she might faint.

"Oh, can't I?" Mary asked. Then she stalked away. Tilly waited no longer than a heartbeat before she ran after her.

Chapter 12

"And then what happened?" Fee demanded. "Don't leave me fluttering in the wind here."

"Then Tilly ran after her as if she thought Mary was going to report her to Bronson," I said. I glanced at my friends. "I think she did it. I think Tilly poisoned her husband or maybe she got her lover to do it for her."

We were upstairs in the apartment Viv and I shared above the shop. Nick was in the kitchen, cooking dinner with Andre acting as his sous chef. Viv, Fee and I were watching them work, helping them in the best way we know how—by staying out of their way. Chicken Balti curry was the dish, and Nick was elbow deep in the spices he used to make it, which smelled like a slice of heaven, while Andre was chopping vegetables and making rice.

Harry had taken Aunt Betty and Freddy home so that she could get started on his grooming for tomorrow. I glanced at the clock. It was almost eight. I knew he was bringing Alistair with him on his way back, but I hadn't had the nerve to mention this to Viv or Fee. I had no idea how this was going to roll out for my friends, especially if we were entering some weird triangle where Alistair liked Viv but Fee liked Alistair and Viv was resistant to liking anyone. I started to have flashbacks to middle school, which for the record were not my favorite years.

"Now, let me get this straight," Nick said. He paused to sprinkle more spices into his very large skillet, before asking, "Swendson cut his hot young wife out of his will?"

"Not completely," I said. "He did leave her the half-built castle and a mountain of debt."

"Sounds like he left her a millstone around the neck," Andre said. "That could be enough to make someone commit murder."

I couldn't argue with his assessment since Harry and I had pretty much concluded the same thing earlier.

"Hoping she would drown?" Viv asked.

"Sure sounds like it," I said.

"But if she'd known, wouldn't she have tried to get him to change the will before she killed him?" Nick weighed in.

"Maybe she did and maybe he refused, so she offed him in anger," Fee said. She sipped her glass of chardonnay and pondered the possibilities.

"Poisoning isn't really a crime of passion," Viv said.

She tapped her forefinger on her chin. "It's more methodical, don't you think?"

"Agreed," Andre said. "It's not like clobbering someone upside the squash with a candlestick in the heat of an argument."

"True," I agreed. "Either way, she's very much a suspect because she was having an affair and she did inherit the castle."

"Are you talking about Tilly Swendson?" Harry asked as he entered the main room of our apartment with Alistair right behind him.

The two of them shed their coats, scarves and gloves. They were both dressed down in jeans and sweaters. Alistair pulled the knit beanie off his head and I saw Fee straighten up beside me. I glanced at her face and saw her grinning at Alistair. Viv was frowning, glancing between Fee and Alistair, and I wondered what she was thinking.

Harry swooped in and kissed me quick, reaching behind me to grab a slice of naan, the bread Nick was prepping to go with dinner. Without looking up from his skillet, Nick slapped Harry's hand away.

"Samosas are over there." He pointed with a wooden spoon at the triangular stuffed pastries at the end of the counter.

"Oooh." Harry left me for the tasty pastry. Completely understandable. I'd already had three.

"How is the curry coming?" Andre asked Nick. "I've got fifteen minutes left on the rice."

"Adding the chicken now," Nick said. His face was turning bright pink from the heat steaming up from the skillet. He dumped a huge bowl of cut-up chicken into the pot. The sizzle was loud and the pungent smell of the curry filling the air made my mouth water.

I turned away to see Alistair hovering over the samosas with Harry. Fee broke into their twosome with a smile up at Alistair and said, "Oy, save some for the rest of us."

Alistair smiled at her and then held one out to her. Instead of taking it in her fingers, Fee parted her lips and Alistair fed the samosa to her. It seemed a surprisingly intimate moment between two people who were not, as far as I knew, a couple. I felt my eyebrows fly up to my hairline and I turned to see what Viv made of all this.

Her face looked completely devoid of expression. That was how I knew she was upset. Viv can put her emotions on lockdown like no one I know. In fact, the stiffer she became the more upset I knew she was. When she lifted her wineglass to her lips, her movements were positively robotic, indicating she was not happy.

"Viv, Scarlett, how about you two set the table?" Nick asked.

"Fine," Viv said. She seemed relieved to leave the tight space of the kitchen.

"Making us work for our supper?" I teased. I took a last sip from my wine. The light fruity chardonnay tingled on my tongue.

Nick glanced from me to Alistair and Fee, who were giggling at each other, to Viv on the other side of the room.

"More like trying to keep my dinner from being up-staged by any drama," he said.

"Ah," I said. "Good call."

I swiveled on my chair and hopped off it to join Viv in the dining room. She was doling out the silverware, so I grabbed a stack of plates from the buffet table against the wall and began to set them at each place. The plates were a mismatched collection of china we'd inherited from Mim and added to from finds at the Saturday market on Portobello Road. There wasn't really anything that uni-fied the plates except for the fact that they were all bone china and we ate off them.

Mim had always served us regular dinners on her mis-matched fine china, saying, "What is the point of having nice things if you never use them?"

Our silverware was the same, a random collection of stainless steel pieces that we had collected as needed. I liked to think that whatever our table looked like to a guest, "boring" would be the last word that leapt to mind.

"So," I said. Viv ignored me.

"Well." I tried again. She still ignored me.

"All right—" I began but she interrupted me.

"Stop." She held up one hand, still holding a fork, as if she could physically deflect any words I might say. "I don't want to talk about it."

"Talk about what?" I asked. Yes, because I'm relent-less like that.

"Them. For the record, I don't care, not even a little."

Her voice was a low growl and she jerked her head in the direction of Fee and Alistair. I glanced at the twosome.

They stood by the counter, smiling at each other and chatting. There was a definite chemistry there as they looked into each other's eyes with obvious interest. Fee's color was heightened and Alistair's eyes sparkled. He looked happier than I'd seen him in a long time.

In my heart, I had always felt like Alistair belonged with Viv but if she wasn't interested then good for him for moving on. Unrequited love is the absolute worst, in my opinion. And good for Fee for not letting a good man go to waste. They'd probably be very happy together.

I tried to tell myself this, except when I glanced over at Viv she looked anything but immune to what was happening. In fact, from the way she was biting her lip, I got the distinct impression she was perturbed by the couple. Huh.

Fee tipped back her head and laughed at something Alistair said. Her corkscrew curls bounced and her long neck was exposed as she leaned back, placing her hand on Alistair's forearm to keep her balance. My gaze darted back to Viv. She was putting the silverware down with a bit more force than was necessary. Quite a bit, in fact.

I heard Alistair burst out laughing. He and Fee were leaning against each other, sharing a laugh and looking as if they'd forgotten the rest of us were even there.

"Excuse me, I'll be right back," Viv said. She dropped the last of the utensils on the table with a clatter, and stomped out of the room to her bedroom. She had taken over Mim's old room, on the far side of the living room, while I still had my old room upstairs. Her door slammed with a resounding *bang*.

Harry joined me at the far end of the table, where I began to fold the cloth napkins into neat rectangles. He leaned close and said, "What do you suppose that is all about?"

He motioned at Alistair and Fee with his head and I shrugged. "She did ask Viv the other day if she fancied him."

"Did Viv say 'no'?"

"Not so much no to Alistair as no to anyone," I said.

"Well, maybe Fee and Alistair are a good fit, then," he said.

"Maybe," I said. But I wasn't convinced. As soon as Viv's door shut, I watched Fee step back from Alistair and the two of them glanced at Viv's closed door and then exchanged a sly knuckle bump. Oh, those crazy kids, what were they up to?

I glanced at Harry to see if he'd seen this exchange, but he had abandoned me and was back at the counter, harassing Nick and Andre while they cooked. Nick slapped his hand away from the naan again and Harry looked pouty. Men and their food, honestly.

"Dinner is served," Nick announced. He dished up the chicken in a large Balti bowl and led the procession of food, with Andre bringing the rice and a vegetable dish, and Harry carrying the naan, to the table.

We all took our seats. Alistair and Fee sat together on

one side while Harry and I took the other. As the chefs, Nick and Andre each took the ends of the table since they were presiding over the meal. The lone seat left was for Viv, next to me, right across from Fee and Alistair. Oh, boy, this was going to be interesting.

"Should I call Viv?" Nick asked.

"No," I said. "She said she'd be right back. I'm sure she'll just be a minute."

We all began to pass the food around and Nick, who was refilling everyone's glass of wine, looked at Alistair and said, "Okay, let's hear the goss, Al. You're the closest to this whole Swendson thing, so do tell. Did Tilly whack her husband?"

"Al?" Alistair's eyebrows rose. He looked at Harry, who was laughing, and asked, "Did he just call me Al?"

"I think it's cute," Fee said.

"Oh, that's a what a grown man wants to be—cute," Alistair said.

He grinned and leaned into Fee in a teasing way. Just then Viv came back into the room. She stagger-stopped at the sight of them sitting side by side and I saw her visibly compose herself, running her palms over her hips before she continued. I could see a shadow of hurt in her eyes, so I jumped into the void, as one does, to distract from her arrival.

"I don't think 'Al' is cute," I said. "Maybe it's my American roots but I always think of Al as a gangster's name."

Alistair squinted one eye and leaned on the edge of the table with one elbow. "'So, I make you laugh, I'm here to amuse you?'" he asked in a spot-on *Goodfellas* accent.

I laughed, ignoring how stiffly Viv sat next to me. Without acknowledging any of us, she began to fill her plate. Harry, not one to pick up on vibes, leaned around me and asked, "All right, Viv?"

The smile she gave him was as vacant as a doll's. It was rather creepy, in fact.

"Of course," she said. "Why do you ask?"

"No reason," Harry said. He sat back with a shiver.

I leaned against him for just a moment but then the Balti curry was coming around and it smelled so good. All thought of my squad and their drama fled as I loaded my plate before handing the bowl to Viv.

Harry was clearly as starved as I was and he tucked into his food, swabbing up the curry with a slice of naan. Andre was doing the same but he hadn't lost the thread of the conversation and turned back to Alistair.

"Have you learned anything from the police, Al . . . istair?" he asked with a grin.

Alistair waved his fork at him in mock warning and then dabbed his mouth with his napkin, before he said, "If they know anything, they are keeping it very close to the vest.

"Technically, anyone who was at the dog show from the time of the cocktail party through the next morning is a suspect," Alistair said. He glanced at me and Harry. "That includes you two."

"But that makes no sense," I said. "Why would we harm Gerry Swendson?"

"To get revenge for Aunt Betty," Alistair said.

"Revenge for what?" Harry asked. He took a sip of wine before continuing. "Because of a bad batch of dog food? It's not like anything bad happened to Freddy."

"Murder does seem a bit extreme," I said. "Besides, isn't there already a lawsuit pending of people who are actively trying to take Swendson down over the quality of the dog food? Why wouldn't we just join that?"

"That lawsuit has been kept pretty hush-hush," Alistair said. "And I don't think your revenge would be over last year's dog food so much as the fact that Swendson tried to have Aunt Betty banned from competing this year."

"Yeah, I did feel a little murdery when I found her looking so sad and stuffed in the corner by the registration table," I admitted.

"The fact is, they don't know what poison killed Swendson yet," Alistair said. "When they do, they'll be able to start scrutinizing suspects more closely. According to Gerry's sister, Mary, he had no known allergies and he wasn't on any medication, so it had to be something that is fairly lethal since it appears he died quite quickly."

"Do you suppose that's why he was stuffed under the dais?" I asked. "Maybe his murderer didn't account for how fast-acting the poison was and they had no choice but to stuff him under the dais to hide him until his body could be disposed of properly."

"This is charming dinner conversation, I'm sure," Viv said. She pushed a piece of chicken across her plate.

I glanced at her, trying to determine if she was joking

or not. Judging by the frown that was curving her mouth down, I was going to guess not. But I wasn't sure it was the conversation that had put her into such a foul mood. Hmm.

"It's no different than what we usually talk about," Fee said. "Is something wrong, Viv?"

Fee tipped her head to the side, specifically Alistair's side, and he looked charmed that her curls brushed his face. Viv glowered. I swear, I felt like I was watching a crazy person poke a bear with a stick, meaning Fee was the crazy person and Viv the bear. Not flattering to either of them but that didn't make it not true.

"Nothing's wrong," Viv said. "I just find the incessant talk about murder tiresome."

"Tiresome?" Nick cried. "Surely you jest."

One of Viv's eyebrows went up. I knew this look. This was most definitely her *no, not jesting* look.

"I mean, look at the suspect list," Nick said, clearly ignoring Viv's desire not to talk about the murder. "You've got the young drunken wife, trying to get away with murder so she can take off with her lover—speaking of which, do we know who that is?"

"No," I said. "I asked a few of the people involved with the dog show but either they don't know or nobody is talking. I'm betting Liza Stanhope knows. She seems the type to know everything about everyone. Too bad she's taken such a dislike of me and Freddy."

"Why do you suppose that is?" Nick asked.

"I get the feeling she doesn't like corgis," I said.

"What?" Andre asked. He sounded appalled. "Who doesn't like corgis? They're like the comedians of all the dog breeds."

"Liza Stanhope doesn't," I said. I turned to Harry. "Don't you agree or do you think it's Aunt Betty that she dislikes?"

"Well, that's even worse," Nick said. "How could anyone not like Aunt Betty? She's adorable."

Harry smiled. "Well, she can be a bit tenacious. She's wanted to win this dog show for four years and she has no trouble badgering people when she doesn't think things are being run properly."

"Like with the dog food?" I asked.

"Swendson was furious with her," Harry said. "I know it's why the detectives are still looking at her." He exchanged a glance with Alistair and it wasn't hard to see that they were worried.

"But the fact that Swendson was found dressed in his clothes for the day and that Aunt Betty was with us all morning gives her an alibi, doesn't it?"

"That depends upon whether it was a fast-acting poison or not," Harry said. "If it was a slow-acting poison, it could have been administered the night before during the cocktail party. That she was having a tiff with him at the party looks bad."

"But that makes no sense," Fee said. "Why would she have a public spat with a person she was planning to murder, yeah? If she was guilty, she wouldn't have brought attention to herself like that."

"Exactly what I said," Alistair said. His look was full of admiration. "Beautiful and smart, too. You're the thinking man's crumpet, Fiona Felton."

Fee's face got heated and she glanced down at her plate as if embarrassed. I glanced at Viv. Now she was stabbing bits of chicken with her fork as if they'd done something to offend her.

"The police seem to think Aunt Betty's intake of gin might have had something to do with her lack of discretion," Harry said. "So, even though it would seem unlikely that she would draw attention to herself, they're not ruling her out, not by a long shot."

"That's rubbish," Andre said. "They're grasping at straws. Anyone can see that the real killers are Penelope and Jasper Young."

My head whipped in his direction. This hypothesis totally worked for me since I loathed those two, but it needed to be fact-based. "How do you figure that?"

"Because they're horrible people," he said. "I think they'd poison the lot of us just to win that stupid crystal bowl."

I laughed. The assessment was certainly apt. Then I remembered that Penelope had said she was going to have to tell DI Bronson what she had overheard, and it was clearly about me. I wondered if I should mention it to the others. Probably, but I didn't want anyone to get upset.

I glanced to my left to see Viv ripping her naan into small pieces. Okay, I didn't want anyone to get more upset than they already were. She was actively avoiding looking across the table to where Alistair and Fee were nudging each other and smiling. A closer look and I could see that the look on Viv's face was one of misery.

I was torn. On the one hand, when I thought about the fist bump I'd seen Alistair and Fee exchange earlier, I was pretty sure they were doing this to nudge Viv, which she deserved for keeping Alistair dangling for so long.

But on the other hand, if I was wrong and in fact Fee and Alistair were really becoming a twosome, then I couldn't deny them the happiness they were finding, and as their friend, I wanted to be happy for them. But coming full circle, Viv was my cousin and she'd been through a rough time. If she felt anything for Alistair, I wanted her to have that opportunity. The tension running across the table from Viv to Alistair felt like a live electric wire. Not knowing what to do, I opted to drink my wine, because wine makes everything better.

"Who else is considered a suspect?" Nick asked. "We've got the young wife, the ambitious dog owners, the people who've filed a lawsuit against the company, Aunt Betty, who else?"

"What about his sister?" Viv asked. She must have realized the murder talk wasn't going to go away. "Mary Swendson was more than his sister, she was his business partner, too." She glanced up at Fee. Her stare was hard and flat. "When you share something like that it's a bond. It requires complete trust. Maybe Gerry did something to betray her trust and she killed him."

Fee quirked one eyebrow up and met Viv's stare. "He betrayed her trust? He's the one who's dead, yeah? Seems to me, killing your brother who is also your business partner is a bigger betrayal of trust than anything he could have done to her."

"Well, we don't know much about their business, do we?" Viv asked.

"Actually," Harry said, but I put my hand on his arm, signaling for him to stop.

"A business relationship is a fragile thing," Viv said. "Spending day in, day out with the same people, you think you know them but maybe you don't."

"Yeah, maybe you don't," Fee agreed. "Maybe there are things more important than business that have to be taken into account."

The two women were staring at each other. I noticed everyone was glancing from them to me as if I was supposed to do something about this. I'm sorry, did I look like I was wearing referee stripes or carrying a whistle? That was a big "hell no." I wasn't going to get into the middle of this mess. I'd either lose a friend or a cousin or both. Nope. I was just going to keep my mouth shut.

"I guess sometimes people just surprise you," Viv said. She took her napkin off her lap and dabbed her mouth. Then she tossed it onto the table and rose from her seat. "Thank you for dinner, Nick, it was wonderful."

"I can see that by the way you've cleared your plate," he said.

Viv had created some sort of portrait art, using the rice and chicken and bits of ripped-up naan. I wasn't sure but it reminded me of Edvard Munch's *The Scream*.

"If you'll all excuse me, I'm not feeling very well," she said. She reached out and patted Nick's arm and then went to pick up her plate.

"Don't," I said. I shooed her away from the table with my hand. "Go rest. I'll wrap up your dinner so you can finish it later if you get hungry."

"Thank you," she said. She left the room, calling over her shoulder, "Good night, everyone."

We all called after her and I glanced at Alistair and saw him watch her leave the room. His eyes looked shadowed with regret but Fee leaned into him and whispered something I couldn't hear. He gave her a small nod and then turned to Harry.

"What do you think our chances are against the Black Hornets, mate?" he asked.

My beloved launched into a very windy monologue about the Hornets' strengths and weaknesses versus their own team's. As riveting as this was, I excused myself to wrap up Viv's dinner. I picked up her plate and brought it to the kitchen, where I covered it with a sheet of cling wrap and put it in the fridge. I stalled, wiping down the counters, hoping that Fee would join me after a bit. Sure enough, she did. She brought both of our wineglasses with her.

She took the bottle of chardonnay that sat on the counter and filled our glasses. She handed me mine and tapped her glass against it and said, "You know I would never do anything to hurt Viv intentionally, yeah?"

"I know," I said. "But I'm pretty sure she's hurting now and it seems pretty intentional."

"Sometimes you have to hold someone's feet to the fire to get them to do what needs to be done," Fee said.

"Is that what you're doing?" I asked. I really hoped it was.

She neither confirmed nor denied. She just said, "Trust me."

"I do," I said. "I definitely do."

"Thank you," she said.

"But—" I began but she shook her head. She wasn't going to tell me any more. She was just going to leave me wondering? It was straight-up cruel. "You're a cold woman, Fiona Felton."

"But effective," she said.

She led the way back to the table and I don't think I imagined it, but with Viv gone there was more space between Fee and Alistair. They seemed to have regained their old friendship with none of the flirty weirdness that had been happening between them before. I noticed Nick glanced at them a couple of times, and I knew he was thinking the same.

"So, what's the plan for tomorrow?" Andre asked. "It's the day they look over the coat, teeth and all of that. Are you and Freddy ready?"

"I don't know, what do you think?" I opened my mouth

and showed him my teeth, scoring a laugh as he choked on his chicken curry.

"Warn a fellow when you're going to do that," he cried. "That's enamel cruelty."

Nick snorted and said, "Tooth to be told, she got you with that one."

I glanced at Harry, who was chuckling. "I'd say she got to the root of it."

"Dental puns, really?" Alistair asked. "Have we not drilled deep enough?"

That set them all off again. Fee was laughing into her napkin along with the others and, per usual, I just couldn't stand to be left out.

"I think we all need to brush up on our puns," I said. I laughed pretty hard at that one, but I was the only one laughing. "Get it? Brush up?"

"Oh, Scarlett." Fee sighed. "May the floss be with you."

The entire room erupted. I gaped at them all. I knew it was a joke to ignore my puns, but seriously, "brush up" had been a good one. I turned and glared at Harry.

"It was a good one," he said. "I even felt my mouth twitch up a bit. Right here." He pointed to the corner of his mouth and his lips curved up a teeny bit. I threw my napkin at him.

Harry laughed and then hugged me. He was big and warm and smelled too good to stay mad at for more than a moment. Dratted man.

"I suppose we should call it a night," Alistair said as they all settled down. "The show starts early tomorrow."

"How are you feeling about it, Scarlett?" Nick asked. His voice was full of genuine concern and I smiled at him.

I gave him a nervous look and admitted, "I'm okay. I just hope I don't let Aunt Betty or Freddy down. He's in the lead. I would hate to muck that up."

"You won't," Harry said. He kissed my forehead and then leaned back to meet my gaze. "You've done amazing and Freddy's in first place. Nothing can stop you now."

Except for the crazed murderer on the loose, I thought. But at least I didn't say it out loud.

Chapter 13

"How do I look?" I asked as I entered the hat shop from our apartment upstairs. I twirled in my sage green Jenny Packham collared day dress with elbow-length sleeves and a flared skirt.

"Like a winner," Harry said. Then he kissed me and my nerves evaporated.

He and Aunt Betty had come by the shop to collect me for the final day of the dog competition. Amen.

"I swear you two are my OTP," Fee said.

"OTP?" Viv asked.

"One true pairing," Fee explained. "The pinnacle of ship."

"Ship?" Aunt Betty asked.

"Short for 'relationship,'" Fee said.

"Kids these days," Aunt Betty said to Harry. "I swear I don't understand a word she's saying."

He laughed. "It's slang, Aunt B, no worries. I don't understand most of it either."

"Thank you, Fee," I said. "We do good ship if I do say so myself."

"Don't give up hope, Fee. Maybe you and Alistair will achieve that sort of pairing," Viv said. I was rather surprised her voice didn't leave behind a scorch mark.

I glanced at Fee but she didn't answer and turned her face away. I got the feeling she was hiding a smile, which bolstered my theory that she and Alistair were in cahoots. Lordy, I hoped this did not backfire on us all.

"We'd best be off," Harry said. He glanced at Viv and Fee. "Are you two going to be there when they announce the winner?"

"Wouldn't miss it," Fee said.

"I suppose," Viv said, sighing. She glanced over the counter at Freddy. "Do me proud, boy."

As we left, I said to Harry, "Did you see that? She actually spoke to him. I really think Viv is coming around on the dog thing."

He gave me a dubious look with one eyebrow lowered but didn't say anything. We left the hat shop and climbed into his car. Freddy and I were in the backseat while Aunt Betty rode in front with Harry. I think Freddy might have been nervous because when I petted him a poof of hair rose up into the air.

A chime sounded and Aunt Betty took her phone out

of her purse. She glanced at the message she had just received and said, "Oh, bother. We need to make a slight detour, Harry."

"What?" he asked. "But the dog show."

"Will have to wait," she said. "My corgi rescue group needs me."

"Now?" he asked. "I don't mean to point out the obvious, because it's obvious, but we're a bit busy at present."

"We're running early. It'll be fine. Besides, it can't be helped," she said. "I take my role as a corgi rescuer very seriously. Miriam was supposed to be on call today but she has the flu and I'm her backup."

"Bloody hell," Harry muttered.

"What was that?" Aunt Betty asked.

"Very well," he said.

"That's what I thought you said," she said.

Harrison followed her directions into Kensington. Parking was nonexistent, so it was decided after much debate that he and Freddy would wait in the car while Aunt Betty and I went on the rescue mission.

I didn't feel dressed for a rescue but rather more for afternoon tea at a place nicer than my own kitchen. I hurried after Aunt Betty, who strode with purpose toward a redbrick town house. My heels slowed me up a bit as I skipped around a couple of icy patches, trying to ignore the chilly draft that seemed determined to go up my skirt.

"The message says that the dog is on the young side, a female, and her name is Bella," Aunt Betty said. She was studying her phone as she approached the steps of number

14. She opened the door to the vestibule and I scooted closer to the heater beside the mailboxes. Aunt Betty scanned the residences and then hit the number for 14-C.

"Hello?" a woman's voice spoke through the intercom.

"Hi, this is Betty Wentworth, I'm with corgi rescue and am here about Bella," she said.

I could hear barking in the background and the woman said, "Bella from hella? Come and get her, she's all yours."

"Oh, dear," Aunt Betty said. The interior door's lock clicked and she pulled it open, holding it for me.

We trudged up the stairs to the second floor, where the apartment was situated. The barking got louder as we got closer.

Aunt Betty raised her fist to knock but the person on the other side must have been waiting because the door was pulled open before her knuckles could connect with the wood.

"Take her," a middle-aged woman with brown hair that was highlighted with streaks of silver said. She was broadly shaped and wore a thick turtleneck under a shapeless cardigan over sweatpants. She had no makeup on, reading glasses perched on her head, her phone in her hand and an air about her that said she'd given up on life and had no intention of reengaging anytime soon.

I wanted to hug her and tell her everything would be okay but since I had no idea what she was dealing with, it seemed inappropriate at best and extremely insensitive at worst. Instead, I followed Aunt Betty into the apartment.

It was barren except for a few boxes. The windows were large, without curtains, making the room airy and bright.

Aunt Betty glanced around. "Where is she?"

The woman ran a hand over her face. "Destroying something, no doubt."

Aunt Betty flashed her an annoyed look and set off into the apartment.

"I'm just trying to get my parents moved into an elderly care facility," the woman said. "They're both in failing health and my dad has dementia."

Her voice broke and she looked like she just needed a good cry. This time I went with my impulse and gave her a half hug.

"There, there . . ." I paused. "I'm sorry, what's your name?"

"Lynn," she said. "Lynn Biscoff."

"Like the cookie?"

She gave me a look. "Yeah, like the biscuit."

"I'm Scarlett, like the color," I said. She gave me a watery smile. "We're here now. We'll take the puppy off your hands."

"I can't thank you enough." Lynn sighed and wiped the tears from her face with the sleeve of her sweater. She picked up a leash from the kitchen counter and handed it to me. "I don't know what my mother was thinking, bringing home a puppy last month. She knew they were moving and she knew the new place didn't take pets."

I nodded. It sounded to me like her mother had gotten

the dog to avoid the move. I didn't say it because I was pretty sure she'd figure it out on her own when she had a minute to think. Besides, we had enough to deal with at the moment.

I heard the scrabble of dog paws on wood and glanced across the empty room to see a puff ball of white and honey, a miniature Freddy, in fact, coming at me. Aunt Betty was hot on her heels.

"Grab her, Scarlett!" Aunt Betty cried.

For the record, I tried. Really, I did. But the dog was half projectile and before I even had my hands out, she rocketed right past me, making me totter on my heels. Aunt Betty blew by me, giving me a none-too-gentle push as she went.

"Cut her off!" she cried.

Aunt Betty went one way around the pile of boxes, and I went the other. Lynn watched, looking too exhausted to move her feet. But to her credit, she crouched down as if Bella might leap into her arms and she'd catch her.

I dropped low and as the puppy came at me, I was certain I'd be able to grab her and said, "I've got her! I've got her!" My arms hugged air. "I don't have her!"

How Bella managed to dash through my feet and race back down the hall, I don't know, but she did. I straightened up, getting a mild head rush, and hurried after her.

"Bella! Come here, Bella!" I cried. "We do not have time for this!"

Aunt Betty was fumbling in her purse, where she

found some dog treats. Not the hard-biscuit kind but the sort that were soft and looked like mini sausages.

"Good thinking," I said.

She winked at me. "She ran into the back bedroom. Let's slip in and close the door. We'll probably have to corner her, as she's either scared out of her mind or thinks this is a game."

"Given her nickname, Bella from hella, I'm betting on game," I said.

We slipped into the bedroom. It, too, was bare except for a pile of bedding in the middle of the floor. The closet doors were open and a quick glance showed that it was empty except for a few sad wire hangers. I scanned the room. There was no sign of the willful puppy.

Then I saw a wriggle out of the corner of my eye. The large fluffy blue blanket moved. I waved at Aunt Betty and pointed at the pile on the floor. She nodded. Silently we crept forward. There was another wriggle and a baby growl. As if the fierce Bella was trying very hard to sound ferocious. It was so stinking cute, I felt my heart go smoosh.

Aunt Betty held the treat out and we closed in on the puppy, coming at her from opposite sides of the blanket. There was a wriggle and a pounce and then a little head popped out from beneath the fluffy comforter. Two big ears, a black nose and a pair of sparkling eyes regarded us. Her tongue slipped out of her mouth as she panted and I got the feeling Bella was delighted with us. Before she could dash away, Aunt Betty held out the treat, which caused Bella to wiggle with excitement. While Bella gingerly took the treat from Aunt Betty's hand, I clipped the leash to her collar.

Aunt Betty and I exhaled simultaneously as if we'd just run a marathon. Aunt Betty glanced at her phone to check the time. "We have to go!"

Not wanting to give Bella the chance to slip out of her collar, I picked her up in a football hold—she was as solid as a ten-pound turkey—and carried her back into the main room.

"You got her!" Lynn clapped her hands in front of her. She smiled at us but then her smile slid away and she asked, "What will happen to her?"

"We'll find her a really good home," Aunt Betty said. "And in the meantime, she'll receive the very best of care as a foster puppy."

Lynn looked relieved. She reached out and rubbed Bella's head. "I'm sorry, little love. You're just too much for my old folks and taking care of them means I can't take care of you."

Bella licked her wrist and Lynn smiled. "She really is a good girl if you can overlook her barking, chewing the furniture, and relentless herding tendencies."

"We'll train that out of her," Aunt Betty said. "Don't you worry."

I looked down at the bundle of fur in my arms. She didn't resemble a problem puppy but I knew I was likely getting snookered by her big brown eyes and her wagging butt. Heaven help me.

My phone buzzed with an impatient text from Harry. He was circling the building for the fourth time and concerned that Freddy was going to miss the dog show.

"Feel free to contact us anytime," I said to Lynn. "And good luck with everything."

"Thanks," she said. She smiled at me. "You, too."

Aunt Betty and I hurried out of the building to see Harrison double-parked right in front. Aunt Betty opened the back door and I slid in with Bella while she climbed in front. We were barely buckled when Harry shot into the traffic, making his way to Finchley Park.

"What are we going to do with the puppy?" he asked. His eyebrows knotted as he took in the sight of Bella, making herself at home on my lap while she chewed on her leash.

"Keep her," I said immediately. I hadn't really thought about it until the words came out but once I heard them out loud I knew it was 100 percent the right decision.

"Ginger, Viv isn't going to let you have a dog at the shop," he said.

"That's why Bella will stay with you at your place," I said.

Freddy sniffed Bella's head and then licked her. She tried to return the favor but I blocked her with my hand, not wanting her to mess up Freddy's perfect look.

"There'll be time for that later," I said. Bella, clearly exhausted from her morning, yawned and fell asleep in my lap almost as fast as I fell in love with her. I let my fingers sift through her soft fur. She was supposed to be with me. I felt it all the way down in my bones.

When I glanced up, Harry was watching me in the rear-view mirror. His eyes were half-amused, half-chagrined.

"So, we have a puppy." He said it as a statement, not a question and I knew I had never loved him more.

"Yes," I said. "We do."

The jostling motion of the car rocked Bella into a deep sleep. So different from the holy terror that had been dodging us in the apartment, she was now as limp as a noodle. I ran my fingers through her soft fur, picked up her feet and checked the pads, played with the tips of her ears. She didn't even move.

Freddy leaned over and gave her a thorough sniffing, from head to foot. Then he flopped down beside me and rested his head on his feet while he watched her. I wondered if he considered her a part of his pack. If so, was she going to be an alpha, beta or omega? Judging by this morning, I was leaning toward alpha.

Harrison found a decent parking spot, and we hustled into the building at Finchley Park. My nerves were shot, frankly, and I was ready for the dog show to be over. But Freddy was a contender, so I knew I had to dig deep and present him to the best of my ability.

Aunt Betty had him looking downright spiffy with a shining coat and polished teeth. We had decided to forgo hats this morning, so he wouldn't have an unfortunate case of hat head before the judging.

I took Freddy's leash and passed off Bella to Harry, who carried her like a sleeping baby in his arms. Ridiculously adorable.

We entered the arena and it was again full to bursting. The murmur of the crowd was restless as people maneuvered their way to their seats. I showed my credentials and was given a program. I gave it a quick glance and noted that Freddy and I were going in front of the judges in an hour. I took a deep breath. This was it.

Once the final scores were up, the top five winners would be invited to a fancy high tea with the judges and the sponsors. I checked the leaderboard, which was on the far wall. Freddy's name was still in the number one spot with Muffin just below him.

I glanced around the room, looking for Richard. There was no sign of him or his bulldog. I did see Penelope Young, however. She was talking to Detective Inspector Bronson and I noticed she pointed in my direction. I saw Bronson turn my way and his gaze was considering. My intuition started to tingle and I knew she was following through with her threat from the day before. She was saying something to Bronson about "what she'd overheard" and it had to do with me. I put my hand on Harry's arm. When he glanced at me, I tipped my head in the detective's direction.

It seemed my instincts were spot-on, because Bronson cut through the crowd and headed our way. He worked through the people and dogs with a singular purpose. I felt myself get nervous even though I knew I had no reason to be. No matter what horrible thing Penelope Young said about me, I hadn't done anything wrong. It would be fine. There was no other acceptable alternative.

"Scarlett, might I have a word with you?" Detective Inspector Bronson asked. His tone was polite, and yet, it didn't really feel like a question I could say "no" to.

I held up the schedule and said, "Freddy and I are in the ring in an hour."

"I only need a few minutes," he said.

"Whatever you need to discuss with Scarlett, you can say to us, too," Harry said.

Bronson met his gaze, glanced down at snoozing Bella and gave a small nod. "If you'll follow me."

"Me, too?" Aunt Betty asked.

"Yes," Harry said. "We all stay together until they discover who murdered Swendson."

We went back to the security office where Bronson had interviewed us before. Freddy took it all in stride, hurrying along on his short legs. I felt my heart do a little hiccup when he looked at me with his earnest face. While I was ready to be done with the dog show, I was really going to miss Freddy, but maybe that's why fate had brought Bella into my life.

"Have a seat," Bronson said.

He circled the desk and waited while Aunt Betty and I took the chairs and Harry stood behind us. Freddy sat in between our feet, looking like he was eager to hear what this was all about.

"It's been brought to my attention—" he began but I interrupted. Rude, I know, but I couldn't help myself.

"By Penelope Young?" I asked.

He nodded. "Yes, she was the one who brought her concerns to me."

"And what concerns were those?" Harry asked. His voice was hard as if he were biting off each word before spitting it out. He kept the volume low, however, and I suspected that had to do with Bella. It hit me then that he was going to make a spectacular dog dad.

"She said that you and Gerry Swendson had an argument the morning of the agility tests, that she couldn't make out what was said but that it was clear you were furious."

"Codswallop," Aunt Betty snapped.

"What she said," I agreed. "I never saw Gerry Swendson the morning of the agility tests. In fact, I didn't even know I'd be competing until we got here and discovered that Liza Stanhope refused to let Aunt Betty enter. That's when I took her place, so why would I have had a problem with Swendson before then?"

"What time did she say this altercation took place?" Harry asked. "Scarlett was with me, then she was at the hat shop, before coming here to the dog show. Since she was with someone at all times, it should be very easy to provide an alibi for her."

"Mrs. Young said that she believed the conversation took place at about eight o'clock in the morning before the dog show was even open to an audience," he said.

I felt my heart plummet into the pointy toes of my shoes. To present Freddy today I had dressed up in a flirty skirt with heels and everything—not for nothing, but I was slaying it. But none of this was going to help me right now because somehow Penelope had managed to pick the one time, eight o'clock, that I had been alone during the morning of the agility tests.

I remembered that I'd left Harry's house to go home at seven thirty but had stopped on my way for coffee and a mince pie, which I had eaten in the bakery, where it was warm. Damn my love of a good pastry.

"You were at the hat shop by eight, right?" Harry asked me. He turned to Bronson. "Her business partner, Vivian Tremont, will confirm her whereabouts that morning."

I turned in my seat and faced Harry, willing him to turn back to me. When he did, I made an imperceptible, I hoped, shake of my head. To his credit, his face remained impassive instead of looking shocked. In fact, if I didn't know better I'd say he wasn't even surprised.

I think this is the best part of finding your soul mate. A real one can read your mind, I swear. As if by unspoken agreement, Harry and I said nothing more to Bronson about it.

There were questions I wanted to have answered first, starting with, Why was Penelope Young lying about seeing me? Was she trying to get me disqualified from the dog show to gain a higher ranking for Henry? Or did she really think she had seen me? Or was she just trying to draw suspicion off herself and her husband, Jasper?

She had to know I was going to call her out. She was putting everything we had strived for in jeopardy. We had worked too hard to get Freddy into the winning position to lose it all now over a bogus accusation.

"So, you have an alibi?" Bronson asked. I don't think I was imagining that he sounded relieved. I figured, compared to most of the other competitors, I was the least annoying.

I shrugged. "Yeah, of course I do. You can call my cousin, Viv, if you want."

I felt Harry get tense beside me. Okay, maybe that had been taking the bluff too far.

"No, that's good enough—for now," he said. He looked discouraged.

"This is a complete waste of time. Do you have any leads, any *real* leads, in the case?" Aunt Betty asked. She stared at Bronson as if she found him lacking, and I saw him shift in his seat.

One corner of his mouth tipped up into a rueful smile. "They're all real. I'm just not sure which one is the truth, including the one that gives Scarlett a motive to have poisoned Swendson."

Chapter 14

"That's cuckoo bananas," I said. "We've already established that I didn't even know I was going to be in the competition. Why would I murder Swendson?"

"Maybe he threatened to toss you out of the competition like he did Betty," Bronson said.

"He didn't, because I never saw him," I said. "Besides, why would I care? It's not as if I know what I'm doing!"

"Possibly you wanted revenge for the bad food he gave Freddy last year."

"I didn't even know Freddy until a few weeks ago," I said.

Bronson stared at me. Clearly, he'd been running these scenarios through his head since talking to Penelope.

"Perhaps you were helping your fiancé exact his revenge on Swendson."

"And why would I want revenge?" Harry asked. The look he sent Bronson was incredulous.

"Because Swendson argued with your aunt the night before the dog show began," he said.

Harry looked at Aunt Betty and then back at Bronson. "So? So they argued? So what? We didn't know that Swendson had her blackballed until registration the following morning, by which time Swendson was already dead."

"Probably by opioid overdose," I said.

Bronson went still. "How did you know that?"

"It was a guess," I said. "Back in the day, when I worked in the hospitality industry at a major resort hotel, I dealt with a few cases where guests had overdosed. One was an old man who'd gotten confused and taken too many pain pills. The other was a young twentysomething woman, who'd taken some pills while drinking with her friends.

"Both cases were awful. The victims' bodies, which I'd only glimpsed while waiting for the paramedics, had the bluish tinge to the lips and fingers, as well as the dried-up spittle from foaming at the mouth, just like Swendson's body. I remember that the girl had been bruised all along one side, and we thought she might have been assaulted but the paramedics said she'd likely had a seizure on the cold hard floor of her bathroom. Was there any bruising on Swendson?"

"I'm sorry, I'm not at liberty to discuss," he began, and I said with him, "an ongoing investigation."

"Right," I said. I met Bronson's gaze. I didn't like what I was about to say but I felt it needed to be clarified. "Swendson didn't commit suicide. Someone slipped him those pills the morning of the show. Someone who wanted him dead."

Bronson tossed down the pen he'd been fidgeting with. "Damn it, that's the same conclusion I keep coming to but *who* and *why*?"

I felt myself relax, as it seemed like he was bumping us down the suspect list, but only a little. There was still a murderer out there, after all.

"Don't you find it interesting that Penelope knew exactly what time to say she saw Scarlett talking to Swendson to put her at the scene before the murder?" Aunt Betty asked. She reached down and patted Freddy thoughtfully. "Why, it's almost as if she knew what time he was murdered."

We all sat silently. I watched Bronson's face. He gave nothing away. "That's assuming that his murder took place in the morning."

"He was found in the clothes he'd chosen that morning," Aunt Betty said. "I heard that his housekeeper verified he was wearing the exact same outfit when he left his house. It has to mean he was murdered that morning."

"How do you know what his housekeeper said?" Bronson asked.

"Gossip." Aunt Betty shrugged. "Tilly let it be known that she spent the night at her mother's because of a headache, how convenient, and she told someone that their housekeeper verified Swendson's attire."

Bronson looked frustrated by the rumor mill. I imagined it didn't make his job any easier.

"Unless Tilly and her housekeeper lied. It could be that she's the one who murdered him and delivered him here, and she's paying off her housekeeper to back her story," I said. "Maybe she murdered him late that night and dragged the body back in a new outfit."

"There's no way she could move him by herself," Harry said. "He's twice as big as she is. If she did murder him at home and bring him here, she had to have help."

"Assisted by some strong *young* people who want to win a dog show more than anything?" I asked. I put the emphasis on "young" just to make sure Bronson didn't miss it.

Bronson looked at each of us. "Thank you for your time. I'll be sure to keep you apprised of anything else we learn."

And just like that we were dismissed. I had kept my cool in the office but now I wanted to get me a piece of Mrs. Penelope Young. How dare she fabricate seeing me talk to Swendson in Finchley Park the morning of the agility tests? I wanted to stomp her, crush her, smash her into bits.

"Ginger, you okay in there?" Harry asked.

I scowled at him. I was pretty sure there was smoke coming out of my ears. I showed my teeth in an attempt at a smile.

"Great, just great," I said.

"That looks even worse," he said.

"He's right," Aunt Betty said. "You have to pull it together. You've got the final competition in thirty minutes. You need to get your game face on."

"Fine," I said. "But if I run into Penelope Young, I might just kick her on principle."

"After the competition," Aunt Betty said. She handed me Freddy's leash. "Now, go freshen up."

I nodded. She was right. Freddy had worked so hard for this. He deserved my commitment to his final competition even if it was just him standing on a table and having his teeth checked.

Harry's phone chimed. He held Bella with one arm while he checked it and said, "That's from Viv. She and Fee are here and they're saving us seats."

Suddenly, I was nervous. Not just a little nervous—oh, no—this was like "teeth clacking, knees knocking, I have to pee really bad" nervous. Freddy was in the lead. He could totally win this thing if the judges found his overall appearance appealing. I glanced down at him and felt as if his entire future was resting on my shoulders.

"I can't do this," I said. Panic was making my voice wobble. I held out my hands for Bella and thrust Freddy's leash at Harry at the same time. "I'll go sit in the stands and you do the dog-show thing."

Harry smiled at me. He shifted Bella and did not take Freddy's leash. "I'm not dressed to present Freddy."

I looked him over in his jeans and sweater. "You look fine to me."

"But you look beautiful," he said.

Well, bless his clearly-love-is-blind, foolish heart. The

fact that he saw me this way made my heart sing, but I still didn't want to do the dog show. There was so much at stake. What if I screwed it up? I didn't want to be responsible for Freddy losing.

"Thank you," I said. "I still think you should take him instead of me."

"Nonsense," Aunt Betty said. "It's just nerves. You'll be fine."

"I don't feel fine," I said.

"Good. Then you'll take it seriously," she said. She made a shooing motion with her hand.

"Don't worry," Harry said. He kissed my forehead. "Trust Freddy. He hasn't steered you wrong yet."

I watched him turn and walk away with Bella and, dang, if that wasn't the cutest thing ever, seeing my man with a puppy in his arms. I wondered what he was going to tell Viv about Bella and then I was pretty happy that I was back here with Freddy instead of breaking it to my cousin that Harry and I had adopted a dog.

Freddy and I went to await our turn in the handlers' room. I tried to walk with a purpose and confidence I didn't feel. I could feel the stares of the other competitors upon us. We were in the lead. The crystal bowl was ours to lose at this point. The thought made me queasy.

Freddy and I found a quiet corner. I could feel my heart trying to punch out past my ribs and my hands were sweating, so I took a moment to breathe in slowly, hold it for four seconds and then exhale slowly, rinse and repeat until I felt like I wasn't going to faint.

One of the PAWS people called, "Freddy and Scarlett Parker."

Freddy perked right up, dancing on his feet as if he'd been waiting his whole life for this. I held his leash close to my side and together we trotted into the arena. The applause was deafening. It was clear Freddy was a favorite. I supposed people were tired of Muffin winning and really, who could blame them?

I refused to look for Harry and the others in the crowd, as it would just make me more nervous, especially if Viv gave me stink eye from one hundred yards for the puppy. Her stink eye is powerful like that. Instead, I focused on our walk across the arena to the judges' table, keeping Freddy on my left, our gaits perfectly in sync.

The head judge was there, Claudia, and she looked as serious as ever. Freddy shot up the ramp onto the cloth-draped table, where he stacked. This was the portion of the event where he had to stand in place while the judges evaluated the overall look of him.

Because the PAWS dog show was a charitable event, they didn't have the same conformation rules as the Westminster dog show. Aunt Betty had explained that each dog was evaluated by its overall appearance, using the standards set for its breed, or in the cases of mixed breeds, its contributing bloodlines. I had done some reading and knew what some of the corgi standards were considered to be. The list was daunting, however, so I'd pretty much forgotten everything but the personality, which was friendly and workmanlike. Corgis were generally never aggressive or anxious. I was hoping this would be a selling point for convincing Viv that Bella could visit the shop during the daytime when Harrison was at work. I glanced at the packed stands. Where were they?

No, no. I shook my head. Now was not the time to think about that. I forced myself to be as still as Freddy. When the judges asked to see his teeth, I moved his lips aside just as Betty had shown me. Freddy was tolerant through all of the manhandling. The judges walked around him in circles, studying his lines. His coat shimmered under the lights, his ears were perfectly matched and up as if he was listening to what they had to say about him.

"Run him around," Claudia instructed.

"Beg pardon?" I asked.

She gestured impatiently with her pen, swinging it in a circle. "Run him around us. I want to see his gait, while walking and running."

"Oh, sure thing," I said. With little urging, Freddy came down the ramp.

I quickly kicked off my heels. I was not going to risk breaking an ankle while trotting a dog around the arena. Freddy stayed beside me and we walked a bit before breaking into a run. True confession. I am not a runner. In fact, I hate it. Unless there is cake at the end of a race, I really don't see the point.

The judges were watching, however, so Freddy and I did our best to look like one functioning unit. We slowed to a walk again and rejoined the judges. Claudia gave me a quick nod. It was the first time I didn't feel disapproval pouring off her toward me. Of course, it might have been a pity nod because I was shoeless, light-headed, sucking wind, and my face likely resembled a small, bitter, root vegetable. Did I mention I hate running?

I slipped on my heels and staggered from the arena to go wait in back with my competition. On my way, I passed Andre, who was looking at the display on his digital camera and shaking with laughter.

"Oh, Scarlett," he said. "I'm sorry, but . . ."

He was laughing too hard to finish the sentence. I took the camera and glanced at the pictures. Oh. My. God. He had caught me in my full glory, red hair streaming behind me while I tried to show off Freddy. My cheeks were blown out like a puffer fish, my face was on fire, and my eyes looked wild.

"You will delete these," I said. "They will never see the light of day."

He glanced at the screen again and started laughing. "But the memes I could make."

"No!"

"All right, all right," he agreed. The next dog was called up and he squeezed my hand. "All photographic evidence aside, you and Freddy did really well out there."

"Uh-huh," I said.

He was gone before I got the second syllable out. I glanced down at Freddy.

"Well, for better or worse, we're done," I said.

I sagged against the wall. I needed to catch my breath. Competitors had been told that after competing in today's event they were to wait in the back room and not sit out in the stands. Partly, it was because it was a packed house but also, I believe, they wanted to build up the suspense.

A vizsla named Tucker was up and he trotted past Freddy and me, looking confident but smelling a bit gassy.

Oof. I looked at Freddy but he didn't seem fazed. Mouth-breathing, I took the opportunity to study the people out in the arena. Behind the judges' table sat Mary and Tilly Swendson, along with Liza Stanhope in the VIP section. What an odd threesome, I thought. Mary was the only one who had seemed to actually mourn her brother, but from what I'd heard about him, I wasn't sure why.

He'd borrowed against the company to build that monstrous castle for his young wife that she was now stuck with and if it was true that she didn't inherit half of the company, she had no way to pay for. It seemed like it must be a punishment for the lover that everyone seemed to know she had. I glanced again at the people sitting in the VIP section. There were several gentlemen, other sponsors and PAWS board members, but none that I could imagine being involved with Tilly. Then again, as I glanced at her and saw that she was drinking a glass of wine and sending scathing glances in Mary's direction, I doubted any sane man would want to take that on. Maybe Gerry Swendson had killed himself to get away from her. It was an uncharitable thought, and I almost felt bad about it. Almost.

I supposed it was possible that Gerry Swendson had

killed himself. Maybe the crushing debt and the pending lawsuit had made him take the first available exit. I glanced at the dais where his body had been found. Except for that problem. The dais. Why was his body hidden beneath it? If it was a suicide, why was there no note?

I shook my head. There were too many people who wanted Swendson dead. It could have been suicide, but I seriously doubted it.

Freddy and I left the arena and made our way through the corridor to the back room. I saw Richard Freestone with Muffin. They looked calm and composed. He certainly didn't seem too upset about the possibility of coming in second this year. I wondered if maybe when all this was over, if Aunt Betty finally won, perhaps she'd give Richard a chance. After all, they were of an age and they both loved dogs. Many relationships started with less.

As I leaned against the wall, I saw the Youngs with Henry. I glared at Penelope. I couldn't help it. That load of bull she'd told Bronson made me think she was trying to deflect suspicion from her and Jasper. Of all the competitors, those two were the worst, and given how mean Henry was, it wouldn't surprise me at all to discover they were murderers. Okay, maybe that was a little dark but why had Penelope gone to Bronson about me? Was she just trying to cause trouble for me or did she have something to hide?

There was only one way to find out. Before I could think it through, I was striding across the room to confront them.

"Oy, Ms. Parker!"

I heard the voice calling my name. I did. But I chose to ignore it. Three days of being stressed out on top of finding a dead body and I was at my end. I wanted to kick some booty and Penelope Young's was as good as any.

"Whoa, whoa, whoa." Richard Freestone popped up in front of me with Muffin at his side. "Is there something I can help you with?"

"Nope," I said. "I'm just going to have a little conversation."

"Really?" he asked. "Because the way you're flexing your fist looks like you have about five points to make. It would be a shame to lose this for Betty over an unnecessary altercation when you and Freddy are so close to a win."

I glanced at him and then down at my fist. I unclenched my fingers and shook out my hand.

"You're right," I said. "Thank you for reminding me of the bigger picture."

"No problem," he said.

"Henry and Penelope and Jasper Young," the PAWS person called from the door.

I watched as Penelope and Jasper made their way over. For once, Henry was walking obediently instead of being dragged. He tried to nip a poodle on his way out the door though, so there was that.

When the door closed behind them, I turned to Richard. "So who do you think killed Gerry Swendson?"

He looked surprised that I'd asked. He blinked and

then he blustered a bit. "I'm not sure what you mean. It's not been declared a murder, has it?"

I gave him an exasperated look. "What do you mean you don't know what I mean? It's all anyone has talked about for two days, you must have some thoughts about it. And of course it was murder. He didn't shove himself under the dais."

"Is that what the police think?" he asked. His eyebrows shot up.

"Yes," I said. I sounded more certain than I actually was, but I wanted information and Richard had been around for years. Surely he had to know something.

"I prefer to leave this sort of thing up to the police," he said. I stared at him. Hard. He sighed. "All right, now that you mention it, it did occur to me that the person with the most motive is probably Tilly."

"Why?"

"Because it's always the spouse," he said.

"All right, but if it wasn't her, then who?" I asked.

"You want me to have a number two?"

"Yes, and a three if you can manage it."

"I can't," he said. "I only offered up Tilly because who else could it be?"

"I'm glad to see you've put so much thought into this," I said. How had he not been consumed by this?

"Again, isn't that what the police are for?" he asked. "That Detective Inspector Bronson scowls his way around the room, sniffing out suspects and motives. I feel like he might be part bloodhound."

"Well, if it helps to track down the killer, I'm all for it," I said. "Also, I don't think it was Tilly."

"Why not?" he asked.

"Because apparently she's not inheriting anything but debt," I said. "It wasn't to her advantage to kill her husband."

"Even if it means she's free to be with her lover?" he asked.

"You knew about that?"

"Everyone knows about that." His tone was dry and I laughed. "I'm only surprised Gerry didn't kill Claudia first."

"Claudia?" I blinked. "The head judge? Why would he?"

"As I said, everyone knows," he said. "Except for Gerry, but maybe he found out and that's why he's dead."

I felt my jaw sag open. I was trying to picture the pampered and pouty Tilly Swendson partnered with the serious and severe Claudia Curtis. It did not compute.

"Wow, I didn't see that coming," I said. "But if everyone knew, that makes it even more unlikely that she killed him. She must have known she'd be the prime suspect."

"If not Tilly, then who do you think killed Swendson?" he asked. "Claudia?"

"No, and for the same reasons I don't believe it was Tilly—it's too obvious," I said. "If I had a clue, I'd be badgering the police to make an arrest. Do you suppose it has something to do with the lawsuit?"

"Lawsuit?" He gave me a cautious look.

"I heard you talking to Liza Stanhope," I said. "I know you know that there's a lawsuit in play from some of last year's competitors, suing Swendson's Dog Food for making their pets sick."

His eyes went wide. "No one is supposed to know about that."

"Well, clearly some people do, if you know, and I know, and Liza Stanhope knows," I said. "Don't you think one of the people in the lawsuit could have gone off the rails and killed Swendson? I mean, people can get pretty crazy about their dogs."

"But murder," Richard said. He bent over and scratched Muffin's ears. The bulldog shook her head and a little slobber settled on Freddy's coat. *Ew.* "That's a hefty price to pay for substandard dog food."

"Like I said, pet owners can be crazy."

"Indeed," he agreed.

The doors opened and Jasper and Penelope entered. Jasper was carrying Henry under his arm like a basketball. I got the feeling the evaluation didn't go so well.

"Muffin and Richard Freestone."

At his name, Richard smiled at me. "Well, that's us. See you on the other side."

"Good luck," I said. I was surprised to find that I meant it. Richard was a nice man and Muffin was a charmer in her own jowly, drooly way. Of course, she was nowhere near as awesome as Freddy but that might have just been me.

"Thanks," he said. "Come on, Muffin."

Freddy and I watched them leave. I glanced across the room and saw Penelope and Jasper hissing at each other.

It looked like there was trouble in Youngville. This did not bother me at all. They were hands down the most obnoxious couple I had ever met and their dog was a bit of a jerk, too. The only reason I didn't hold him responsible was because I was certain he was a product of his environment and if he was in a different home, he'd likely be a perfectly lovely Jack Russell.

As I watched, he lifted his leg and peed in the water dish of the whippet beside him. Okay, nature versus nurture, it was a toss-up.

Chapter 15

I sat alone while Richard was gone. I wondered about his point that Tilly was probably the killer. He was right. All the true-crime shows say it's usually the spouse who commits the murder. But in this case, with the half-built castle and all the debt, it would have been so financially damaging for her to have Richard die instead of just divorcing him, why would she do it? Unless it wouldn't be.

If it was common knowledge that she was cheating, the question was, Did they have a prenuptial agreement? If they did, maybe she would have lost everything, including the half-built castle, in a divorce. A luxury property even deep in debt might have been better than nothing.

I glanced at the clock. I figured we had a few minutes until they finished judging the last of the competitors, so

I took Freddy out to the designated area to do his business. I wondered how Bella was behaving and realized that walking a dog every day was going to become part of my life. Weird.

We had just come back into the room when Liza Stanhope entered from the opposite side of the room. She clapped to get everyone's attention and the conversations slowly wound down to a dull murmur.

"Attention, everyone, if you'll kindly file into the arena, we are about to announce the winners." She cupped her mouth with her hands to increase her volume but, truly, her voice was shrill enough to carry without the assist.

She glanced around the room and I saw her and Richard exchange a look. I wondered what it meant. Was that Liza signaling to Richard that he had won again? It wasn't out of the realm of possibility. Our scores had been so close. Oh, no, I felt my stomach cramp.

I looked down at Freddy. Had I let him down? Was he going to be disappointed not to win the coveted crystal bowl of kibble? And even worse, Aunt Betty was going to be upset. She wanted this so badly. I didn't know how I would face her if we lost.

"Come on." The woman behind me nudged me none to gently. "Let's go."

"Sorry," I said. Why was I apologizing? I had no idea. It's my default setting. All day long people swirl around me and I say, "I'm sorry," as if I have anything to do with their missing the crosswalk light, their coffee being too hot, or the drizzle of rain falling from the sky impeding their progress.

The woman nudged me again, harder this time, and asked, "Were you planning to move today or Thursday?"

I looked in front of me at the line of people and dogs surging toward the door. There was literally no place for me to go.

"Sorry," I said. Damn it.

The woman looked annoyed. I turned my back to her. I didn't need that sort of bad juju when I was potentially facing a crushing defeat. Inch by inch handlers and their dogs moved to the door. Finally, we were in the hallway and then out in the arena.

The crowd was restless, clearly the excitement was reaching a fevered pitch. They had us stand in a circle on the edge of the arena. Freddy and I were in between a fluffy white terrier named Kirbie and a small black and white shih tzu named Rylie. The terrier was so excited it was practically vibrating, while the shih tzu lay down on the floor and stretched out as if it was so over the whole dog show thing. Talk about your opposites. Freddy took it all in stride, sitting beside me like a proper gentleman.

I didn't look out at the crowd because, at the moment, I didn't want to know where my people were. If we lost, I didn't want to see Aunt Betty's disappointment. It would crush me.

The podium, the same one Gerry Swendson had been found beneath, had three spots at different heights for the three finalists, with another two places on the floor for the third and fourth runners-up.

I glanced across the arena to where Penelope and Jasper stood with Henry. I hoped with every fiber of my being that they didn't rank in the top five. Anyone else would be okay but not those two.

Mary Swendson was standing with Claudia and Liza. The three women had their heads pressed together and they seemed to be having an intense discussion. I wondered if there had been a tie. That wasn't going to go over well, because I know that I for one was not planning on sharing the crystal bowl if I won. It was mine, all mine . . . er . . . I mean it was Freddy's, all Freddy's.

I watched the heated discussion. Claudia was shaking her head while Mary and Liza looked at her. Finally, Claudia crossed her arms over her chest and glared. Whatever hill she was planting her flag on, it was clear she wasn't budging. Given how stern she'd been, I didn't think it boded well for Freddy. I sighed. He'd been the runner-up before. This was his year. He had to take at least second or third. Preferably second. But even if he did, it was cold comfort, knowing he was so close.

With a sharp word at Mary, Liza turned on her heel and stomped away. She took a spot behind the judges' table in the VIP section, and I saw her riffling through paperwork as if she was looking for something. There was an air of desperation about her. Interesting.

Finally, Mary Swendson shook off Claudia and stepped up to the mic in front of the dais. She addressed the crowd in her usual no-nonsense fashion that I'd come to like.

"Good evening, everyone. In memory of my brother, I am happy to invite our head judge, Claudia Curtis, up to announce this year's winner of the PAWS dog show. I know it was a difficult decision for our judges"—she paused and looked pointedly at Claudia before continuing—"with so many fabulous dogs in the competition, and I want to personally thank each and every one of you for making this dog show the signature event that it is. The commitment you have to your canines and the world of dogs is unparalleled and Swendson's Dog Food is, as always, thrilled to partner with PAWS in making a difference in animal shelters all over the country."

Everyone cheered and Mary stepped back to make room for Claudia.

She cleared her throat once, then again, and announced the fourth runner-up. I watched as a German pointer named Archer came forward with his handler. Next was a Doberman called Kit. They were each given a medal on a ribbon and a small bouquet of wildflowers.

"You've got the makings of champions," Claudia said. "I hope we'll see you next year." She congratulated all of the participants for an excellent showing and then got down to business.

"Our second runner-up is a standard poodle, Lucy, and her handler, Chris Hansen," she said. The audience broke into applause and a man with long hair and wearing a Hawaiian shirt under his suit jacket crossed the arena, stepping out with a pretty, black standard poodle, who trotted to the podium as if this was what she was born to do.

"Bloody American," the woman beside me muttered. *Oh, dear.*

They stepped up on the podium on the lowest step. A medal on a ribbon was put around both of their necks and a bouquet of yellow calla lilies was handed to the man.

Okay, so we weren't in third. Did that mean we were second? Did we even make it to the podium? My heart was thumping hard in my chest and my palms were sweating. I swallowed and tried to do my breathing exercises but I couldn't focus.

I glanced up into the stands, needing something. No, not something. I needed my people. This was excruciating. I wanted to win so badly. I scanned the crowd. To my surprise they were all together. Aunt Betty and Harry, who was still holding Bella. Viv and Fee, with Nick sitting in between them and Alistair on the other side of Fee. Uh-oh. I wondered how that was going.

They were all watching Claudia, and I could tell they were just as stressed as I was. Nick was chewing a thumbnail. Alistair was fidgeting with the watch on his left wrist. Fee was twisting one of her corkscrew curls around her index finger. Viv was biting her lip. Aunt Betty was sitting on the edge of her seat and had her hands clasped together in front of her chest as if praying. I glanced at Harry. I knew his go-to anxiety gesture was to run his hands through his hair. His fingers always left big trails that I liked to smooth out. He wasn't doing that right now, however. Instead, he was smiling at me. His bright green eyes were sparkling and as our gazes met and held, he reached down and waved the sleeping Bella's paw at me.

The adorableness of it filled my heart and squeezed out my fear. Yes, it would be cool to win the show but there was so much more important stuff in my life, not the least of which was all of the people sitting up there together. I grinned at Harry and gave him a wink. His smile deepened and I knew right then that everything was going to be just fine.

I heard the *click* of a camera shutter and saw Andre standing nearby. He gave me a thumbs-up, and I turned my attention back to Claudia. She glanced at Liza, who was still riffling through paperwork on the judges' table. Liza glanced up at her and shrugged. It was an annoyed and impatient gesture. Two of the other judges frowned at Liza and then at Claudia. One of them made a rolling motion with his hand to indicate Claudia should finish up.

Claudia took a deep breath and turned to face the crowd. She lifted the mic to her mouth and said, "Our first runner-up is Muffin and her handler, Richard Freestone."

Richard stood still for a moment as if caught by surprise. He glanced down at Muffin and patted her head. Andre snapped pictures as Richard and Muffin stepped out of line. Richard smiled and waved to the crowd, who cheered with great enthusiasm. It was clear that Richard was just fine with his first-runner-up win. He smiled at me as he walked past and I smiled in return but it felt forced.

There was no way to know if Freddy and I had won—not until they said the name.

I watched as Richard and Muffin got their medals and a large silver plate with Muffin's name engraved on it. It felt as if time were moving backward. How long could this possibly take? I really thought I might faint. Freddy must have sensed my distress because he rose on his hind feet and licked my hand. It brought me back, and I forced myself to breathe slow and steady. It wouldn't do to pass out before the event was over.

When Claudia approached the mic, I stood frozen, my breathing shallow, my heart stuttering, my insides quaking. I'm a pretty emotional person so I knew I had to prepare for the worst so I didn't make a scene, meaning I'd burst into big gut-wrenching sobs as tears gushed out of my eyeballs if we didn't win.

"And the winner of the nineteenth annual PAWS dog show is . . ." She paused and I thought I'd burst into flame. "Freddy and his handler, Scarlett Parker!"

I'd like to report that I was totally cool and gave a regal nod before stepping forward. Yeah, no, I lost my everloving mind. I shouted and jumped up and down. I clapped like I was a GIF of joy. Freddy did the same, except for the clapping, and then I scooped him up and hugged him while he licked my face. The crowd seemed delighted with our lack of restraint and the cheers and applause were deafening.

Andre popped up right in front of us and snapped a million pictures as we mugged and then ran to the podium. Yes, we ran and jumped and cheered all the way to Claudia, who, to my surprise, actually smiled at our unabashed enthusiasm. When she went to pet Freddy, he got up on his back legs and hugged her with his front feet as if he knew she was the key to his win.

We circled the podium and climbed the short steps to the top. I searched the crowd, again, for our people. It wasn't hard. Viv and Fee were standing on their seats, waving their arms in the air, Alistair had both his arms up, looking ready to catch either or both of them should they tumble. Nick was applauding with arms long and his hands out in front of him, as if it were the Oscars. Harry was grinning at me and clapping around an armful of Bella, who amazingly slept through it all. And then there was Aunt Betty. She had her hands to her face and I knew she was weeping with tears of joy. Freddy, her dog, had won.

It hit me then that it didn't seem right that I should be here. The years of training, the losses, the bond between canine and handler, that was all hers. The only reason I'd been able to step in at the last second was because she had trained Freddy so well. This moment on the podium was hers. It should be her with the ribbon and the flowers and the big crystal bowl.

I didn't think it through, nothing new there, I just looked at Freddy and said, "Sit."

He sat, still wagging, and I ran down the podium steps and across the floor, up the stairs to the bleacher where Aunt Betty stood with the others. I held out my hand. She stared at me for a moment and I said, "This is your win. Come on."

She wiped her face with the heels of her hands. She took a breath, grinned and then put her hand in mine. The noise of the crowd ratcheted up to deafening as I escorted her across the floor and then assisted her up the podium steps.

Freddy jumped up to greet her and she bent down and hugged him. She let go and commanded that he sit and he did. He was positively aquiver to have her beside him and I was so glad I'd thought of it. This was Aunt Betty's moment absolutely.

When Aunt Betty bent down to receive her medal and flowers, she looked humbled. I noted that Richard wasn't watching her during her moment of glory, and I found that odd. He'd said that he cared for Betty, that he hoped she won so he could ask her out. He didn't look like that now. Instead, his fingers tightened on the flower stems he was holding so tightly that his knuckles were white. Had he lied to me? Had he feigned an interest in Aunt Betty? If so, why? To make himself more likable? To what purpose?

In contrast, I noticed that the other runners-up were grinning and applauding for Aunt Betty. Chris Hansen, the one with the poodle, even leaned over to say something that made her laugh. I glanced back at Richard. He wasn't sharing in the joke. Instead, his gaze was intently focused on Liza. She was still digging through the paperwork on the judges' desk. His gaze then shifted to Claudia, who straightened her spine and stared back at him as if challenging him.

When Mary and Tilly Swendson came forward, Tilly looked pale and rather sickly, while Mary seemed pleased. There was a small skirmish with the crystal bowl as Tilly held on to it, glancing at Liza, while Mary tried to present it to Aunt Betty. Finally, Mary wrenched the bowl from Tilly's grasp and handed it up to Aunt Betty.

With a look of triumph, Aunt Betty held it up over her head, Andre took a million pictures and the crowd cheered with terrific enthusiasm. I clapped and stomped my feet and let out a series of "woo-hoos" until I was practically hoarse.

It was one of the greatest moments of my life made even more special when Harry joined me behind the podium with a sleeping Bella snuggled up under his coat. This. This was what we'd been trying to achieve, and Freddy and Aunt Betty looked amazing up there on the podium, soaking in all the glory that was their due.

I was pretty sure my heart was going to explode out of my chest.

"You did it," Harry whispered in my ear. I turned to smile up at him.

"Freddy did it," I said. "I just followed him, trying not to hold him back."

"Doesn't matter," he said. "You were amazing. If you hadn't stepped up, Aunt Betty wouldn't be having her moment."

See? This is why I love this guy. He's always in my corner. Always.

Andre was working the scene, taking pictures of the five winners with their dogs. Everyone was smiling, except Richard. I supposed losing was better in theory than in actuality. I imagined he'd get over it soon enough. There was always next year.

After pictures, the winners and their guests were invited to high tea in one of the smaller banquet rooms in the building. Personally, I was starving and the thought of a chicken or egg salad sandwich, preferably with curry, and some macarons was taking over my brain with an insistence that was impossible to ignore.

The audience was filing out of the building and the crowd noise lessening. In my mind, I hurried them all along with a mental shooing of my hands. *Go, go, go. People need to eat. And by people, I mean me.*

Nick, Viv, Fee and Alistair were making their way toward us. They'd been chosen as our guests for the celebratory high tea held after the winners were announced. I noticed that Fee had her hand on Alistair's elbow and he was leaning over her in the solicitous way a boyfriend does. Hmm. Behind them Viv and Nick followed. Nick was chatting away but Viv looked distracted. Her gaze kept landing on Fee's hand on Alistair's arm and then flitted away, then returned and then darted away again. I got the feeling she was trying to figure out what it meant, but also, she didn't want to know. Poor Viv. She was going to lose a good guy all because she'd been too afraid to try.

The arena was half-empty when they reached us, with just the hangers-on lingering, to get pics with their favorite dogs, when Liza erupted from the judges' table as if she'd been shot out of a cannon. She clutched two papers in her hand and she strode to the front of the podium with purpose, as if she was about to stop a crime.

"Wait!" she cried. Her voice was as shrill as a police whistle. "Stop! I said stop!"

Everyone froze and turned toward her as if in slow motion. The looks of shock on the faces of the people in the arena were identical to what I was sure was on my face. What the heck was the woman doing? Stop what? Surely she couldn't mean the trophy ceremony.

Claudia stepped forward, clearly trying to head Liza off. She reached the small podium with the mic a second before Liza did and shook her head as if to signal that Liza should stop whatever she was doing immediately. I glanced at Mary Swendson. She was frowning, looking confused, while Tilly's eyes were wide with what looked to be hope. What was going on?

A glance at Richard and the other winners showed that they looked bewildered as well. The only one who didn't look surprised was Aunt Betty. Instead she looked braced as if she'd been expecting something like this.

She held the crystal bowl in her arms and I saw her fingers tighten on the rim as she stared at Liza. If looks could dematerialize a body, Liza would have evaporated into mist on the spot. Sadly, she didn't.

Instead, after a quick hissed conversation, Liza wrestled the mic out of Claudia's hand. Well, she tried to, but Claudia put up a pretty good fight. Undaunted, Liza began to speak into the mic while bent over and struggling with Claudia in a tug-of-war over the microphone, which had them knotted up and walking sideways like a crab following a receding wave into the sea.

"I'm sorry but there's been a mistake," Liza said. Her voice was ragged as she struggled to keep her mouth close enough to the mic for her voice to project throughout the arena. "Freddy has two applications filled out with different handlers listed—this is a clear violation of competition rules. He is disqualified. I repeat, Freddy is disqualified. The winner of the PAWS dog show for the fourth year in a row is Muffin and her handler, Richard Freestone!"

Chapter 16

Pandemonium broke out! The arena erupted into shouts of outrage and indignation. That was mostly our group. Nick was shouting and gesturing as if directing traffic, and Fee was right there beside him. Alistair had his hands on his hips and was striding forward, clearly attacking the situation from a lawyerly perspective. Harry reached out and grabbed his arm, halting his progress. Viv crossed her arms over her chest and glared at Liza as if trying to determine where exactly she wanted to stick her with some long, lethal hatpins. Oh, dear.

I hated that I was caught off guard, but honestly, I couldn't believe what was happening. It was such a load of rubbish. Liza had done this on purpose, first by telling Aunt Betty that her registration papers would continue to be "misplaced" and then by letting me register in her place. It was almost as if she'd been planning this all along. I felt Aunt Betty's gaze meet mine, and I knew she was thinking the same thing. We'd been set up.

All of a sudden, I felt a chill in my bones. The note Aunt Betty had received threatening Freddy. Had that been Liza's doing?

The sound of boos began to increase in volume, and I noticed several of the PAWS volunteers, situated around the arena, were voicing their displeasure. No one liked to see an award get taken away by a technicality, and I wondered if Liza had factored the negative reaction into her plan. Claudia let go of her abruptly and Liza staggered. She glared at her volunteers, but they didn't quiet down. She turned her back to them and shrugged. Liza Stanhope clearly did not care how this played out. She strode to the podium and tried to forcibly take the crystal bowl out of Aunt Betty's hands.

"Oy!" Harry hefted Bella up and into my arms before hurrying to Aunt Betty's side to give her a hand. He looked back at Alistair and shouted, "Go wide!"

Alistair took off at a run. Freddy was growling at Liza from his spot on the dais. If I didn't know better, I'd think he was protesting her attempt to take his award away.

"Let go!" Aunt Betty said. "It's my award. Freddy won it fair and square. I don't want to hear your nonsense about some clerical error."

"It is not nonsense," Liza huffed. She doubled down, putting her weight into tugging the bowl from Aunt Betty.

Harry wasn't having it, however, and he grabbed the bowl from the bottom and used Liza's momentum to push her away and then pull the bowl out of her hands.

"Hey!" she protested.

It was too late. Harry jumped off the podium and launched the bowl into the air. I felt my heart surge up into my throat and as one every single person in the arena gasped. Out of nowhere, two steady hands appeared and snatched the bowl. The person tucked and rolled and bounced back up on his feet with the bowl perfectly intact. Alistair!

I sagged in relief, realized I was squeezing Bella too hard and loosened my grip. Her big brown eyes popped open and I said, "It's okay, baby girl."

"Your timing is impeccable, just like on the pitch," Harry said. He clapped Alistair on the back as they walked toward the podium, where Aunt Betty stood, glaring at Liza.

Detective Inspector Bronson strode forward. It was clear he'd been watching everything. The look on his face was severe and it was my fondest hope that he'd arrest Liza for being, well, a horrible human seemed legit.

Mary Swendson stepped forward. She gently took the mic from Claudia, who still clutched it in her hands.

"Ladies and gentlemen, please, let's all calm down and in an orderly fashion proceed to the high tea that's been arranged for our winners," she said. "Anything that needs to be sorted can be done so over tea and scones. Correct, Detective Inspector?"

Bronson hesitated for a moment. He surveyed the room and then he nodded. I suspected he just wanted to contain the crazy so he could get to the bottom of things.

Mary gestured for the PAWS volunteers to lead the way. Slowly the winners climbed off the dais. Harry assisted Aunt Betty down and we clustered around her as the other guests joined their winners and in staggered groups we headed toward a door at the end of the arena.

"Excuse me." Liza stopped in front of Alistair with her hands out.

"May I be of assistance?" Alistair asked. His expression was bland.

"Yes, you can give me that," she snapped. She lunged for the bowl but Alistair held it over his head, which was too high for even the tall Liza to reach, as evidenced by her jumping swipes acquiring nothing. Although, I did give her props for trying.

"Liza, what are you doing?" Claudia snapped. "Control yourself. We'll figure this out at the tea."

"What's there to figure out?" Liza asked. "She"—she pointed to Aunt Betty—"is not the winner and neither is she." She pointed at me.

I passed Bella to a startled Viv and stepped forward so that I was nose to chin with Liza. "But he is!" I snapped and pointed to Freddy. "And you're not going to take it away from him."

She stepped back and stared down her nose at me. "We'll see."

I don't think I ever wanted to punch anyone so much in

my life. Yes, this even superseded my desire to put a hurt on Penelope Young, and that was saying something.

In the tea room, the professional catering crew that had been hired for the event stood along one wall as if uncertain what to do. Mary signaled to them to commence serving, for which I was grateful because I was starving.

Alistair stayed by Aunt Betty's side and held on to the crystal bowl for her. Liza looked like she'd snatch it from him if he loosened his hold even a little. Harry flanked him, obviously offering his friend backup.

Our group found our table and we all sat, with Harry and Alistair sitting on each side of Aunt Betty. I noticed the other competitors had large entourages and tables all to themselves as well. Richard had a group of young women with him, they were all taking pictures with him and Muffin, and I got the feeling that they were his online followers as opposed to actual friends. I deduced this from the painful conversation I was overhearing—all right, eavesdropping on.

"Mr. Freestone, how old are you?" one of the young women asked. She was a doe-eyed ingenue, who looked barely legal. "I only ask because in your profile picture, you look so much younger."

She bit her lip as if embarrassed by her own honesty. I wanted to turn and tell her that he was old enough to be her father but I didn't. Mostly because Viv had set Bella down and she was busily investigating the area. I wondered if she was hungry or had to go outside. Poor thing.

Richard answered her in a low tone that I couldn't quite

make out over the conversation of the rest of the room. Whatever he'd said made her giggle and I had a feeling it was a pivot, not revealing his true age but mentioning his social media prowess.

I glanced at the door and noticed that Detective Inspector Bronson was watching a heated exchange between Liza and Claudia. I was certain Liza was pressing her case to have Aunt Betty and me disqualified and Richard moved into first place. I glanced at Richard's table and saw him smile at his bevy of beauties and then look at Liza with a cold, calculated stare.

It hit me then that all of his talk about being in the dog show for Betty was a load of bunk. He had a table full of hot young things, he had a huge career as the winner of the PAWS dog show every year, and his lack of involvement when Liza tried to strip Aunt Betty of her award proved that he'd just been trying to sweet-talk me with a pledge of affection for Aunt Betty.

That pompous blowhard, as Aunt Betty had called him, didn't care one tail wag about Aunt Betty as a woman, a competitor or a friend. I watched as his entourage fussed over him and Muffin, pouring his tea and plating his tiny sandwiches. I wanted to throw something at him, preferably a teapot. I'd been so gullible when he said he cared about her, romanticizing something between him and Aunt Betty, when he was probably just looking for information. Ugh.

Liza had said he had a fortune in endorsements. If it was true that Swendson was trying take over PAWS by getting rid of Liza and hiring new people, it might have meant Swendson was looking for a return on his investment. He may have wanted Muffin and Richard to not win again so as to keep the contest fresh. Was this common knowledge? Did Mary, Claudia or Tilly know? Suddenly I felt as if I was in the dog show version of *Game of Thrones*, where everyone lied and had hidden motives and who knew who would be the victor in the end?

"Bella, no, that's not yours," Viv scolded the puppy.

I glanced under the tablecloth and saw Bella chewing on Viv's purse strap. It was covered in drool and the leather had multiple puncture wounds. Nuts! This was not going to help me convince Viv to let her spend her days with us.

I looked over to the side of the room where Mary, Claudia and Liza stood, still arguing about the end result of the dog show. It didn't appear they were going to come to terms. Detective Inspector Bronson stepped back, obviously not wanting to mediate the outcome.

"Alistair, maybe you could go work your lawyerly magic," Harry said. "I have a feeling they're not getting anywhere over there."

It was true. The finger-pointing and gesturing between Liza and Claudia was still happening, while Mary and now Tilly, too, stood watching them as if unsure of whose side to take.

"I was just thinking that," Alistair said. Deftly he reached for a mini egg salad sandwich on the three-tiered plate on the table and popped it into this mouth before he went to join the discussion. He was gone only a few minutes. Both women seemed happy to unload onto a new person.

When Alistair returned his expression was grim. "Aunt Betty, do you remember signing a waiver when you registered?"

"Yes, it's standard," Aunt Betty declared.

Alistair turned to Viv. He looked professional, as always, but there was a flash in his eyes, a look of longing so strong I felt it pull at my heart strings. I glanced at Fee. She was watching him with interest—not of a romantic sort but more like she was curious about the situation.

"Do you remember signing a waiver, Viv?"

"There was a waiver? What waiver?" she asked. "The woman at the registration didn't give me any forms to sign other than the registration paper."

"It doesn't matter," Aunt Betty said. "I already filled out the waiver when I registered Freddy the first time, so he should be covered."

"Not if your first registration is deemed ineligible," Alistair said.

"Which it was," Liza snapped as she strode toward our table. "Your first registration doesn't count. I don't care if this idiot"—she gestured to me and my mouth fell open in shock—"did let you stand on the podium in her stead, she was the registered handler and the release form was to be filled out by her. As it states in the bylaws, any missing paperwork will be considered a disqualifier from the competition."

Harry was half out of his seat, ready to take her down for insulting me, bless him, but I grabbed his arm and pulled him back into his seat.

"But Ginger, she—" he protested.

"It's okay. Let's see how this plays out," I said.

"As the head judge, I say that's ridiculous," Claudia said. She stood beside Liza, glaring at her. "I don't understand why you're being like this. Freddy is the winner and any registration issues are on us, don't you agree, Mary?"

Mary Swendson approached the two women, looking very grave. She glanced between them and sighed. "Actually, I'm with Liza on this, Claudia. Rules are rules. If we bend the rules this time, we'll have to bend the rules all the time. I hate to say this, especially over a paperwork glitch, but the first-place finish belongs to Mr. Freestone."

Aunt Betty gasped. Our table, being on the rowdy side, broke into a chorus of arguments, with everyone shouting and no one listening. It rather reminded me of social media these days. A whole lot of yelling into the void. So tiresome. Bronson, who'd been observing the situation, hurried across the room.

Aunt Betty looked stricken as Liza reached for the crystal bowl, but Alistair was there to intercept it. "Not so fast," he said.

Harry began to stand as if he'd take on the women in defense of Aunt Betty. Admirable, but it wasn't going to help at the moment. Again, I pulled him back down.

Claudia raised her hands, indicating that everyone should calm down. It didn't work. Frustrated, she reached into her pocket and pulled out a silver whistle. She gave three short blasts, and the room instantly got quiet, except for Bella, who let out a mournful baby howl as if the whistle had hurt her ears.

Viv scooped her up from beneath the table and comforted her. I caught a grin from Fee, who noticed, too.

Once the room was silent, Mary glanced at Aunt Betty and then at Freddy and said, "I am so sorry."

I got the feeling she was apologizing more to Freddy than Aunt Betty. I was not having it. Neither was Aunt Betty. She rose from her seat with all the dignity of the Queen and tossed her napkin onto the table.

"You can take your apology and stuff it," she snapped. Bright splotches of color shone on her cheeks and her eyes crackled with a furious light. She rounded on Richard, marching toward his chair as if she intended to do him some harm. "This is your fault. I don't know how and I don't know why but you and your followers have completely corrupted the dog show, making a mockery of it. I'm sure you're quite pleased with yourself but someday someone is going to take you down and I just hope I'm there to see it."

"Now, Betty, my dear, I know you're upset." Richard held up his hands as if he was afraid he was going to have to ward her off. If he continued to use that condescending tone, he was going to have to fight me off. What an asshat.

It was then that I noticed Detective Inspector Bronson was pacing around the tables, watching the drama unfolding as if it were an episode of *Broadchurch*. He was studying all the players, obviously looking for something.

"To lose the dog show has to hurt," Richard continued. "Of course, I wouldn't know since I've never lost." He gestured to Alistair to bring the crystal bowl to him. Alistair ignored him.

"You did lose," Aunt Betty said. "The points were clear, Muffin lost to Freddy this year, and you can pretend that isn't so but the numbers don't lie."

"And yet, I'm the winner and you're the loser," he said. His look was smug. "Despite the best efforts of your pack. You should choose your allies more wisely."

Aunt Betty took a swipe at Richard, slapping his shoulder. Harry stepped forward and pulled Aunt Betty back. She was wagging a finger at Richard and said, "I know you're responsible for this. Somehow, you orchestrated this whole thing. I know it. I just don't know how to prove it. Too bad it wasn't you who was poisoned."

We all gasped. Had our sweet Aunt Betty really said such a mean-spirited thing? Detective Inspector Bronson strode forward and asked, "What was that, Ms. Wentworth?"

Betty turned and glared at him. "Don't look so shocked. He's got something on them, something on all of them." She gestured at Liza, Claudia, Mary and Tilly.

Both Liza and Mary looked extremely offended. Claudia, on the other hand, looked thoughtful, while Tilly looked guilty. Huh.

"Ms. Wentworth, I have to say this outburst makes it look like you'd stop at nothing to win first place in the dog show," Bronson said. "Perhaps it's best if you come with me."

"Now, wait one moment," Alistair said. He stepped forward, still holding the bowl. "That's my client."

"You're welcome to join us," Bronson said. "We're going to have another little chat about poison."

"That's ridiculous," Harry protested. "Look at her. She's tiny. Even if she did poison Swendson, which she didn't, how could she possibly have stuffed his body under the podium? She wouldn't even be able to heft one of his legs."

Bronson crossed his arms over his chest and gave him a hard stare. "I imagine she had help."

Harry put a hand over his chest. "Me?"

"Why don't you both come with me?" Bronson asked. "And bring your lawyer, too. You're going to need him."

Bronson reached out for Betty's arm, but Freddy jumped up between her and Bronson and began to growl and show his teeth.

"Restrain him," Bronson said. "Or I'll contact the animal warden to take him."

"You wouldn't dare," Aunt Betty said. She looked shocked.

"Try me," Bronson said. "You had motive and opportunity and this display of anger just shows that you're unstable." It looked like the mild-mannered detective inspector we'd gotten used to had some bite with his bark.

"What a load of tosh!" Fee said. She rose from her seat and crossed her arms over her chest and glared. "Just because a woman is rightly upset does not mean she's unstable."

"Precisely," Viv said. "Why shouldn't Aunt Betty be upset when everyone is trying to take away an award she won outright? Of course she's upset. If she were a man, you wouldn't say she was unstable. You'd say she was being assertive."

Bronson pinched the bridge of his nose, as if trying to activate some patience.

"They're not wrong," I said. I felt the need to add my opinion as the person who'd been in the dog show and as a woman. "You can't go after Aunt Betty just because she is furious. She deserves to be angry."

"Be that as it may," Bronson said. "Whether she was treated unjustly or not, she just threatened the winner in the same manner Gerry Swendson was killed, so now there is reason to believe she may have committed a crime and for that I have to take her in for questioning."

"Your reason is based solely on her refusal to give up an award she won fair and square," I said. "You'd be better served to be asking why it's so important to these people to take the award away from her, don't you think?"

As if he understood, Freddy growled at Bronson again, this time showing some teeth. I quickly stepped forward and took charge of Freddy's leash. Things were getting out of control and I blamed Liza and her histrionics for it. There was no need for her to take away Freddy's award, not here, not now, but she was set on it. The question was *why*.

Richard hadn't seemed upset to be runner-up and the crowd, while it favored Muffin, had been duly charmed by Freddy. I had been in charge of Freddy's social media since the dog show began, and I had seen the dramatic increase in his popularity. The hats had been a big part of it, but it was mostly Freddy and his natural charm.

So why were Mary and Liza so intent on having Richard win again? I glanced at him. He was sipping his tea as if he didn't have a care in the world. Almost as if this kerfuffle didn't bother him in the least because he knew absolutely that things were going to go in his favor in the end. Huh.

Muffin had almost a million followers on her social media pages. She was a force in the dog world. It was well known that Richard didn't have a regular job. He didn't need to, as the endorsements kept him and Muffin living well above where he'd been when he adopted her four years ago. Could Mary's and Liza's determination to give him the award be because of the publicity Muffin generated for the event every year? Was the whole stupid thing rigged?

As I watched, Richard dabbed his lips with his napkin and then reached for another cucumber sandwich. He'd said he had feelings for Betty and yet when they were about to tear the award from her and give it to him, he'd said not a word. In fact, he'd been rather rude to her, proving my theory that he'd been faking his affection for Aunt B.

242

And as he sat there, unmoved by the chaos around him, I got the distinct feeling that he was in a position of power, which could mean only one thing. He knew who had killed Gerry Swendson, and he was using it as leverage to get what he wanted, which was the win in the PAWS dog show.

It was all so obvious now. The murderer had to be in the room, and if Bronson took Aunt Betty and Harry away for questioning, the real murderer would get away with it. I glanced at Tilly, Mary, Liza and Claudia. Richard had said Aunt Betty needed a better pack. Were these women *his* pack?

There was no question that all four women stood to gain from Gerry's death in some way. Tilly could sell her half castle and move on with her lover. Mary would get complete control of the company. Liza wouldn't have to deal with Gerry's insane demands as a sponsor anymore. And Claudia could run the judging as she chose without his interference, without him telling her who would be the winner. She was the only one who was standing strong for Freddy. Was it because she'd gotten rid of Gerry and now felt she could declare the winner? It had to be one of these women, but which one?

"Detective Inspector Bronson, Aunt Betty didn't poison Gerry Swendson, and I can prove it," I said. My voice was loud. I didn't care. Everyone in the room slowly turned to face me. "The murderer is here in the room. In fact, she's standing right there."

I pointed in the general direction of the women who

were still clustered around Alistair, who was holding the big crystal bowl. They each reacted as if I'd hit them with a Taser and at once they started protesting. The only one who didn't was Claudia.

Instead, she just shook her head. "I had no reason to murder Gerry."

It was true that of the four of them she was the least suspect, but I was going to keep poking until someone gave in. I glanced at Harry, who was watching me with equal parts admiration and trepidation, as if he was thrilled that I was going to crack the case and worried that it was going to blow up on me at the same time. I felt the same way.

I rose from my seat and began to walk around the room, circling the tables. Most people had stopped moving. They were watching me as if I were a snake winding my way through the crowd, looking to strike. Freddy stayed beside me as if he, too, knew this was our do-or-die moment.

The only person who was oblivious to me was Richard. He had moved on to the dessert tier of the high tea and was loading his plate with the tiny pastries. I had a sudden urge to slap the small pear tart out of his hands but I resisted.

"I appreciate what you're trying to do," Bronson said. "But if we had any evidence against another person in this room, we would have arrested them by now."

I ignored him and kept walking.

"I did some reading the other night," I said. "And I learned quite a few things about fentanyl poisoning."

Bronson's eyebrows lifted. "How did you know . . . ?"

"I found the body," I said. "I saw the blue lips, the dried foam on the skin around his mouth, and the bruising where he'd banged his head against something hard during a seizure. Which, as we discussed before, is consistent with an opioid overdose."

Bronson nodded. "I'll give you that."

"Of course, it's easy to buy fentanyl on the street," I said. "But what if the murderer didn't have to because they were already on fentanyl as a prescription for pain?"

I noticed several people in the room went still. It made me realize that the global discussion about the opioid epidemic was spot-on. There were a lot of people popping the prescription pain pills, which was no doubt making it difficult for the police to narrow down the killer.

"Just because someone is on a prescription doesn't mean they're the killer," Bronson said.

"I know," I agreed. "But it does give them means and, as you said, if motive and opportunity were indicators of guilt then motive, opportunity and means must surely tip the scale."

"Enough," Liza Stanhope snapped. "Take that woman and her nephew away! They are clearly guilty of doing anything they can to win this competition and since Gerry was determined to ban her after her wild accusations about his dog food, it gives her more than enough reason to have killed him."

"More reason than a woman who was about to be replaced as the chairman of PAWS by Gerry Swendson?" I asked.

Liza gasped. It was a direct hit. The conversation I'd overheard between her and Richard was proving valuable. I glanced at Richard. He was still eating, completely unconcerned by my big reveal.

"I heard you and Richard talking," I explained. "Richard said Gerry was hoping to replace you after seventeen years so that the spotlight was more on him than on the winning dog. That's why you had to get rid of Aunt Betty and Freddy, initially, because if you didn't Swendson was going to have you removed from PAWS."

Liza tossed her jet-black hair and jutted out her chin. "You can't prove anything."

"Oh, can't I?" I asked. Actually, I couldn't but I hoped if I kept talking the facts would all weave themselves together.

I turned to Bronson. "Did you know that Gerry was so deep in debt that there was no way he was going to be able to finish building the castle he had promised his new young wife unless he started to cut corners in the dog food business?"

"We knew he was in financial straits, yes," Bronson said.

"I heard that Mary was in charge of the production of the dog food," I said. "That she scrupulously maintained the highest of standards except for last year right after the award show, when seemingly a very bad batch of Swendson's Dog Food came out and made Freddy, here, very sick."

"Another reason for your aunt Betty to be considered a suspect," Bronson said.

"Perhaps, or maybe it's more likely that the person

whose reputation was tarnished by the bad food would have cause to murder the person who chose substandard ingredients for the food just to cut costs so he could finish building his castle," I said.

"That's a lie!" Mary cried. "I would never harm my brother. Ever."

Her face was red and she looked upset. Good. People made mistakes when they were upset.

"Perhaps not," I said. I glanced at Tilly. "After all, it would require knowing someone who had access to fentanyl in order to slip it to your brother, say, in his morning coffee?"

Tilly's face went red then pale then red again. "I had nothing to do with it."

She didn't meet my eyes and I saw that Bronson was frowning.

"That's right," I said. "You had an alibi. You left the cocktail party and went to your mother's because you had a headache, but your housekeeper assured you that Mr. Swendson had left your home in good spirits and wearing the clothes he was found in. You said you didn't see your husband from the time you left the cocktail party until his body was found."

"That's right," she said. "I've already endured hours of questioning. I'm innocent."

"But is your lover?" I asked.

Tilly went pasty white again. I could feel my friends watching me but I didn't meet any of their gazes because I didn't want to lose the rhythm I had going.

"He had nothing to do with it," Tilly said. "He's been questioned as well and he is innocent."

"He?" I asked. I turned to Claudia and lifted my eyebrows. "Funny. You don't look like a he to me."

Claudia gasped. She glanced quickly at Tilly, who shook her head, but it was too late. They'd given themselves away.

I turned to look at Bronson. For the first time, I could see I had his full attention. He glanced at the four women and then at me.

"What are you saying?" he asked.

"I'm saying that Gerry wasn't killed by one person, he was killed by a pack," I said.

Chapter 17

The room was silent. Freddy and I continued walking until we were back at the table with all of our friends: Andre, Nick, Alistair, Fee, Viv, Aunt Betty and Harry.

"On my first day in the dog show, I met Mary. When we talked, she advised me that if I was going to be successful in the show with Freddy, he had to know I was part of his pack," I said. "That, in fact, I needed to be his alpha. She said the dog hierarchy is alpha, beta and omega, with the alpha the dominant above all others, the beta subservient only to the alpha, and the omega subservient to everyone."

"What does this have to do with anything?" Mary said. "I see no reason to—"

"Hush," I said. "I'm talking, not you."

Mary closed her mouth. So, not the alpha, then. I glanced at the other three. None of them spoke. In fact, they looked as if they were barely breathing.

It hit me then, who the alpha was, who had, in fact, been pulling the strings all along.

"The alpha is the dog that the other dogs try to please," I said. Bronson was watching me, his eyebrows meeting in the middle in a hard line of concentration. "Say, you're at a dog park, you'll note that the alpha dog doesn't greet the other dogs. They come to him."

Freddy and I walked past our table. We moved to stand beside Bronson, and I gestured by tipping my head that he should walk with us.

"The alpha wields all the power," I continued. "The alpha directs the actions of all the others, especially when there is a threat to the pack. The threat, in this case, was Gerry Swendson. He had to be removed."

Bronson nodded. He was beginning to understand.

"Gerry interfered in the production of the dog food," I said. "He cut corners and costs, trying for fast profit. The year's supply of dog food that was given to the winning dogs last year was a prototype of what Gerry wanted to produce. It made the dogs sick and there was a lawsuit, still pending, I believe."

I glanced at Mary. She stood frozen, staring down at the floor, much like a puppy being chastised.

"He tarnished the reputation of the company he and Mary had built. She had to be furious with him, not only as a dog lover but as a business owner."

"She has an alibi," Bronson said.

"Of course she does," I said. "Also, she's not the alpha or the beta, but rather the omega."

Mary's head snapped up. There was anguish in her eyes. I felt no remorse.

"Gerry also wanted to change the direction of the dog show," I said. "He wanted the sponsor to receive more publicity than the winning dog. He felt that switching out the chairman of PAWS would achieve that end. I believe he was hoping to get someone *young*er into the position."

Bronson looked at me with interest. "Any proof of that?"

"No, only the taunting comments overheard in the competitors' waiting room," I said.

"I have listened to quite enough," Liza said. "If you would just hand over the crystal bowl, we will award it to Mr. Freestone and enjoy our tea. Honestly, this display of poor sportsmanship is unseemly."

I raised my eyebrows and looked at Bronson and said, "There's your beta."

A smile tipped the corner of his mouth. "Please continue."

"Severe headaches caused by a pinched nerve in the back," I said. "There's not much that can help except a very potent pain medicine. Of course, patient-doctor confidentiality being what it is, I suppose it would be hard to find out who might have suffered a spinal injury that caused severe headaches with the only relief being a prescription for the very dangerous opioid."

"I have been clear of all medications for months," Tilly

said. The words burst from her as if she'd been trying to hold them in but couldn't anymore. "I don't use. I haven't since, well, since . . ." Her gaze shifted to Claudia, who looked at her as if she just wanted to hug her.

"Let me guess, omega, right?" Bronson asked.

I nodded. "There can only be one alpha. I believe Swendson was it, until he got removed. There's a new alpha now, and he's the one who called for the murder of Gerry Swendson, and he's sitting right here."

I paused beside Richard's seat. Muffin was sitting in the chair beside him. Richard was nibbling on a pink petit four with cream filling. His entourage was speechless, their mouths hanging open as if they couldn't believe he was the mastermind behind the murder of Gerry Swendson.

He didn't bother to acknowledge me or Bronson. In fact, he just kept eating. When he finished, he licked the pink icing off his fingers and then wiped them on his napkin.

"Well, this has been entertaining," he said. "Who knew we were going to have dinner and a show?"

He started to rise from his seat and Bronson said, "Not so fast."

Richard completely ignored him. He held his gaze and continued straightening to a standing position. Then he very purposefully checked the time on his watch. It was a Rolex, proving once again that he was making a fortune from Muffin's popularity. The gold watch band was a little loose and he shook it to move the clock face to the middle of his wrist. He looked pointedly at the time and then at Bronson.

"You have absolutely no reason to keep me. This fictional story, while amusing, is exactly that, fiction, created by a loser who is bitter because she didn't win. The trophy is mine. The title of champion is mine. Now, if you'll excuse me, I'll collect my winner's cup and go. Muffin, come."

He was going to leave! But every instinct I had was screaming that he had engineered the whole thing, Gerry's murder, Freddy's loss of the competition on a technicality, all of it.

I whirled around and faced the women. "If you don't speak up now, he walks and you get charged with murder. Is that what you want?"

I saw Claudia and Tilly exchange a glance. Liza and Mary looked confused as if they'd been under a spell but it was finally lifting.

"Richard told me that Gerry was planning to have me removed as a judge because he found out about me and Tilly," Claudia said. "I didn't care. I told her to be strong and that after the dog show, she could leave Gerry and come live with me, but then Gerry was murdered and we thought it best to wait.

"When I arrived at the dog show on the morning of the agility tests, Richard was there and he told me that Gerry had committed suicide by taking Tilly's medication. He said that because of her relationship with me, no one would believe it was suicide and that Tilly would be charged for his murder if we didn't hide the bottle and the body. He made me help him hide the body under the dais, but he kept the bottle."

She looked bitter and it was then that I knew she had taken a hell of a risk to keep insisting that Freddy won the dog show when Richard was holding this over her head.

"Definitely an alpha," I muttered. Claudia met my gaze with a sad smile.

Everyone turned to Tilly to see if she would verify the story. She was sitting at a table, having collapsed into a seat, and was openly sobbing. Her hands were shaking as tears slid down her face, ruining her makeup and making her look even younger than she was.

"It's okay, Mrs. Swendson," Bronson said. "Just tell us what happened."

"Several months ago, at a press event for Swendson's, Richard asked me for some of my pain medication," Tilly said. "I was still using pretty heavily back then, and I didn't think it through. He said he had wrenched his back and was in horrible, crippling pain. I didn't want to think of anyone else suffering like that, so I thought I was helping him by giving him my prescription. I forgot all about it, because I was trying to get clean for Claudia. I've been off the meds and sober for months, ever since we . . ." She glanced at Claudia with so much love wrapped up in vulnerability that I felt my own throat get tight. "On the morning of the agility tests, Richard used those same pills to kill Gerry by crushing them up and putting them into his coffee."

"Why?" Bronson asked. "Why did Richard want Swendson dead?"

"Gerry was going to do everything he could to make

sure Muffin didn't win this year. He hated that Muffin's celebrity eclipsed the dog show, which he paid a fortune to sponsor. He felt that it was unfair that the dog gets so much attention, and he hated that Richard made a fortune off the show while Gerry was spiraling into debt and probably going to lose everything.

"When Richard found out what Gerry was doing, he decided to kill him. When I threatened to go to the police and tell them, Richard said he still had the bottle my pills had come in and that he had carefully preserved my fingerprints on it. He said he'd out me and my lover and turn over the bottle to the police if we didn't help him. Claudia wanted to go to the police, but I was terrified and begged her not to."

Bronson turned to Liza. He didn't say a word. He just stared. She folded like a cheap suit.

"I didn't know what he was capable of, I swear," she said. "I'm as much a victim as Tilly and Claudia. Gerry was angry with me. He said he was going to have me removed from PAWS because he wasn't seeing enough return on his investment in his sponsorship of the dog show. I complained to Richard via text, saying I wished Gerry would just drop dead. It was just an angry message. I didn't mean it. Richard said not to worry, that he would take care of it. He tried to convince me that Swendson had committed suicide, but I never believed it. Not really."

"Why didn't you come to the police?" Bronson asked. He looked peeved and I couldn't blame him. What a waste of time.

"Because Richard told me that if I expressed any concern about Swendson's death other than as a tragic suicide, he would feel compelled to come forward with my text expressing my wish that Swendson would drop dead," Liza said. She cast a glance at the table where all of Richard's followers sat. "I've built PAWS up from nothing, I couldn't let him take it all away. When Richard demanded to win the competition, I felt like I had to do what he wanted or he'd try and make it look like I was the killer. He said he could do it. I panicked."

"And you," Bronson said to Mary. "How could you let your brother's killer roam free?"

"I didn't know!" Mary's voice was low and full of slow-burning fury when she spoke. She glanced at the others and snapped, "How could you? How could you know he was the killer and do nothing?"

"Oh, please," Claudia chided her. "How did you not figure it out? You knew he was manipulating all of us, including you."

"I thought he was just trying to win the competition," Mary said, seething. She turned back to Bronson. "Richard threatened me. He told me he would use Muffin's considerable influence to destroy my brand if I didn't guarantee him the win at the dog show, but that was it. I honestly thought my brother had committed suicide. He was always so overly dramatic that I thought maybe this time, he'd just gone too far. I didn't know Richard murdered Gerry. If I had, I would have—"

"You would have what?" Tilly snapped. She glanced at

her sister-in-law in disgust. "You knew he was drugging me, using my accident as an excuse to hook me on opioids, and you did nothing."

Mary glanced away. Guilt bowed her shoulders. "You're right. I should have done something to help you, and we all should have done something to stop him." She raised her head and glared at Richard.

"This has all been very entertaining," Richard said. "But it seems to me that all we have here is a bit of gossip. You have absolutely no proof."

"Actually, I do," I said.

Richard gave me a look of derision as if I was unworthy of his notice. I turned to Tilly and asked, "Did Gerry own a Rolex watch by any chance?"

"Yes, I gave him one for our wedding. How did you know?" she asked.

I glanced back at Richard. His affection for pretty things was about to get him in very deep trouble.

"I saw it on Mr. Swendson's wrist on the night of the cocktail party," I said. "And I just saw it again on Mr. Freestone's wrist when he checked the time."

Detective Inspector Bronson stepped forward just as Richard bolted for the exit. Thankfully, Harry and Alistair were able to run him to ground like a rugby ball.

They tackled him hard and snatched him up by the arms, carrying him so he was forced to walk on his tip-toes to Bronson with Muffin trotting along beside him, having no idea that her human was going to be gone for a very long while.

"It's not his, it's mine, you're mistaken, you can't prove anything," he argued. "Unhand me, you thugs!"

I turned to Bronson and said, "Every Rolex has a serial number that corresponds to its production date. If Tilly has the certificate of authenticity, it will prove that this watch belonged to Swendson."

"I do have it," Tilly said. "It's in our jewelry safe, I'm sure of it."

The detective inspector grinned, looking like he'd just won the big crystal bowl full of kibble.

"Mr. Freestone," Bronson said. "I'm sure this will come as no surprise, but you're under arrest for the murder of Gerry Swendson."

Chapter 18

The tea was anticlimactic after that. Aunt Betty posed with her trophy with the other winners, all of whom moved up a peg since Richard and Muffin were removed. Two of Richard's followers offered to take care of Muffin for him, which was a step up in the world for Muffin.

It was decided that Freddy, despite the paperwork issue, would keep his first-place finish. Andre took loads of pictures, and then we all staggered back to the hat shop to drink some champagne and reflect on the events of the day.

Nick poured everyone a glass and offered a toast to Freddy. Raising his glass, he said, "Here's to you, old chap. You were in it to win it and indeed you did. With some help from your friends and your excellent lid. At first it looked dicey, and was off to a rocky start, but you won them all over with your bum in the shape of a heart. To Freddy."

"Hear! Hear! To Freddy," we said in a chorus, and clinked glasses.

The bubbles were delightful and refreshing after a day that left me parched. Fee made up a plate of cheese and crackers and various fruits. It wasn't a meal though and I knew we were going to have to do something about that. Personally, all I wanted was a pie from Pizza Express and bed. This had absolutely been one of the most exhausting days of my life.

A cream-and-tan-colored fur ball dropped at my feet. Poor Bella looked flat-out exhausted with her snout on my shoe and her upper and lower legs splayed as if she didn't even have the energy to curl up into a ball.

"Aw," I said.

"Poor thing," Viv said. She was standing beside me, smiling down at the puppy. "We need to make her a proper bed in our living room upstairs. Do you think she'd like that old quilt of Mim's? The one with the flowers on it?"

I stared at her. I didn't want to get my hopes up. Very carefully, I said, "Are you saying what I think you're saying?"

Viv sighed. "I don't like to go back on the things that I say, you know that."

"I do," I said.

"But when you handed her to me today, well, she yawned and her little pink tongue curled up, and she's just so soft, and she has no one. I mean, what will happen to her if we don't take her in?"

My heart started to flutter. "I imagine she could find a good home. Of course, she might just as easily land in a bad home."

"Exactly," Viv said. She looked at me with a frown. "Damn you, you made me care."

"I'm sor—" I began to speak but then I noticed that she wasn't looking at me but rather past me at Alistair, where he was standing with Harry.

Oh, man, here I was again. To meddle or not to meddle? To be clear, in case there is any doubt, when these are my choices, I always choose to meddle.

I glanced back at Viv. "It's not too late. If you care, you should tell him."

"And just ignore that he and Fee seem to have found each other?" she asked. "I could never do that. Never."

I glanced across the room where Fee was chatting with Nick, Andre and Aunt Betty. She was laughing and petting Freddy, where he sat between her and Nick, basking in their affection. I mulled over our dinner party and how Fee had told me that she'd never do anything that would hurt Viv, and then I remembered the covert knuckle bump I'd seen Fee and Alistair exchange at the dog show. They were up to something; I was sure of it.

"What if they're just really good friends?" I asked.

Viv was staring down at Bella, looking forlorn. When

she glanced up, she looked resolved. "No, it's more than that. They seem enthralled with each other, and look at them. Why wouldn't they be? I mean, Fee is gorgeous and Alistair . . ."

"Yes?" I asked, hoping that I'd hear some acknowledgment of what a great guy he was.

"It doesn't matter," Viv said.

"It matters to me."

Viv started and stared at me with wide eyes. I looked past her and, sure enough, there was Alistair.

"Please tell me that's Harry," she whispered.

"Sorry," I said.

She closed her eyes, looking pained. Then she blew out a breath and made her face a pleasant mask.

"Don't do that," I said. "This is your chance. Tell him how you feel."

"Go away, Scarlett," she said. Her voice was high, almost piercing. "And take him with you."

"No," I said. "At least to the second part."

I bent over and scooped up Bella. Good grief, I was sure she'd gained a pound since we'd found her that morning. She relaxed against me like a boneless blob. I crossed the room to join Harry and passed her off, feeling my heart do a silly cartwheel when he cradled the puppy in his solid arms. What is it about a man with a puppy or a kitten that renders a woman brainless?

"What's going on over there?" he asked.

"I am hoping a moment of truth," I said. "Although whether it's going to make any diff—"

"What?" Viv cried. "How dare you?"

I turned around and saw her toss the contents of her champagne glass into Alistair's face. He blinked and shook the fizzing beverage off his face. I glanced at the others, watching from the other side of the room. Nick, Andre and Aunt Betty looked shocked, but Fee was smiling. Harry grabbed a kitchen towel from the counter and tossed it at his friend. Alistair snatched it out of the air without even looking.

"Refreshing," he said. He wiped off his face and hair.

"Don't," Viv said. "Don't make light of this."

"Ah, Viv," he said. "I've never made light of how I feel about you, but a man can only hear 'no' so many times before he has to quit for his own sanity. So, tell me, should I quit on you?"

Viv glanced from him, to me, to Fee, and back to him. She looked agitated and uncertain, both unfamiliar looks for Viv, and she nodded.

"You could have something really special with Fee, she's a wonderful woman, and I won't mess that up for you," she said.

Alistair looked rueful. He glanced past Viv at Fee and said, "Should we tell her?"

Fee stood and walked toward them.

"Tell me what?" Viv asked. "Oh, no, please tell me you're not getting married. I mean, if that's what you want that's great, but it . . . oh, God, can I leave now?"

"No, you can't," Fee said. She took Viv's hand in hers and gave it a squeeze. "Alistair is my friend and that's all

263

he is, yeah?" She lowered her head so that she was looking Viv right in the eyes.

"What are you saying?" Viv asked.

Fee sighed. "I'm saying that sometimes people don't appreciate what they have until it's gone, and I didn't want that to happen to you."

Viv was silent. She glanced back and forth between them. She looked incredulous, possibly furious, and her entire body was quivering like a plucked harp string. "Are you telling me that you set me up?"

Alistair put a hand on the back of his neck. "I take full responsibility."

"Piffle," Fee said. "It was my idea. Don't you dare go taking all the credit for it."

"I thought I was being noble by taking all of the wrath," he said.

"There's no wrath," Fee said. "I did her a favor. She was never going to give you the time of day until she was forced to realize that you weren't going to be available forever." She turned back to Viv. "He really wasn't. Men like him are few and far between. It was killing me to watch you muck it up."

"You are my millinery assistant," Viv said. "You are employed here to work on hats, not my love life."

"I don't mind," Fee said. "I can do both."

"Fee, this is completely—" Viv began but Alistair interrupted.

"Brilliant," he said.

Viv was blinking and blustering as if she wasn't sure

whether to protect herself in a cloak of outrage or acknowledge that her friend had given her the push she needed. The entire room was quiet, waiting for her to process.

She looked from Alistair to Fee and then she broke into an exasperated grin. "Yes, it was brilliant except when he asked me out just now I tossed my champagne on him in a show of solidarity to you. You might have explained first."

"Sorry," Fee said, not sounding sorry at all. She hugged them both and then stepped away.

"Can I take this to mean that if I ask you out again, right now, you'll say 'yes'?" Alistair asked.

"No," Viv said. "I won't."

The confusion and dismay that swept across both Fee's and Alistair's faces was crushing. I reached for Harry's hand and squeezed his fingers with mine. This was awful. All of our friendships were going to become super awkward and then everything would unravel as Alistair didn't come around anymore and Fee went off and found a new place to work. My stomach turned and I felt like I was going to be sick. I glanced at the couch and saw that Nick, Andre and Aunt B looked stricken.

"Ah, I see," Alistair said. "You don't forgive us or, more accurately, you really have no interest in dating me ever in this life."

"Wrong again," Viv said with a shake of her head. "You asked if I would say 'yes' to a date right now."

"And you're saying 'no,'" Alistair said. His words were short and sharp with his disappointment.

"Yes," she said. "But only because I think it's high time I asked you out on a date, don't you?"

Alistair went completely still. I squeezed Harry's fingers and felt the return pressure of his fingers around mine. Did this mean what I thought? Could she? Would she?

"Alistair, for the life of me, I can't figure out why you're still interested in me," Viv said. "But I've realized lately, with some help from a friend, how much you mean to me and I'd very much like to take you out on a date. Will you join me for dinner tomorrow, say, at seven o'clock?"

A smile, as slow as a sunrise over the London skyline, spread across Alistair's lips. He took Viv's fingers in his and kissed the back of her hand in a gesture as gallant and romantic as any woman could ever dream of and said, "I'd be delighted."

Aw. I sighed and Harry hugged me to his side and whispered, "Thank goodness. I was worried my best man and your maid of honor would spend our wedding ceremony glaring at each other. Speaking of which, I don't think I can wait until summer, let's move the date up."

"Okay," I said, because I'm easy like that.

Fee, unable to contain herself any longer, began to jump and clap. This woke up Bella, who demanded to be put down so that she could run around the room with Freddy, who was barking as if he, too, knew that something big had just happened.

Nick and Andre began to applaud and we all joined in. Viv blushed, which became deep pink when Alistair leaned down and kissed her quick. With her fingers over her lips and a bemused smile on her face, she said, "Is there any more champagne? I seem to have spilled mine."

We were bustling around Mim's Whims the next morning when Detective Inspector Bronson stopped by. He informed us that after an intense interrogation and under the advice of his lawyer, Richard Freestone confessed to the murder of Gerry Swendson. Apparently, Gerry had discovered that Richard was manipulating his way into winning the dog show, by bribing judges and so forth, and planned to boot him out of this year's competition. Richard couldn't have that so he arrived early on the morning of the agility tests and murdered Gerry by crushing pills of the opioid and slipping them into Gerry's coffee. Of course, he couldn't resist Gerry's Rolex and helped himself to it as the man lay dying.

Richard had thought he'd have time to arrange the body and make it look like a suicide, but Gerry died within minutes, forcing him to alter his plan. According to Claudia, he'd thought they could hide the body under the dais and then sneak it out later under the cover of darkness after the dog show, but Freddy had put a stop to that.

Claudia and Tilly knew that Richard had murdered Gerry, so they were trying to lessen their charges for accessories after the fact by agreeing to testify against him. Bronson thought they might get off completely since they hadn't planned the murder and were brought into it only after it had been committed. Since I felt that all the blame was Richard's, I hoped they weren't charged, which I told Bronson in no uncertain terms.

Aunt Betty stopped by the shop with Freddy in the afternoon, much to Bella's delight. Betty had been called to an emergency meeting of PAWS, where Liza was removed by the board as the chairman of PAWS, but mercifully they didn't hire Penelope Young to replace her. They offered the position to Betty instead. She was thinking it over.

When Harry arrived after work to join us for dinner, he told us that the business world was abuzz with the news of Swendson's Dog Food. Investors were selling all of their stocks, as it appeared the scandal would likely cause Mary to lose the pending lawsuit over the quality of the dog food and the business would have to declare bankruptcy.

I tried to feel sorry for the people involved but I just couldn't manage it. So much drama and for what? A crystal bowl and the title of best in show. It just didn't seem worth it.

Bella became the hat shop dog and while Viv followed her around with a handheld vacuum to suck up the fur she left behind—on everything—the two of them developed an understanding.

Bella was allowed to spend her days with us so long as she wore the hats that Viv designed for her. Thankfully, Bella took to this new modeling career like a champ, because after the dog show, we did start a line of hats for dogs that proved to be insanely popular.

I even added a section to our webpage that showcased Bella in girl dog hats and Freddy in boy hats. Andre took the pictures for us and they came out ridiculously cute. We even did a portrait of Freddy in a top hat and Bella in a bridal veil. Harry didn't like that one. He said Bella was entirely too young to consider marriage. Unsurprisingly, she has become a daddy's girl and positively throws herself at Harry when he arrives to pick us up at the end of the day.

Viv remained aloof with the puppy, refusing to think of her as anything other than an employee, or so I thought. This belief was blown wide open when I came home from a dinner out with Harry and found Viv and Alistair asleep on our sofa with Bella snuggled up in between them. None of them awoke when I entered the room, so I left them to it. It was clear that our entire hat shop crew had gone to the dogs.

Keep reading for an excerpt from
Jenn McKinlay's new romantic comedy . . .

Paris Is Always a Good Idea

Available Summer 2020 from Jove!

"I'm getting married."

"Huh?"

"We've already picked our colors, pink and gray."

"Um . . . pink and what?"

"Gray. What do you think, Chelsea? I want your honest opinion. Is that too retro?"

I stared at my middle-aged widowed father. We were standing in a bridal store in central Boston on the corner of Boylston and Berkeley Streets and he was talking to me about wedding colors. *His* wedding colors.

"I'm sorry, I need a sec," I said. I held up my hand and blinked hard, while trying to figure out just what the hell was happening.

I had raced here from my apartment in Cambridge after

a text from my dad had popped up on my phone, asking me to meet him at this address because it was an emergency. I was prepared for heart surgery not wedding colors!

Suddenly, I couldn't breathe. I wrestled the constricting wool scarf from around my neck, yanked the beanie off my head, and stuffed them in my pockets. I scrubbed my scalp with my fingers in an attempt to make the blood flow to my brain. It didn't help. *Come on, Martin*, I coached myself, *pull it together.* Lastly, I unzipped my puffy winter jacket to let some air in, then I focused on my father.

"What did you say?" I asked.

"Pink and gray, too retro?" Glen Martin, aka Dad, asked. He pushed his wire-frame glasses up on his nose and looked at me as if he was asking a perfectly reasonable question.

"No, before that." I waved my hand in a circular motion to indicate he needed to back it all the way up.

"I'm getting married!" His voice went up when he said it and I decided my normally staid fifty-five-year-old dad was somehow currently possessed by a twentysomething bridezilla.

"You okay, Dad?" I asked gently, not wanting to set him off. "Have you recently slipped on some ice and whacked your head? I ask because you don't seem to be yourself."

"Sorry," he said. He reached out and wrapped me in an impulsive hug, another indicator that he was not his usual buttoned-down mathematician self. "I'm just . . . I'm just so happy. What do you think about being a flower girl?"

"Um . . . I'm almost thirty." I tipped my head to the side and squinted at him.

"Yes, but we already have a full wedding party, and you and your sister would be really cute in matching dresses, maybe something sparkly."

"Matching dresses? Sparkly?" I repeated. I struggled for air. It was clear. My father had lost his ever-lovin' mind. I should probably call my sister. Dad needed medical attention, possibly an intervention. Oh, man, would we have to have him committed?

I studied his face, trying to determine just how crazy he was. The same brown-green hazel eyes I saw in my own mirror every morning held mine, but where my eyes frequently looked flat with a matte finish, his positively sparkled. He really looked happy.

"You're serious," I gasped. I glanced around the bridal store that was stuffed to the rafters with big, white, fluffy dresses. None of this made any sense and yet here I was. "You're not pranking me?"

"Nope." He grinned again. "Congratulate me, peanut, I'm getting married."

I felt as if my chest were collapsing into itself. Never, not once, in the past seven years had I ever considered the possibility that my father would remarry.

"To who?" I asked. It couldn't be . . . nah. That would be *insane*.

"Really, Chels?" Dad straightened up. The smile slid from his face and he cocked his head to the side, which was his go-to disappointed-parent look.

I had not been on the receiving end of this look very often in life. Not like my younger sister, Annabelle, who seemed to thrive on "the look." Usually, it made me fall right in line but not today.

"Sheri. You're marrying Sheri." I tried to keep my voice neutral. Major failure, as I stepped backward, tripped on the trailing end of my scarf, and gracelessly sprawled onto one of the cream-colored velvet chairs that were scattered around the ultra feminine store. From the look on my father's face, I thought it was a good thing I was sitting because if he answered in the affirmative I might faint.

"Yes, I asked her to marry me and to my delight she accepted," he said. Another happy stupid grin spread across his lips as if he just couldn't help it.

"But . . . but . . . she won you in a bachelor auction two weeks ago!" I cried. "This is completely mental!"

The store seamstress, who was assisting a bride up on the dais in front of a huge trifold mirror, turned to look at us. Her dark hair was scraped up into a knot on top of her head and her face was contoured to perfection. She made me feel like a frump in my Sunday no-makeup face. Which, in my defense, was not my fault because when I'd left the house to meet Dad, I'd had no idea the address he'd sent was for Bella's Bridal. I'd been expecting an urgent care. In fact, I wasn't sure yet that we didn't need one.

Glen Martin, Harvard mathematician and all-around nerd dad, had been coerced into participating in a silver fox bachelor auction for prominent Bostonians by my sister, Annabelle, to help raise funds for the Boston Children's Hospital. I had gone, of course, to support my sister and my dad and it had mostly been a total snoozefest.

The highlight of the event being when two socialites got into a bidding war over a surgeon and the loser slapped the winner across the face with her cardboard paddle. Good thing the guy was a cosmetic surgeon because there was most definitely some repair work needed on that paper cut.

But my father had not been anywhere near that popular with the ladies. No one wanted a mathematician. No one. After several minutes of excruciating silence, following the MC trying to sell the lonely gals on my dad's attempts to solve the Riemann hypothesis, I had been about to bid on him myself, when Sheri, a petite brunette, had raised her paddle with an initial bid. The smile of gratitude Dad had sent Sheri had been blinding, and the next thing we knew a flurry of bids happened, but Sheri stuck in there and landed the winning bid for four hundred thirty-five dollars and fifty cents.

"Two weeks is all it took," Dad said. He shrugged and held out his hands like a blackjack dealer showing he had no hidden cards, chips or cash.

I clapped a hand to my forehead. "It takes more time to get a first paycheck on a new job than you've spent in this relationship. Is it even considered a relationship at the two-week mark?"

"I know it's a surprise, Chels, but when—" he began but I interrupted him.

"Dad, a bachelor auction is not the basis for a stable, long-lasting relationship."

"You have to admit it makes a great story," he said.

"No, I don't! What do you even know about Sheri? What's her favorite color?"

"Pink, duh." He looked at me with a know-it-all expression more commonly seen on a teenager than a grown-ass man.

"Who are you and what have you done with my father?" I wanted to check him for a fever, maybe he had the flu and was hallucinating.

"I'm still me, Chels," he said. He gazed at me gently. "I'm just a happy me, for a change."

Was that it? Was that what was so different about him? He was happy? How could he be happy with a woman he hardly knew? Maybe . . . oh, dear. My dad hadn't circulated much after my mom's death. Maybe he was finally getting a little something and he had it confused with love. Oh, God, how was I supposed to talk about this with him?

I closed my eyes. I took a deep breath. Parents did this all the time. Surely I could manage it. Heck, it would be great practice if I ever popped out a kid. I opened my eyes. Three women were standing in the far corner in the ugliest chartreuse dresses I had ever seen. Clearly, they were the attendants of a bride who hated them. And that might be me in sparkly pink or gray if I didn't put a stop to this madness.

"Sit down, Dad," I said. "I think we need to have a talk."

He took the seat beside mine and looked at me with the same patience he had when he'd taught me to tie my shoes. I looked away. Ugh, this was more awkward than when my gynecologist told me to scoot down, repeatedly. It's like they didn't know a woman's ass needs some purchase during an annual. *Focus, Martin!*

"I know that you've been living alone for several years." I cleared my throat. "And I imagine you've had some needs that have gone unmet."

"Chels, no—" he said. "It isn't about that."

I ignored him, forging on while not making eye contact because, Lordy, if I had to have this conversation with him, I absolutely could not look at him.

"And I understand that after such a long dry spell, you might be confused about what you feel, and that's okay," I said. Jeebus, this sounded like a sex talk by Mr. Rogers. "The thing is, you don't have to marry the first person you sleep with after Mom."

There, I said it. And my wise advice and counsel was met with complete silence. I waited for him to express relief that he didn't have to get married. And I waited. Finally, I glanced up at my father, who was looking at me with the same expression he'd worn when I found out that he was actually the tooth fairy. Chagrin.

"Sheri is not the first," he said.

"She's not?" I was shocked. Shocked, I tell you.

"No."

"But you never told me about anyone before," I said.

"You didn't need to know," he said. "They were companions, not relationships."

"They?!" I shouted. I didn't mean to. The seamstress

sent me another critical look and I coughed, trying to get it together.

Dad shifted in his seat, sending me a small smile of understanding. "Maybe meeting here wasn't the best idea. I thought you'd be excited to help plan the wedding but perhaps you're not ready."

"Of course I'm not ready," I said. "But you're not either."

"Yes, I am."

"Oh, really? Answer me this, does Sheri prefer dogs or cats?"

"I don't—" He blinked.

"Yes, because it's only been two weeks," I said. "You remember that lump on your forehead? It took longer than two weeks to get that biopsied but you're prepared to marry a woman you haven't even known long enough for a biopsy."

My voice was getting higher and Dad put his hands out in an *inside voice, please* gesture. I would have tried but I felt as if I was hitting my stride in making my point. I went for the crushing blow.

"Dad, do you even know whether she is a pie or cake sort of person?"

"I . . . um . . ."

"Do you realize you're contemplating spending the rest of your life with a person who might celebrate birthdays with pie?"

"Chels, I know this is coming at you pretty fast," he said. "I do, but I don't think Sheri liking pie or cake is really that big of a deal. Who knows, she might be an ice cream person and ice cream goes with everything."

"Mom was a cake person," I said. There. I'd done it. I brought in the biggest argument against this whole rushed-matrimonial insanity. Mom.

My father's smile vanished as if I'd snuffed it out between my fingers like a match flame. I felt lousy about it, but not quite as lousy as I did at the thought of Sheri, oh, but no, becoming my stepmother.

"Your mother's been gone for seven years, Chels," he said. "That's a long time for a person to be alone."

"But you haven't been alone . . . apparently," I protested. "Besides, you have me and Annabelle, who is always in crisis, so I know she keeps you busy."

His smile flickered. "She does at that."

"So, why do you need to get married?" I pressed.

Dad sighed. "Because I love Sheri and I want to make her my wife."

I gasped. I felt as if he'd slapped me across the face. Yes, I knew I was reacting badly, but this was my father. The man who had sworn to love my mother until death do they part. But that was the problem, wasn't it? Mom had died seven years ago and Dad had been alone ever since, right up until he met Sheri Armstrong two weeks ago when she just kept raising her auction paddle for the marginally hot mathematician.

I got it. Really, I did. I'd been known to have bidding fever when a mint pair of Jimmy Choos showed up on eBay. It was hard to let go of something when it was in your grasp, especially when another bidder kept raising the stakes. But this was my dad, not shoes.

One of the bridal salon employees came by with a tray of mimosas. I grabbed two, double-fisting the sparkling beverage. Sweet baby Jesus, I hoped there was more fizz than pulp in them. The fizzing bubbles hit the roof of my mouth and I wished they could wash away the taste of my father's bad news but they didn't.

"Listen, I know that being the object of desire by a crowd of single, horny women is heady stuff—"

"Really, you know this?" Dad propped his chin in his hand as he studied me with his eyebrows raised and a twinkle in his eye.

"Okay, not exactly, but my point, and I have one, is that you and Sheri aren't operating in the real world here," I said. "I understand that Sheri is feeling quite victorious having won you but that doesn't mean she gets to wed you. I mean, why do you have to marry her? Why can't you just live in sin like other old people?"

"Because we love each other and we want to be married."

"You can't know this so soon," I argued. "It's not possible. Her representative hasn't even left yet."

My father frowned, clearly not understanding.

"The first six months to a year, you're not really dating a person," I explained. "You're dating their representative. The real person, the one who leaves the seat up and can't find the ketchup in the fridge even when it's right in front of him, doesn't show up until months into the relationship. Trust me."

"What are you talking about? Of course I'm dating a person. I can assure you, Sheri is very much a woman," he said. "Boy howdy, is she." The tips of his ears turned red and I felt my gag reflex kick in.

"Dad, first *ew*," I said. "And second, a person's representative is their best self. After two weeks, you haven't seen the real Sheri yet. The real Sheri is hiding behind the twenty-four/seven perfect hair and makeup, the placid temper, the woman who thinks your dad jokes are funny. They're not."

"No, no, no." He shook his head. "I've seen her without makeup. She's still beautiful. And she does have a temper, just drive with her sometime. I've learned some new words. Very educational. And my dad jokes are, too, funny."

I rolled my eyes. I was going to have to do some tough love here. I was going to have to be blunt.

"Dad, I hate to be rude, but you're giving me no choice. She's probably only marrying you for your money," I said. I felt like a horrible person for pointing it out, but he needed protection from gold diggers like Sheri. It was a kindness, really.

To my surprise, he actually laughed. "Sheri is more well off than I am by quite a lot. I'm the charity case in this relationship."

"Then why on earth does she want to marry *you*?" I asked.

The words flew out before I had the brains to stifle

them. It was a nasty thing to say. I knew that, but I was freaked out and frantic and not processing very well.

"I didn't mean that the way it sounded," I began but he cut me off.

"Yes, you did."

He stood, retrieving his coat from a nearby coatrack. As he shrugged into it, the look of hurt on his face made my stomach ache. I loved my father. I wouldn't inflict pain upon him for anything, and yet, I had. I'd hurt him very much.

"You did mean it and, sadly, I'm not even surprised. I mistakenly hoped you could find it in your heart to be happy for me," he said. "I have mourned the loss of your mother every day since she passed and I will mourn her every day for the rest of my life, but I have found someone who makes me happy and I want to spend my life with her. That doesn't take away what I had with your mother."

"Doesn't it?" I argued. How could he not see that by replacing my mother he was absolutely diminishing what they'd had? "Sheri's going to take your name, isn't she? And she's going to move into our house, right? So, everything that was once Mom's—the title of Mrs. Glen Martin and the house where she loved and raised her family—you're just giving to another woman. The next thing I know you'll tell me I have to call her Mom."

A guilty expression flitted across his face.

"No," I snapped. "Absolutely not."

"I'm not saying you have to call her that, it's just Sheri's never had a family of her own and she mentioned in passing how much she was looking forward to having daughters. It would be nice if you could think about how good it would be to have a mother figure in your life again."

"I am not her daughter, and I never will be," I said. My chest was heaving with outrage. "How can you even pretend that all of that isn't erasing Mom?"

Dad stared down at me with his head to the side and the right eyebrow arched, a double whammy of parental disappointment. He wrapped his scarf about his neck and pulled on his gloves.

"Listen, I don't know if Sheri will take my name. We haven't talked about it," he said. "As for the house, I am planning to sell it so we can start our life together somewhere new."

I sucked in a breath. My childhood home. Gone? Sold? To strangers? I thought I might throw up. Instead, I polished off one of the mimosas.

"Sheri and I are getting married in three months," he said. "We're planning a nice June wedding and we very much want you to be a part of it."

"As a flower girl?" I scoffed. "Whose crazy idea was that?"

"It was Sheri's," he said. His mouth tightened. "She's never been married before and she's a little excited. It's actually quite lovely to see."

"A thirty-year-old flower girl," I repeated. I was like a dog with a bone. I just couldn't let it go.

"All right, I get it. Come as anything you want, then,"

he said. "You can give me away, be my best man, be a bridesmaid, or officiate the damn thing. I don't care. I just want you there. It would mean everything to Sheri and me to have your blessing."

I stared at him. The mild-mannered Harvard math professor who had taught me to throw a curveball, ride a bike and knee a boy in the junk if he got too fresh had never looked so determined. He meant it. He was going to marry Sheri Armstrong and there wasn't a damn thing I could do about it.

"I don't know, Dad," I said. "I don't think I can be a part of . . . this." I couldn't even make myself say the word "wedding."

My father turned up his collar, bracing for the cold March air. He looked equal parts disappointed and frustrated. "Suit yourself."

He turned away and I sat frozen. I hated this. I didn't want us to part company like this but I couldn't change how I felt. I waited, feeling miserable, for him to walk away, but instead he turned back toward me. Rather than being furious with me, which would have allowed me to dig in my heels and push back, he looked sad.

"What happened to you?" he asked. "You used to be the girl with the big heart who was going to save the world."

I didn't say anything. His disappointment and confusion washed over me like a bath of rank sludge.

"I grew up," I said. But even in my own ears I sounded defensive.

He shook his head. "No, you didn't. Quite the opposite. You stopped growing at all."

"Are you kidding me? In the past seven years, I have raised millions to help the fight against cancer. How can you say I haven't grown?" I asked. I was working up a nice froth of indignation. "I'm trying to make a difference."

"That's your career," he said. "Being great at your profession doesn't mean you've grown personally. Chels, look at your life. You work seven days a week. You never take time off. You don't date. You have no friends. Heck, if we didn't have a standing brunch date, I doubt I'd ever see you except on holidays. What kind of life is that?"

I turned my head to stare out the window at Boylston Street. I couldn't believe my father was belittling how hard I worked for the American Cancer Coalition. I had busted my butt to become the top corporate fund-raiser in the organization, and with the exception of one pesky co-worker, my status was unquestioned.

He sighed. I refused to look at him. "Chels, I'm not saying what you've accomplished isn't important. It's just that you've changed over the past few years. I can't remember the last time you brought someone special home for me to meet. It's as if you've sealed yourself off since you mother—"

I whipped my head in his direction, daring him to talk about my mother in the same conversation where he announced he was remarrying.

"Chels, you're here!" a voice cried from the fitting room entrance on the opposite side of the store. I glanced away from my dad to see my younger sister, Annabelle, standing there in an explosion of hot pink satin and tulle trimmed with a wide swath of sparkling crystals.

"What. Is. That?" I looked from Annabelle to our father and back. The crystals reflected the fluorescent light overhead, making me see spots, or perhaps I was having a stroke. Hard to say.

"It's our dress!" Annabelle squealed. Then she twirled. The long tulle skirt fanned out from the form-fitting satin bodice and Annabelle's long dark curls streamed out around her. She looked like a demented fairy princess. "Do you love it or do you love it?"

"No, I don't love it. It's hideous!" I cried. The seamstress glared at me, looking as if she was going to take some of the pins out of the pincushion strapped to her wrist and come stab me a few hundred times. I lowered my voice, a little. "Have you both gone insane? Seriously, what the hell is happening?"

Annabelle staggered to a stop. She reeled a little bit as she walked toward us, looking more like a drunk princess than a fey one.

"How can you be happy about this?" I snapped at her. I gestured to the dress. "Have you not known me for all of your twenty-seven years? How could you possibly think I would be okay with this?"

Annabelle grabbed the back of a chair to steady herself. "By 'this' do you mean the dress or the whole wedding thing?"

"Of course I mean the whole wedding thing," I

growled. "Dad is clearly having some middle-aged crisis and there's you just going along with it for a sparkly dress. Damn it, Annabelle, couldn't you for once get your head out of your ass and think about someone other than yourself?"

"Chelsea." Dad's voice was low with warning. "Don't speak to your sister that way."

Annabelle blinked at me, looking surprised and a little hurt. "I am thinking about someone. I'm thinking about Dad. I kind of feel like I have a vested interest, given that it was my auction that brought Dad and Sheri together."

"Because you, like Dad, have gone completely mental!" I snapped. "Two weeks is not long enough to determine whether you should marry someone or not. My God, it takes longer to get a passport. What are you thinking, supporting this insanity?"

"Chels, that's not fair and you know it," Dad said.

My expression must have been full-on angry bear because he changed tack immediately, his expression softening.

"When did you stop letting love into your heart?" he asked. His voice was gentler, full of parental concern, which rolled off my back like water off a duck. He didn't get to judge me when he was marrying a person he barely knew. "Is this really how you want to live your life, Chels, with no one special to share it with? Because, I don't."

I turned back to the window, refusing to answer. With a sigh weighty with disappointment, he left. I watched his reflection in the glass grow smaller and smaller as he departed. I couldn't remember the last time we had argued, leaving harsh words between us festering like a canker sore. Ever since Mom had died, the awareness of how precious life was remained ever present and we always, always, said "I love you" at the end of a conversation, even when we weren't getting along.

I thought about running after him and saying I was sorry, that I was happy for him and Sheri, but it would be a lie and I knew I wasn't a good enough actress to pull it off. I just couldn't make myself do it. Instead, I tossed back my second mimosa because mimosas, unlike family, were always reliable.

Ready to find
your next great read?

Let us help.

Visit prh.com/nextread